THE HUMANS WERE HAVING A BALL
WHEN THE ALIEN PREPARED TO TELEPORT

. . .and then he arrived, firing the first of his twenty-round magazine.

The human nearest to Ferad flew apart, two-thirds of the mass of his thorax having been converted to super-hot steam. . .The thickly-packed humans were trying to surge away from the gun like the waves of compression and rarefaction in a gas . . . Ferad shot into fleeing backs trapped by the press of bodies.

Sopasian had suggested a bomb, but Sopasian had missed the point. What Ferad brought to the gala was personal death, an attack that went on and on and on in the safest place in the world, the victims would have said a moment before.

None of them were armed. The ballroom was like a nursery tunnel, females and infants and all of them helpless as the veriest newborn—but it had to be done.

DAVID DRAKE

HAMMER'S
AT ANY PRICE
Slammers

BAEN
science fiction
BOOKS

AT ANY PRICE

This is a work of fiction. All the characters and events portrayed in this book are fictional, and any resemblance to real people or incidents is purely coincidental.

A Baen Book

Baen Publishing Enterprises
260 Fifth Avenue
New York, N.Y. 10001

First printing, September 1985
Second printing, May 1986

ISBN: 0-671-55978-8

Cover art by Paul Alexander

Printed in the United States of America

Distributed by
SIMON & SCHUSTER
TRADE PUBLISHING GROUP
1230 Avenue of the Americas
New York, N.Y. 10020

DEDICATION

For Janet Morris

The same thing in a forty-four

FERAD'S BODY SCALES were the greenish black of extreme old age, but his brow horns —the right one twisted into a corkscrew from birth—were still a rich gray like the iridium barrel of the powergun he held. The fingertips of his left hand touched the metal, contact that would have been distracting to most of his fellows during the preliminaries to teleportation.

Molt warriors had no universal technique, however, and Ferad had grown used to keeping physical contact with the metallic or crystalline portion of whatever it was which he intended to carry with him. He was far too old to change a successful method now, especially as he prepared for what might be the most difficult teleportation ever in the history of his species—the intelligent autochthones of the planet named Oltenia by its human settlers three centuries before.

The antechamber of the main nursery cave

had a high ceiling and a circular floor eighteen meters in diameter. A dozen tunnel archways led from it. Many young Molt warriors were shimmering out of empty air, using the antechamber as a bolthole from the fighting forty kilometers away. The familiar surroundings and the mass of living rock from which the chamber was carved made it an easy resort for relative youths, when hostile fire ripped toward them in the press of battle.

The vaulted chamber was alive with warriors' cries, fear or triumph or simply relief, as they returned to catch their breath and load their weapons before popping back to attack from a new position. One adolescent cackled in splendid glee though his left arm was in tatters from a close-range gunshot: in his right hand the youth carried both an Oltenian shotgun and the moustached head of the human who had owned it before him. The ripe sweat of the warriors mingled with propellant residues from projectile weapons and the dry, arch-of-the-mouth taste of iridium from powerguns which still glowed with the heat of rapid fire.

Sopasian, Ferad's junior by a day and his rival for a long lifetime, sat eighteen meters away, across the width of the chamber. Each of the two theme elders planned in his way to change the face of the three-year war with the humans. Sopasian's face was as taut with strain as that of any post-adolescent preparing for the solo hunt which would make him a warrior.

Sopasian always tried too hard, thought Ferad as he eyed the other theme elder; but that was what worked, had always worked, for Sopasian. In his right hand was not a gun bought from a human trader or looted from an adversary but rather a traditional weapon: a hand-forged dagger, hafted with bone in the days when Molt warriors fought one another and their planet was their own. While Ferad stroked his gunbarrel to permit him to slide it more easily through the interstices of intervening matter, Sopasian's left hand fiercely gripped a disk of synthetic sapphire.

The two elders had discussed their plans with the cautious precision of mutually-acknowledged experts who disliked one another. Aloud, Ferad had questioned the premise of Sopasian's plan. Consciously but unsaid, he doubted his rival or *anyone* could execute a plan calling for so perfect a leap to a tiny object in motion.

Still deeper in his heart, Ferad knew that he was rotten with envy at the very possibility that the other theme elder would succeed in a teleportation that difficult. Well, to be old and wise was not to be a saint; and a success by Sopasian would certainly make it easier for Ferad to gain his ends with the humans.

The humans, unfortunately, were only half the problem—and the result Sopasian contemplated would make his fellow Molts even more intransigent. Concern for the repercussions of his plan and the shouts of young warriors like those who had made the war inevitable merged with the background as Ferad's mind tried to grip the electrical ambience of his world. The antechamber itself was a hollow of energy—the crystalline structure of the surrounding rocks, constantly deforming as part of the dynamic stasis in which every planetary crust was held, generated an aura of piezoelectrical energy of high amplitude.

Ferad used the shell of living rock as an anchor as his consciousness slipped out in an expanding circle, searching to a distance his fellows—even Sopasian—found inconceivable. For the younger warriors, such a solid base was almost a necessity unless their goal was very well-known to them and equally rich in energy flux. As they aged, male Molts not only gained conscious experience in teleportation but became better attuned to their planet on a biological level, permitting jumps of increasing distance and delicacy.

In circumstances such as these, the result was that Molts became increasingly effective warriors in direct proportion to their growing distaste for the glory which had animated them in their hot-blooded youth. By the time they had reached Ferad's age. . . .

The last object of which Ferad was aware within the antechamber was an internally-scored five-centimeter disk, the condensing unit for a sophisticated instrument display. The disk came from a disabled combat car, one of those used by the mercenaries whom the human colonists had hired to support them in their war with the Molts.

Sopasian held the crystal in his left hand as his mind searched for a particular duplicate of it: the location-plotter in the vehicle used by Colonel Alois Hammer himself.

"Largo, vector three-thirty!" called Lieutenant Enzo Hawker as Profile Bourne, his sergeant-driver, disrupted the air-condensed hologram display momentarily by firing his powergun through the middle of it.

A bush with leaves like clawing fingers sprawled over a slab of rock a few meters from the Slammers' jeep. Stems which bolts from the submachinegun touched popped loudly, and the Molt warrior just condensing into local existence gave a strangled cry as he collapsed over his own human-manufactured powergun.

"Via!" the little sergeant shouted as he backed the air-cushion jeep left-handed. "Somebody get this rock over here. Blood and martyrs, that's right on top of us!"

An infantryman still aboard his grounded skimmer caught the shimmer of a Molt teleporting in along the vector for which Hawker had warned. He fired, a trifle too early to hit the attacker whose imminent appearance had ionized a pocket of air which the detection apparatus on the jeep had located. The cyan bolt blew a basin the size of a dinnerplate into the rock face on which the Molt was homing. Then the ten-kilo shaped charge which Oltenian engineers had previously placed shattered the rock and the autochthone warrior himself into a sphere of flying gravel and less recognizable constituents.

Ducking against the shower of light stones, a pair of Oltenians gripping another shaped charge and the bracket that would hold it two meters off the ground scuttled toward the slab on which Bourne's victim quivered in death. A trooper on the right flank of the company, controlled by the other detection jeep, missed something wildly and sent a bolt overhead with a hiss-*thump!* which made even veteran Slammers cringe. The two locals flattened themselves, but they got to their feet again and continued even though one of the pair was visibly weeping. They had balls, not like most of the poofs.

Not like the battalion supposedly advancing to support this thrust by a company of Hammer's infantry reinforced by a platoon of Oltenian combat engineers.

"Spike to Red One," said Hawker's commo helmet—and Bourne's, because the tall, heavy-set lieutenant had deliberately split the feed to his driver through the intercom circuits. Profile was the team's legs; and here on Oltenia especially, Hawker did not want to have to repeat an order to bug out. "Fox Victor—" the Oltenian battalion "—is hung up. Artillery broke up an outcrop, but seems like the Molts are homing on the boulders even. There's some heavy help coming, but it'll be a while. Think you might be able to do some good?"

"Bloody buggerin' *poofs*," Sergeant Bourne muttered as he bent in anticipation of the charge blasting the nearby slab, while the pipper on the map display glowed on a broad gully a kilometer away as "Spike"—the company commander, Henderson—pinpointed the problem.

The pair of detection jeeps were attached to the infantry for this operation, but Hawker's chain of command was directly to Central—Hammer's headquarters—and the idea wasn't one that Henderson was likely to phrase as an order even to someone unquestionably under his control. The Slammers had been on Oltenia for only a few days before the practice of trusting their safety to local support had proven to be the next thing to suicide.

But the present fact was that the company was safe enough only for the moment, with the larger crystalline rocks within their perimeter broken up. The autochthones could—given time to approach the position instead of teleporting directly from some distant location—home in on very small crystals indeed. Unless somebody shook lose Fox Victor, the troopers in this lead element were well and truly screwed.

Hawker rubbed his face with his big left hand, squeezing away the prickling caused by Bourne's nearby shots and the nervous quiver inevitable because of what he knew he had to say. "All right," he muttered, "all right, we'll be the fire brigade on this one too."

A hillock six hundred meters distant shattered into shellbursts turbid with dirt and bits of tree. Waves quivered across the ground beneath the jeep for a moment before the blast reached the crew through the air. Bourne cursed again though the artillery was friendly, the guns trying to forestall Molt snipers by pulverizing a site to which they could easily teleport. The attempt was a reminder that no amount of shelling could interdict all outcrops within the line-of-sight range of a powergun.

"Want an escort, Red One?" asked the company commander, flattened somewhere beside his own jeep while his driver's gun wavered across each nearby spray of vegetation, waiting for the warning that it was about to hold a Molt warrior.

"Profile?" asked Lieutenant Hawker, shouting over the fan whine rather than using the intercom.

"What a bloody copping *mess*," grunted the sergeant as his left hand spun the tiller and the fans spun the jeep beneath them. "Hang on," he added, late but needlessly: Hawker knew to brace himself before he said anything that was going to spark his driver into action. "No, we don't want to bloody babysit pongos!" and the jeep swung from its axial turn into acceleration as smooth as the brightness curve of rheostat-governed lights.

"Cover your own ass, Spike," Hawker reported as the jeep sailed past a trio of grounded infantrymen facing out from a

common center like the spokes of a wheel.
"We'll do better alone."

The trouble with being a good all-rounder
was that you were used when people with
narrower capacities got to hunker down and
pray. The other detection team, Red Two,
consisted of a driver possibly as good as
Bourne and a warrant officer who could
handle the detection gear at least as well as
Hawker. But while no one in the Slammers
was an innocent about guns, neither of the
Red Two team was the man you really
wanted at your side in a firefight. They
would do fine, handling detection chores
for the entire company during this lull while
the autochthones regrouped and licked their
wounds.

Red One, on the other hand, was headed
for the stalled support force, unaccompa-
nied by skimmer-mounted infantry who
would complicate the mad dash Profile intended to make.

Shells passed so high overhead that they
left vapor trails and their attenuated howl
was lost in the sizzle of brush slapping the
jeep's plenum chamber.

"Gimme the push for Fox Victor," Hawker
demanded of Central, as his right hand
gripped his submachinegun and his eyes
scanned the route by which Bourne took
them to where the supports were bottle-
necked.

The Slammers lieutenant was watching
for Molts who, already in position, would
not give warning through the display of his

detection gear. But if one of those bright-uniformed, totally-incompetent Oltenian general officers suddenly appeared in his gunsights. . . .

Enzo Hawker might just decide a burst wouldn't be wasted.

The gorgeous clothing of the officers attending the Widows of the War Ball in the Tribunal Palace differed in cut from the gowns of the ladies, but not in quality or brilliance. General Alexander Radescu, whose sardonic whim had caused him to limit his outfit to that prescribed for dress uniforms in the *Handbook for Officers in the Service of the Oltenian State*, knew that he looked ascetic in comparison to almost anyone else in the Grand Ballroom—his aide, Major Nikki Tzigara, included.

"Well, the lily has a certain dignity that a bed of tulips can't equal, don't you think?" murmured the thirty-two-year-old general as his oval fingernails traced a pattern of lines down the pearly fabric of his opposite sleeve.

Nikki, who had added yellow cuffs and collar to emphasize the scarlet bodice of his uniform jacket, grinned at the reference which he alone was meant to hear in the bustle of the gala. From beyond Tzigara, however, where he lounged against one of the pair of huge urns polished from blue john—columnar fluorspar—by Molt craftsmen in the dim past, Major Joachim Steuben asked, "And what does that leave me, General? The dirt in the bottom of the pot?"

Colonel Hammer's chief of base operations in the Oltenian capital flicked a hand as delicately manicured as Radescu's own across his own khaki uniform. Though all the materials were of the highest quality, Steuben's ensemble had a restrained elegance—save for the gaudily-floral inlays of the pistol which was apparently as much part of the Slammers dress uniform as the gold-brimmed cap was for an Oltenian general officer. In fact, Major Steuben looked very good indeed in his tailored khaki, rather like a leaf-bladed dagger in an intarsia sheath. Though flawlessly personable, Steuben had an aura which Radescu himself found at best disconcerting: Radescu's mind kept focusing on the fact that there was a skull beneath that tanned, smiling face.

But Joachim Steuben got along well in dealing with his Oltenian counterparts here in Belvedere. The first officer whom Hammer had given the task of liaison and organizing his line of supply from the starport had loudly referred to the local forces as poofs. That was understandable, Radescu knew; but very impolitic.

Nikki, who either did not see or was not put off by the core of Joachim which Radescu glimpsed, was saying, "Oh, Major Steuben, *you* dirt?" when the string orchestra swung into a gavotte and covered the remainder of the pair's smalltalk.

Every man Radescu could see in the room

was wearing a uniform of some kind. The regulars, like Nikki Tzigara, modified the stock design for greater color; but the real palm went to the "generals" and "marshals" of militia units which mustered only on paper. These were the aristocratic owners of mines, factories, and the great ranches which were the third leg of human success on Oltenia. They wore not only the finest imported natural and synthetic fabrics, but furs, plumes, and—in one case of strikingly poor taste, Radescu thought—a shoulder cape flayed from the scaly hide of an adolescent Molt. Officers of all sorts spun and postured with their jeweled ladies, the whole seeming to the young general the workings of an ill-made machine rather than a fund-raiser for the shockingly large number of relicts created in three years of war.

Radescu lifted his cap and combed his fingers through the pale, blond hair which was plastered now to his scalp by perspiration. The second blue john vase felt cool to his back, but the memories it aroused increased his depression. The only large-scale celebrations of which the autochthones, the Molts, had not been a part were those during the present war. While not everyone—yet—shared the general's opinion that the war was an unmitigated disaster, the failure of this gathering to include representatives of the fourteen Molt themes made it less colorful in a way that no amount of feathers and cloth-of-gold could repair.

A gust of air, cool at any time and now

balm in the steaming swamps, played across the back of Radescu's neck and the exposed skin of his wrists. He turned to see a scarlet Honor Guard disappearing from view as he closed a door into the interior of the Tribunal Palace. The man who had just entered the ballroom was the Chief Tribune and effective ruler of Oltenia, Grigor Antonescu.

"Well met, my boy," said the Chief Tribune as he saw General Radescu almost in front of him. There was nothing in the tone to suggest that Antonescu felt well about anything, nor was that simply a result of his traditional reserve. Radescu knew the Chief Tribune well enough to realize that something was very badly wrong, and that beneath the wall of stony facial control there was a mind roiling with anger.

"Good evening, Uncle Grigor," Radescu said, bowing with more formality than he would normally have shown his mother's brother, deferring to the older man's concealed agitation. "I don't get as much chance to see you as I'd like, with your present duties."

There were factory owners on the dance floor who could have bought Alexander Radescu's considerable holdings twice over; but there was no one with a closer path to real power if he chose to travel it.

"You have good sense, Alexi," Antonescu said with an undertone of bitterness that only an ear as experienced as Radescu's own would have heard.

The Chief Tribune wore his formal robes

of office, spotlessly white and of a severity unequalled by even the functional uniform of Joachim Steuben . . . who seemed to have disappeared. Another man in Grigor Antonescu's position might have designed new regalia more in line with present tastes or at least relieved the white vestments' severity with jewels and metals and brightly-patterned fabrics rather the way Nikki had with his uniform (and where *was* Nikki?). Chief Tribune Antonescu knew, however, that through the starkness of a pure neutral color he would draw eyes like an axe blade in a field of poppies.

"It's time," Antonescu continued, with a glance toward the door and away again, "that I talk to *someone* who has good sense."

On the dance floor, couples were parading through the steps of a sprightly *contre-danse*—country dance—to the bowing of the string orchestra. The figures moving in attempted synchrony reminded Alexander Radescu now of a breeze through an arboretum rather than of a machine. "Shall we . . . ?" the general suggested mildly with a short, full-hand gesture toward the door through which his uncle had so recently appeared.

The man-high urns formed an effective alcove around the door, while the music and the bustle of dancing provided a sponge of sound to absorb conversations at any distance from the speakers. Chief Tribune Antonescu gave another quick look around him and said, gesturing his nephew closer,

"No, I suppose I need to show myself at these events to avoid being called an unapproachable dictator." He gave Radescu a smile as crisp as the glitter of shears cutting sheet metal: both men knew that the adjective and the noun alike were more true than not.

"Besides," Antonescu added with a rare grimace, "if we go back inside we're likely to meet my esteemed colleagues—" Tribunes Wraslov and Deliu "—and having just spent an hour with their inanity, I don't care to repeat the dose for some while."

"There's trouble, then?" the young general asked, too softly in all likelihood to be heard even though he was stepping shoulder to shoulder as the older man had directed.

There was really no need for the question anyway, since Antonescu was already explaining, "The great offensive that Marshal Erzul promised has stalled. Again, of course."

A resplendent colonel walked past, a young aide on his arm. They both noticed the Chief Tribune and his nephew and looked away at once with the terrified intensity of men who feared they would be called to book. Radescu waited until the pair had drifted on, then said, "It was only to get under way this morning. Initial problems don't necessarily mean—"

"Stalled. Failed. Collapsed totally," Antonescu said in his smooth, cool voice, smiling at his nephew as though they were discussing the gay rout on the dance floor. "According to Erzul, the only units which haven't fallen back to their starting line decimated are those with which he's lost contact entirely."

"Via, he *can't* lose contact!" Radescu snapped as his mind retrieved the Operation Order he had committed to memory. His post, Military Advisor to the Tribunes, was meant to be a sinecure. That General Radescu had used his access to really study the way the Oltenian State fought the autochthones was a measure of the man, rather than of his duties. "Every *man* in the forward elements has a personal radio to prevent just that!"

"Every man alive, yes," his uncle said. "That was the conclusion I drew, too."

"And—" Radescu began, then paused as he stepped out from the alcove to make sure that he did not mistake the absence of Major Steuben before he completed his sentence with, "and Hammer's Slammers, were they unable to make headway also? Because if they were . . ." He did not go on by saying, ". . . then the war is patently unwinnable, no matter what level of effort we're willing to invest." Uncle Grigor did not need a relative half his age to state the obvious to him.

Antonescu gave a minute nod of approval for the way his nephew had this time checked their surroundings before speaking. "Yes, that's the question that seems most frustrating," he replied as the *contre-danse* spun to a halt and the complex patterns dissolved. "Erzul—he was on the screen in person— says the mercenaries failed to advance, but he says it in a fashion that convinces me he's lying. I presume that there has been another failure to follow up thrusts by Hammer's units."

The Chief Tribune barked out a laugh as humorless as the stuttering of an automatic weapon. "If Erzul were a better commander, he wouldn't *need* to be a good liar," he said.

The younger man looked at the pair of urns. At night functions they were sometimes illuminated by spotlights beamed down on their interiors, so that the violet tinge came through the huge, indigo grains and the white calcite matrix glowed with power enchained. Tonight the stone was unlighted, and only reflections from the smooth surfaces belied its appearance of opacity.

"The trouble is," Radescu said, letting his thoughts blend into the words his lips were speaking, "that Erzul and the rest keep thinking of the Molts as humans who can teleport and therefore can never be caught. That means every battle is on the Molts' terms. But they *don't* think the way we do, the way humans do, as a society. They're too individual."

The blue john urns were slightly asymmetric, proving that they had been polished into shape purely by hand instead of being lathe-turned as any human craftsman would have done. That in itself was an amazing comment on workmanship, given that the material had such pronounced lines of cleavage and was so prone to splinter under stress. Even the resin with which the urns were impregnated was an addition by the settlers to whom the gift was made, preserving for generations the micron-smooth polish which a Molt had achieved with no tool but the palms of his hands over a decade.

But there was more. Though the urns were asymmetric, they were precise mirror images of one another.

"If we don't understand the way the Molts relate to each other and to the structure of their planet," said Alexander Radescu with a gesture that followed the curve of the right-hand urn without quite touching the delicate surface, "then we don't get anywhere with the war.

"And until then, there's no chance to convince the Molts to make peace."

The ambience over which Ferad's mind coursed was as real and as mercurial as the wave-strewn surface of a sea. He knew that at any given time there were hundreds, perhaps thousands, of his fellows hurling themselves from point to point in transfers which seemed instantaneous only from the outside. There was no sign of others in this universe of stresses and energy, a universe which was that of the Molts uniquely.

That was the key to the character of male Molts, Ferad had realized over the more than a century that he observed his race and the human settlers. Molt females cooperated among themselves in nurturing the young and in agriculture—they had even expanded that cooperation to include animal husbandry, since the human settlement. The prepubescent males cooperated also, playing together even when the games involved teleportation for the kilometer or so of which they and the females were capable.

But with the hormonal changes of puberty, a male's world became a boundless, vacant expanse that was probably a psychological construct rather than a 'real' place—but which was no less real for all that.

In order to transport himself to a point in the material landscape, a Molt had to identify his destination in the dreamworld of energy patterns and crystal junctions that depended both on the size of the object being used as a beacon and on its distance from the point of departure. Most of all, however, finding a location depended on the experience of the Molt who picked his way across the interface of mind and piezoelectrical flux.

That focus on self deeply affected the ability of males to consider anything *but* individual performance. Hunters, especially the young who were at pains to prove their prowess, would raid the herds of human ranchers without consideration of the effect that had on settler-autochthone relations. And, even to the voice of Ferad's dispassionate experience, it was clear that there would be human herds and human cities covering the planet like studded leather upholstery if matters continued as they began three centuries before.

But while the war might be a necessary

catalyst for change, no society built on continued warfare would be beneficial to Man or Molt.

The greater questions of civilization which had been filling Ferad's time in the material world were secondary now in this fluid moment. Crystals which he knew—which he had seen or walked across or handled—were solid foci within the drift. They shrank as the theme elder's mind circled outward, but they did not quickly lose definition for him as they would have done decades or a century earlier.

The psychic mass of the powergun Ferad held created a drag, but his efforts to bring the weapon into tune with his body by stroking the metal now worked to his benefit. He handled the gun in teleporting more easily than he did its physical weight in the material world. His race had not needed the bulk and power of human hunters because their pursuit was not through muscular effort and they struck their quarry unaware, not aroused and violent. Besides that, Ferad was very old, and gravity's tug on the iridium barrel was almost greater than his shrunken arms could resist.

He would hold the weapon up for long enough. Of that he was sure.

Ferad's goal was of unique difficulty, not only because of the distance over which he was teleporting but also due to the nature of the objects on which he was homing. He had never seen, much less touched them; but an ancestor of his had spent years pol-

ishing the great urns from solid blocks of
blue john. That racial memory was a part
of Ferad, poised in momentary limbo between the central cave system of his theme
and the Tribunal Palace in Belvedere.

A part of him like the powergun in his
hands.

"Shot," called the battery controller
through the commo helmets, giving Hawker
and Bourne the warning they would have
had a few seconds earlier had the rush of
their passage not shut off outside sounds as
slight as the first pop of the firecracker
round. The initial explosion was only large
enough to split the twenty-centimeter shell
casing short of the impact point and strew
its cargo of five hundred bomblets like a
charge of high-explosive buckshot.

"Via!" swore the sergeant angrily, because
they were in a swale as open as a whore's
cunt and the hologram display which he
could see from the corner of his eye was
giving a warning of its own. The yellow
figures which changed only to reflect the
position of the moving jeep were now replaced by a nervous flickering from that
yellow to the violet which was its optical
reciprocal, giving Lieutenant Hawker the
location at which a Molt warrior was about
to appear in the near vicinity. It was a lousy
time to have to duck from a firecracker
round.

But Via, they'd known the timing had to
be close to clear the ridge before the jeep

took its position to *keep* the bottleneck open. Bourne knew that to kill forward motion by lifting the bow would make the slowing jeep a taller target for snipers, while making an axial 180 turn against the vehicle's forward motion might affect the precision with which the Loot called a bearing on the teleporting autochthone. The driver's left hand released the tiller and threw the lever tilting the fan nacelles to exhaust at full forward angle.

His right hand, its palm covered with a fluorescent tattoo which literally snaked all the way up his arm, remained where it had been throughout the run: on the grip of his submachinegun.

"Splash," said the battery controller five seconds after the warning, and the jeep's inertia coasted it to a halt in the waving, head-high grain. A white glow played across the top of the next rise, mowing undergrowth and stripping bark and foliage from the larger trees. The electrical crackle of the bomblets going off started a second later, accompanied by the murderous hum of an object flung by the explosions, a stone or piece of casing which had not disintegrated the way it should have—deadly in either case, even at three hundred meters, had it not missed Bourne's helmet by a hand's breadth.

"Loot!" the driver called desperately. The burring fragment could be ignored as so many dangers survived had been ignored before. But the Molt warrior who by now was in full control of his body and whatever weapon he held, somewhere beyond the waving curtain of grain. . . . "Which *way*, Loot, which way!"

"Hold it," said Lieutenant Hawker, an order and not an answer as he jumped to his full meter-ninety height on the seat of the jeep with his gun pointing over the driver's head. There was a feral hiss as Hawker's weapon spewed plastic casings from the ejection port and cyan fire from the muzzle. Profile Bourne's cheeks prickled, and a line of vegetation withered as the burst angled into the grain.

There was a scream from down-range. The sergeant slammed his throttle and the nacelle angle into maximum drive even as his teammate dropped back into a sitting position, the muzzle of his powergun sizzling as it cooled from white to lambent gray. The scream had been high-pitched and double, so that the driver did not need to hear Hawker say, "*Cop*! It was a female and a kid, but I thought she had a bloody satchel charge!"

It wasn't the sort of problem that bothered Bourne a whole lot, but he didn't like to see the Loot so distressed.

The reason Fox Victor was having problems—beyond the fact that they were poofs who couldn't be trusted in a rainstorm, much less a firefight—was obvious on this, the reverse slope of the gully which formed the actual chokepoint for the support column. Low retaining walls curved back into the sloping hillside like arms outstretched by the arched opening in their center: the entrance to what the Oltenians called a Molt nursery cave.

In fact, the underground constructs of which this was a small example were almost never true caves but rather tunnels carved into igneous and metamorphic rocks of dense crystalline structure. The sedimentary rocks which could be cut or leached away into caves by groundwater were of no use as beacons for teleporting autochthones—and thus of no use in training young Molts to use their unique abilities.

By being surrounded from earliest infancy with living rock whose crystals were in a constant state of piezoelectrical flux, Molts—male and female alike—began to teleport for short distances before they could crawl. As they grew older, prepubescents played in the near vicinity of their nurseries and gained a familiarity with the structure of those rocks which was deeper than anything else they would meet in life.

And when called to do so by military need, Molt warriors could home on even the smallest portions of the particular locality in which they had been raised. Shelling that broke up the gross structure of a slab did not affect the ability of warriors to concentrate, though the damage would ordinarily have at least delayed younger Molts trying to locate it for teleportation. The result, at least for poofs without the instruments to detect warriors before the shooting started, would be disastrous.

Now, while the pair of Slammers were flat out with nothing but a 15 slope to retard the jeep, the possibility of a Molt teleporting to point-blank range beside them was the least of Profile Bourne's worries. The bolt that snapped into the hillside thirty meters away, fluffing and dimming shell-set grass-fires in its momentary passage, was a more real danger. The microfragments from the firecracker round had cleared the crest and face of the ridge, but a Molt somewhere out there, far from the immediate battle scene, continued to snipe at the jeep undeterred. The autochthones were not, in the main, good marksmen, and the vehicle's speed made it a chance target anyway to a gun-man a kilometer distant.

But the chance that let the bolt blow a divot from the soil and splinters from the rock close beneath might easily have turned the jeep into a sizzling corona as electrical storage cells shorted through driver and pas-senger. It was nothing to feel complacent about, and there was no way to respond while the jeep was at speed.

If only they were about to join one of the Slammers' tank companies instead of a poof battalion! Snipers would learn that they, like dogs, got one bite—and that a second attempt meant the ground around them glowed and bubbled with the energy re-leased by a tank's main gun or a long burst from a tribarrel.

That didn't, of course, always mean that the first bite had not drawn blood. . . .

A less skilled driver would have let his
jeep lift bow-high at the crest where the
ridge rolled down its other slope. Bourne
angled his fan nacelles left, throwing the
vehicle into a sideslip which cut upward
velocity without stalling the jeep as a target silhouetted in two directions. The grass
and low brush of the crest were scarred by
the bomblets, and a lump half-hidden by
the rock which had sheltered it might have
been a warrior caught by the shrapnel.

While Bourne concentrated on his own
job, Lieutenant Hawker had been on the
horn with the poof battalion commander,
their Central-relayed conversation audible
to the driver but of no particular interest.
All Sergeant Bourne cared was that the
Oltenian troops not add their fire to that of
the Molts already sniping at the jeep. Men
so jumpy from being ripped without recourse
might well fire at any target they could hit,
even when the intellectual levels of their
brains knew that it was the wrong target.

"Profile, a hundred and fifty!" the lieutenant ordered. His left arm reached out
through the flashing hologram display in
the air before him, converting its digital
information into a vector for his driver's
gun.

The sergeant grounded the jeep in a stony
pocket far enough below the crest to be
clear of the Molt marksman who had fired
as they climbed the back slope. Molts could
teleport in within touching distance, but
this time that was the plan; and the rocks

jumbled by a heavy shell provided some cover from distant snipers.

Bourne did not fire. He knew exactly where the Molt was going to appear, but spraying the area a hundred and fifty meters down the wash would have been suicidal.

Like most of Hammer's troopers, Sergeant Bourne had seen the wreckage Molt warriors made of Oltenian assaults. He hadn't really appreciated the ease with which disaster happened until he saw what now took place in the swale.

The watercut depression in a fold between crystalline ridges was now studded with rubble cracked from both faces by armor-piercing shells and the blazing remains of half a dozen Oltenian vehicles. The human bodies blended into the landscape better than did equipment marked out by pillars of smoke and sometimes a lapping overlay of kerosene flames, though the corpse half-way out of the driver's hatch of an armored car was obvious with his lifted arms and upturned face—brittle as a charcoal statue.

The single firecracker round had been intended only to clear the Molts briefly from the area. A poof armored car and armored personnel carrier were trying to make a dash across the gully during the lull, however, instead of waiting for the Slammers to get into position as Hawker had directed. Some might have said that showed exemplary courage, but Profile Bourne couldn't care less about fools who died well—which was all this crew was managing.

The automatic weapon in the car's turret traversed the slope toward which the vehicle advanced, making a great deal of dust and racket without affecting in the least the warrior who must have teleported directly between the car and the personnel carrier. Bourne didn't fire at the Molt, knowing that the armored vehicles shielded their attacker and that the poofs across the swale would respond to the submachinegun's 'attack' on their fellows, no matter *how* good their fire discipline might be.

"Via! Three more, Profile," Lieutenant Hawker said, his pointing arm shifting 15 to the right as the swale rang with the sound of a magnetic limpet mine gripping the steel side of the vehicle against which it had been slapped.

Rock broken by heavy shells, brush smoldering where the bursting charges of the antipersonnel bomblets had ignited it. No target yet, but Profile loosed a three-round burst to splash the boulders twenty meters from the oncoming APC and warn the poofs.

The armored car dissolved in a sheet of flame so intense that the shock wave a fraction of a second later seemed a separate event. A trio of Molts froze out of the air where Hawker had pointed and Bourne's own shots had left glazed scars on the stone a moment before.

He had a target now and he fired over open sights, two rounds into the back of the first warrior and three at the second who leaped up into the last bolt when molten stone sprayed from the boulder sheltering him. A storm of fire from at least twenty Oltenian guns broke wildly on the general area. The Loot was shouting, "*Close Profile!*" his big arm pointing behind the jeep, but nothing this side of Hell was going to keep Bourne from his third kill—the Molt crouched behind his steaming powergun, firing into the APC as fast as his finger could pull the trigger.

Only when that Molt crumpled did the sergeant spin to shoot over the racked electronics modules replacing the jeep's back seat. Bourne lifted the heat-shivering muzzle of his gun even as his finger took up slack in the trigger. If he had fired as he intended into the center of mass of the warrior coalescing a meter away, the satchel charge the Molt was clutching to his chest would have gone off and vaporized the jeep. Instead, the distorted face of the autochthone dissolved in a burst so needlessly long that even Profile knew that he had panicked.

"Seventy-five," the Loot was saying, and Bourne rotated toward the new target while the decapitated remains of his previous victim toppled backwards. In the swale below, the APC crackled with what sounded like gunfire but was actually the explosion of ammunition within its burning interior. Seventy-five meters, a rough figure but there was a tangled clump of ground cover at about that distance in the direction the Loot was pointing, a flat-topped block jutting like a loggia garden into the gully. Bourne squeezed off what was intended to be a two-round burst alerting the poofs deployed on the further side.

There was a single cyan flicker from the submachinegun—he'd emptied the magazine on the previous Molt, leaving only one lonely disk in the loading pan.

Cursing because the warrior homing on the block was going to get a shot in for sure and the Loot was already pointing another vector, the sergeant swapped magazines. His eyes were open and searching the terrain for the new target, two hundred meters to the front and closer to the Oltenian battalion than to the jeep. The right handgrip enclosed the magazine well, and a veteran like Bourne had no need to look down for hand to find hand in an operation as familiar as reloading.

He had no need to worry about the warrior his shot had marked, as it turned out.

The standard poof shoulder weapon, a stubby shotgun, did not, with its normal load of flechettes, have the range of the target. The outside surface of the guntube could be used as the launching post for ring-airfoil grenades, however, like the one which hurled a pair of Molts in opposite directions from its yellow flash in the center of the target. Turret guns from armored vehicles were raking the blasted area as well, even hitting the corpses as they tumbled.

Could be some a' the poofs had sand in their craws after all.

A powergun too distant to be a target for

Bourne under these circumstances was emptied in the direction of the jeep as fast as some warrior could pull the trigger. The bolts weren't really close—some of them were high enough for their saturated blue-green color to be lost in the sunlight. The trio that spattered rock eighty meters from the jeep—forty meters, twenty—were not less terrifying, however, for the fact that the next three missed by more than the sergeant could track.

Bourne's burst toward the Loot's latest warning was careless if not exactly frightened. He couldn't see anything and it was less of a threat than the snipers now ranging on them anyway. . . and then, when the Molt leaped into his vision while poof guns chopped furiously, the sergeant realized that the warrior was hiding from *him*, from the jeep, and fatally ignoring the Oltenians.

"Fox Victor," Lieutenant Hawker ordered, "roll 'em," and the bolt that shattered a boulder into fist-sized chunks ringing on the jeep came from the angle opposite the previous sniper.

"Loot, it's—" the driver said, reaching for the throttle left-handed. A hilltop barely visible puffed white, shells answering a satellite report of sniping, but that alone wouldn't be enough to save their ass. The trucks and armored vehicles of the poof battalion were rumbling from cover; a couple autochthones fired at them, missing badly. Via! If they could miss the broad, flat sides of an

APC, how did they get so bloody close to the sheltered jeep?

"Right," said Hawker as he glanced at his display, still and yellow as it vainly awaited more teleporting autochthones, "let's ro—" and the last word was swept away by his driver's fierce acceleration out of the pocket of stone which had become an aiming point for the enemy far-off.

The Loot was on Central's push, now, calling for panzers and a salvo of artillery, while Bourne jinked back up and away and the air winked with ill-aimed sniper fire. The bastards didn't need to be good, just lucky, and the bolt that fried sod a millisecond before the jeep's skirts whisked across it was almost lucky enough. Central was answering calmly, dryly—*their* butts weren't on the line!—but that wasn't something the sergeant had time for anyway. They'd done their job, done it bleedin' *perfectly*, and now it looked like they'd be lucky to get out with a whole skin.

Well, that was what happened when you tried to support the poofs.

As the jeep topped the ridge a second time but in the opposite direction, a bolt snapped past it from the far side of the grain field and coincidentally a truck blew up in the swale behind. The detection team could not prevent the support battalion from taking casualties when it traversed open ground. What the Loot's warnings—and Profile's own submachinegun, its barrel reeking with sublimed iridium and the finish it

burned from the breastplate to which the
elastic sling held it—*had* accomplished was
to eliminate the warriors who knew the terrain so well that they could place themselves within millimeters of an opponent in
the gully. There were surely other Molts
with a nursery association with this area,
but the autochthones—thank the Lord!—
didn't have the organization to make a
massed response to a sudden threat.

They didn't need to, of course, since a
handful of warriors could stall a poof battalion, and weeks of long-range sniping
eroded the Slammers' strength to no human purpose.

The shock wave from a six-tube salvo
skewed the jeep even though the shells im-
pacted on the far side of the ridge and none
closer than a half kilometer to the course
down which Bourne was speeding to escape. The Loot was having the Slammers'
hogs blast clear the flanks of the Oltenian
battalion, crumbling rocks that would otherwise stand as beacons for Molts bouncing
closer to shoot down the axis of the swale.
The poofs should've done that themselves,
but their artillery control wasn't up to civi-
lized standards, and their gun crews minced
around in a funk fearing a Molt with a
satchel charge would teleport aboard an
ammo transporter. Which had happened of-
ten enough to give anybody the willies, come
to think.

The warrior who had snapped shots at
them earlier now had at least a pair of

supporters—one of whom was too bloody good. Bourne spun and braked his vehicle, fearing the brief pause during which their original downhill velocity was precisely balanced by thrust in the new direction. Lord help 'em if the Loot's request for heavy armor didn't come through the way the artillery support had done.

Though Colonel Hammer didn't leave his people hanging if there was any way around it.

The dark arch of the nursery tunnel into which Bourne headed the jeep was a perfect aiming point—hitting the center of a large target is easier than nailing a small one. The sergeant expected the entrance to be criss-crossed by the dazzling scatter of bolts squeezed off with all the care of which Molt marksmen were capable. He figured he had no hope save the autochthones' bad aim or bad timing. That there were no shots at all was as pleasant a surprise as he'd had since the night a whore tried to kill him with what turned out to be an empty gun. . . .

The tunnel was three meters wide and of simple design, an angled gallery rather than a labyrinth of interconnected chambers. The same purpose was achieved either way: the encouragement of the very young to teleport to points separated from them by solid barriers.

The same stone angles were just what the doctor ordered to block sniper fire—and as for anybody teleporting directly into the cave, they were cold meat as soon as the Loot's equipment picked them up.

"Safe!" the driver cried happily as he yanked the tiller left at the first 60 ⌐break, an edge of polished black granite that had not been dulled by rubbing shoulders as it would have been in a structure occupied by humans.

The warrior just around that corner pointed his Oltenian shotgun squarely at Profile's face.

Molt cave systems were not unlighted—the autochthones actually saw less well in dim conditions than humans did. The roof of this particular tunnel was painted with a strip of—imported—permanent fluorescent, powered by the same piezoelectrical forces which made the rock a beacon for teleporters. It gave off only a pale glow, however, inadequate for irises contracted by the sun outside, so it was in the jeep's front floods that the Molt's eyes gaped. His shadow against the gleaming stone was half again his real height, and the muzzle of the gun seemed broad as the tunnel.

Bourne fluffed his front fans to full screaming lift with his right hand.

He could have shot, have killed the warrior. Man and Molt were equally surprised, and Profile Bourne's reflexes were a safe bet against just about anybody's in those situations.

And then the charge of flechettes, triggered by the warrior's dying convulsion, would have shredded both men from the waist upward.

Lieutenant Hawker shouted as he fired through the hologram display which had failed to warn him. The Molt was already within the tunnel before the jeep entered, so there were no indicia of teleportation for the apparatus to detect. They should have thought of that, but the lightning-swift danger of the snipers outside had made the cave mouth a vision of safety like none since Mother's bosom.

That was the sort of instinctive error that got your ass killed, thought Hawker as his energy bolts scarred long ovals across the ceiling's fluorescence, ricocheting further down the tunnel in diminishing deadliness, and the Molt's shotgun blasted deafeningly into the uplifted skirt and plenum chamber of the jeep.

The screech of the jeep striking and skidding along the tunnel wall at a 45 ˡangle was actively painful to Profile Bourne. You didn't get to be as good a driver as he was without empathy for your vehicle, and the shriek of metal crumpling was to the sergeant comparable to skidding along a hard surface himself. But he'd done that too, thrown himself down on gravel when shots slammed overhead. You do what you gotta do; and anyway, the Molt's body when the jeep hit it provided a pretty fair lubricant.

Their forward velocity had been scrubbed off by the contact rather than killed by the vectored fans in normal fashion. Bourne chopped the throttle so that the braking thrust would not slam them back against the far wall. The jeep slumped down onto its skirts again, its back end ringing on the stone a moment before the whole vehicle came to rest.

The sergeant knew that he ought to be watching the next angle in case another warrior, prepared by the racketing death of the first, came around it shooting. Instead he closed his eyes for a moment and squeezed his hands together hard enough to make the thin flesh start up around the print of each fingertip. Lord, he'd almost pissed himself!

When he opened his eyes, he saw the tiny, glittering dimple in the steel flooring just between his boots. It was a flechette from the shotgun charge which had come within a millimeter of doing the warrior's business—or half of it—despite the fact that the roof of the plenum chamber was in the way.

Lord and martyrs!

"Lord and martyrs," muttered Lieutenant Hawker as he stepped out of the vehicle, and curst if he didn't seem as shook as the driver felt. "Don't worry, got it on aural," he added with a nod toward the hologram display and a left-handed tap on the earpiece of his commo helmet. The data relayed through the headset was less instantly assimilable than what his eyes could intake through the holograms—but there were only two directions from which an attack could come in the tunnel.

Anyhow, Profile figured that he needed to walk out the wobbles he could feel in his legs. Maybe the Loot was the same.

Before the sergeant left the jeep, he switched off the headlights which would otherwise be only a targeting aid to whatever Molts were around. The rock quivered when he stepped onto it, an explosion somewhere, and he cursed or prayed—who knew? —at the thought that another salvo of penetrators on the back slope of the ridge might bring the bloody ceiling down and accomplish what the autochthones had failed to do. What the hell, nobody'd ever told him he'd die in bed.

Bourne skidded at his first step. He glanced down, thinking that the stone beneath his boots must have a glass-smooth polish. It wasn't that—and the Molt with the shotgun deserved worse, it'd been too cursed quick for him.

The two Slammers used handsignals at the next angle, five meters further down the tunnel. They could as easily have subvocalized the plan on the intercom, but Profile's quick tap on his own breastplate and the Loot's grimace of acceptance was all that it took anyway.

Bourne put a single shot against the facing wall, the bolt crackling like shattered brick as it bounced from the stone. A fraction of a second later, the sergeant himself went in low.

The shot might have drawn a reflexive return from anyone poised to meet them

around the angle—but there was no one, no
adult at least: they were in the nursery itself, a circular room no wider than the tunnel from which it was offset to the left, just
around the second angle. There were eighteen reed and moss creches like the pips on
an instrument dial, and about half of them
still squirmed with infant Molts.

"S'all right, Loot!" Bourne shouted as he
rolled into a sitting position; and for all the
encouragement of his words, his ankles were
crossed in a firm shooter's rest beneath him.
"All clear, just the babes."

The flash of the shot was still a retinal
memory to Bourne as he glanced around
the chamber, blinking as if to wash the
spreading orange blot from the black surface of his eyeballs. The scars of the ricochet were marked by powdered stone at a
constant chest height along the circular wall.
No significant amount of energy would have
sprayed the infants, but they were mewing
fearfully anyway.

The Loot came in behind the muzzle of his
gun—you didn't leave decisions of safety to
somebody else, even Sergeant Bourne, not
in a place like this.

The Molt in the creche closest to Bourne
teleported neatly into his lap, scaring the
sergeant into a shout and a leap upward
that ended with the infant clamped hard
against him and the muzzle of Lieutenant
Hawker's submachinegun pointed dead on.
The little Molt squealed even more loudly.

"Let's get the cop outa here before the

locals put a flame gun down the tunnel and investigate later," Hawker said as he ported his weapon again, making no apology for aiming it toward a teleporting autochthone, even one in Bourne's lap. "Doesn't seem those Molts'll snipe at us here, what with the little ones in the line of fire."

"Right," said his driver, kneeling to put the infant back in its—his? her?—creche. There were air shafts cut from the chamber's ceiling to the surface twenty or thirty meters above. Through them now sank, competing with the powergun's ozone prickliness, not only the ash and blast residues of the shelling but the stomach-turning sweetness of diesel fumes. The vehicles of Fox Victor had gained the ridge and should by now be advancing down the reverse slope, covered by shellfire against likely sniper positions.

"No, here," said Lieutenant Hawker, reaching out with a left hand that seemed large enough to encircle the infant Molt which he took from Bourne. "You need to drive. We'll clear these out and then get a squad a' engineers to blow the place before it causes more trouble."

Little bastards looked less human than the adults, Bourne thought as he strode quickly back to the jeep, calm again with the tension of battle released by two sudden shocks within the tunnel. You could only be so scared, and then it all had to let go—or you cracked, and Profile Bourne didn't crack. The limbs of the young Molt were very small, more like those of a newt or lizard than of a human baby. Even as adults, the autochthones were shorter and more lightly built than most humans, but after a few years of age there was no difference in proportions.

"I suppose it's because the ones that crawl least do the other—teleport—better," said the Loot as he swung his big frame into the seat behind the displays, still holding the infant Molt. Via, maybe he *could* read his driver's mind; they'd worked through some curst tight places in the past few years. But it was a natural thing to wonder about if you saw the little ones up close like this, and the Loot was smart, he figured out that sort of thing.

Right now, the only thing Bourne really wanted to figure out was how to find a quiet spot where nobody would try to blow him away for a while. He'd given enough gray hairs to this buggering planet and its buggered poof army already!

There was a centimeter's clearance front and rear to turn the jeep in the tunnel's width, but the sergeant did not even consider backing after he tested his eyeball guestimate with a brief tap on the throttle as he twisted the tiller to bring the vehicle just short of alignment. Sure that it was going to make it, he goosed the fans again and brought the detection vehicle quickly around, converting spin into forward motion as the bow swung toward the first angle and the entrance. If it could be done with a ground effect vehicle, Profile would do it without thinking. Thinking wasn't his strong suit anyway.

The mercenaries' commo helmets brightened with message traffic as the jeep slid back down the initial leg of the gallery. Even a satellite relay squarely overhead didn't permit radio communication when one of the parties was deep beneath a slab of rock. Ground conduction signals were a way around that, but a bloody poor one when all your troops were mounted on air cushion vehicles.

Might be nice to have a portable tunnel to crawl into, now and again. When some poof circus needed to have its butt saved again, for instance.

The tunnel mouth gave them a wedge of vision onto the far slope, expanding as the jeep slid smoothly toward the opening where the driver grounded it. Sparkling chains of fire laced the air above the valley, bubbling and dancing at a dozen points from which snipers might have fired earlier.

" 'Bout bloody time!" the driver chortled, though support from the Slammers' big blowers had come amazingly quickly, given the care with which the expensive vehicles had to travel on this hostile terrain. "About *bloody* time!"

The tribarreled powerguns raking Molt hiding places with counterfire cycled so quickly that, like droplets of water in a fountain, the individual cyan flashes seemed to hang in the air instead of snapping light-quick across the valley. Afterimages strobed within Bourne's dark-adapted eyes: on a sunny day, the bursts of two-centimeter fire imposed their own definition of brightness. Snipers were still safe if they fired and fled instantly; but if a warrior paused to take a breath or better aim, heat sensors would lock on the glowing barrel of his powergun and crisscrossing automatic fire would glaze the landscape with his remains.

The support was combat cars, not the panzers—the tanks—that Bourne had been hoping for. This'd do, but it'd be nice to see a whole bloody hillside go up in a blue flash!

Lieutenant Hawker, holding the Molt, stepped from the jeep and the tunnel mouth, his gun hand raised as if he were hailing a cab in a liberty port. It wasn't the safest thing in the world, on this world, to do, what with autochthones still firing at the oncoming poof battalion and those locals themselves dangerously trigger-happy. Still, the Molts had proven unwilling to shoot toward their infants, and the poofs were more likely to pitch a bunker-buster into the tunnel mouth than they were to shoot at a Slammer in battledress, three times the size of any Molt who ever lived. Shrugging, Bourne butted the jeep a couple meters further forward to take a look himself.

The leading elements of Fox Victor had reformed on the ridge crest and were advancing raggedly abreast in a mounted assault line. There were thirty or so vehicles in the first wave, armored cars and APCs with a leavening of all-terrain trucks taking the place of armored vehicles destroyed earlier in the operation.

The nearest vehicle was one of the light trucks, this one equipped with a pintle-mounted machinegun instead of carrying a squad of engineers with blasting charges the way the mercenaries had hoped. The Loot signalled it over peremptorily while his tongue searched the controller of his commo helmet for the setting that would give him Fox Victor's intervehicle push—Hawker's previous radio contact had been with the battalion commander, pointless right now.

The truck, still fifty meters upslope, wavered in its course and did not immediately slow; its driver and vehicle commander, as well as the rest of the six Oltenians aboard, obviously had doubts about the idea of halting on open ground pocked with glassy evidence of Molt gunfire. They *did*, however, turn squarely toward the entrance of the nursery tunnel while the independent axles permitted the four wheels to bobble in nervous disorder over the irregularities of the terrain.

Most important, nobody took a shot at the two Slammers. Profile's tattooed gun-hand had swung his own weapon minutely to track the Oltenians; now he relaxed it somewhat. Allies, sure, but curse it, they only had to *look* like they were planning to fire and they were *gone*. . . .

The truck braked to a halt beside the notch in the slope which formed the tunnel entrance. Everybody aboard but the gunner leaped out with the spraddle-legged nervousness of dogs sniffing a stranger's territory. Dust, thrown up by treads that were woven in one piece with the wheel sidewalls from ferrichrome monocrystal, continued to drift downhill at a decreasing velocity.

"Who'n blazes're you!" demanded the close-coupled Oltenian captain who presumably commanded more than the crew of this one truck. Additional vehicles were rolling over the ridge, some of them heavy trucks; and, though the artillery was still crunching away at distant locations, fire from the combat cars in crest positions had slackened for lack of targets.

"We're the fairy godmothers who cleared the back slope for you," said Lieutenant Hawker, pumping his submachinegun toward, and by implication over, the ridge. "Now, I want you guys to go in there and bring out the rest of these, the babies."

He joggled the Molt infant that his left hand held to his breastplate; the little creature made a sound that seemed more like a purr than a complaint. "We get them out—there's maybe a dozen of 'em—and we can pack the tunnel with enough explosives to lift the top off the whole bloody ridge. Let's see'em use it to snipe from then!"

"You're crazy," said one of the poofs in a tone of genuine disbelief.

"We aren't doing any such thing," agreed his captain. "Just shove the explosives in on top—there'll be plenty room still."

"They're *babies*," Lieutenant Hawker said with the kind of edge that made Bourne smile, not a nice smile, as he checked the damage to the jeep's front skirt. "I didn't risk *my* hide to get a lot of lip from you boys when I saved your bacon. Now, hop!"

Lord knew what the chain of command was in a ratfuck like this situation, but it was a fair bet that the Loot couldn't by protocol give direct orders to a higher-ranking local. Hawker didn't wear rank tabs, nobody did when the Slammers were in a war zone; and no poof with a lick of sense was going to argue with somebody the size and demeanor of the mercenary officer. The captain's short-barreled shotgun twitched on his shoulder where he leaned it, finger within the trigger guard; but it was to the locals around him that he muttered, "Come on, then," as he strode within the lighted tunnel.

The skirt wasn't damaged badly enough to need replacement, but Profile hoped he'd have a chance soon to hose it down. The slime which glittered with Molt scales was already beginning to stink.

The Loot talked to Central, business that Bourne's mind tuned out as effectively as a switch on his helmet could've done. It was relaxing, standing in the sunlight and about as safe as you could be on this bloody planet: there were still the sounds of combat far away, but the jeep was now lost in the welter of other military vehicles, a needle among needles. The Molts were reeling, anyway, and the few hundred casualties this operation had cost them must be a very high proportion of the fighting strength of the theme involved.

Lieutenant Hawker was absently stroking the back of the infant with the muzzle of his submachinegun. In the minutes since the gun was last fired, the iridium had cooled to the point that the little Molt found its warmth pleasurable—or at least it seemed to: its eyes were closed, its breathing placid.

Echoes merged the shots in the tunnel into a single hungry roar.

"Loot, the—" the sergeant began as he knelt beside the skirt, the jeep between him and the gunfire, his own weapon pointed back down the tunnel. He meant a teleporting warrior, of course, but the detector holograms had been within the driver's field of vision and they were calm with no yellow-violet flicker of warning.

Besides, the squad of Oltenians was coming back down the gallery talking excitedly, two of them supporting a third who hopped on one leg and gripped the calf of the other with both hands. But that was only a ricochet; you couldn't blaze away in a confined space and not expect to eat some of your own metal.

Bourne stood up and let his sling clutch the submachinegun back against his breast-

plate now that he knew there was no problem after all. Wisps of smoke eddied from
the barrels of the shotguns, residues of flash
suppressant from the propellant charges. The
air in the nursery chamber must be hazy
with it. . . .

"What in the name of the *Lord* have you
done?" Lieutenant Hawker asked the captain in a tone that made Profile Bourne
realize that the trouble wasn't over yet after all.

"It's not your planet, renter," the captain
said. His face was spattered with what
Bourne decided was not his own blood. "You
don't capture Molts, you kill'em. Every
cursed chance you get."

"C'mon, somebody get me a medic," the
wounded man whined. "This hurts like the
very blazes!" The fabric of his trousers was
darkening around his squeezing hands, but
the damage didn't seem to Bourne anything
to lose sleep over.

"I told you . . . ," the Loot said in a breath-
less voice, as though he had been punched
hard in the pit of the stomach. The big
mercenary was holding himself very straight,
the infant against his breastplate in the crook
of one arm, towering over the captain and
the rest of the poofs, but he had the look
of a man being impaled.

A four-vehicle platoon of the combat cars
which had been firing in support now kicked
themselves sedately from the ridgeline and
proceeded down the slope. Dust bloomed
neatly around the margin of the plenum

chamber of each, trailing and spreading behind the big, dazzle-painted iridium forms. A powergun bolt hissed so high overhead that it could scarcely be said to be aimed at the cars. Over a dozen tribarrels replied in gorgeous fountains of light that merged kilometers away like strands being spun into a single thread.

"When you've had as many of your buddies zapped as we have," said a poof complacently to the Slammer who had earned his commission on Emporion when he, as ranking sergeant, had consolidated his company's position on the landing zone, "then you'll understand."

"Blood and martyrs, Loot!" said Profile Bourne as he squinted upslope. "That's Alpha Company—it's the White Mice and Colonel Hammer!"

"The only good Molt," said the captain, raising overhead the shotgun he held at the balance and eyeing the infant in Lieutenant Hawker's arms as if it were the nail he was about to hammer, "is a dead—"

And the Loot shot him through the bridge of the nose.

Bloody hell, thought Bourne as he sprayed first a poof whose gun was half-pointed, then the one who leaped toward the truck and the weapon mounted there. Had he reloaded after popping the round into the nursery chamber?

Bourne's first target was falling forward, tangled with the man the Loot had killed, and the second bounced from the side of the truck, the back of his uniform ablaze and all his muscles gone flaccid in mid-leap. A bolt that had gotten away from Bourne punched a divot of rock from the polished wall of the tunnel.

"Profile, that's *enough*!" the Loot screamed, but of course it wasn't.

The Oltenian with a bit of his own or a comrade's shot-charge in his calf was trying to unsling his shotgun. Everything in the sergeant's mind was as clear and perfect as gears meshing. The emotion that he felt, electric glee at the unity of the world centered on his gunsight, had no more effect on his functioning than would his fury if the submachinegun jammed. In that case, he would finish the job with the glowing iridium barrel as he had done twice in the past. . . .

The submachinegun functioned flawlessly. Bourne aimed low so that stray shots would clear the Loot, lunging to try to stop his subordinate; and as the trio of poofs doubled up, the second burst hacked into their spines.

This close, a firefight ended when nobody on one side or the other could pull a trigger anymore. The Loot knew that.

Combat cars whining like a pair of restive banshees slid to a dynamic halt to either side of the tunnel archway. The central tribarrel, directly behind the driver's hatch, and one wing gun of each bore on the detection team from close enough to piss if the wind were right. Despite the slope, the cars were not grounded; their drivers held them amazingly steady on thrust alone, their skirts hovering only millimeters above the rocky soil. The offside gunner from either car jumped out and walked around his vehicle with pistol drawn.

Lieutenant Hawker turned very slowly, raising his gunhand into the air. The infant Molt clutched in the crook of the other arm began to greet angrily, disturbed perhaps by the screams and the smell of men's bodies convulsing without conscious control.

A dead man's hand was thrashing at Profile's boot. He stepped back, noticing that the hair on the back of his left hand, clutching the foregrip of his weapon, had crinkled from the heat of the barrel.

"I want you both to unsnap the shoulder loop of your slings," said a voice, clear in Bourne's ears because it came through his commo helmet and not over the rush of the big fans supporting tonnes of combat car so close by.

There was no threat in the words, no emotion in the voice. The quartet of tribarrels was threat enough, and as for emotion—killing wasn't a matter of emotion for men like Profile Bourne and the troopers of Headquarters Company—the White Mice.

Lieutenant Hawker took a long look over his shoulder, past his sergeant and on to the Oltenian vehicles already disappearing over the far ridge—their path to Captain Henderson's infantry cleared by the risks the detection team had taken.

"Aye, aye, Colonel Hammer," Hawker said to the wing gunner in the right hand car, and he unsnapped his sling.

The hologram display began to flash between yellow and violet, warning that a Molt was about to appear.

"Nikki, I've been looking for you the past half hour," said General Radescu no louder than needful to be heard over the minuet that the orchestra had just struck up. His young aide nonetheless jumped as if goosed with a hot poker, bumping the urn that he had been peering around when Radescu came up behind him.

"Alexi, I—" Major Nikki Tzigara said, his face flushed a darker red than the scarlet of his jacket bodice. There were white highlights on Nikki's cheekbones and brow ridge, and the boy's collar looked too tight. "Well, it's a. . . ." He gestured toward the whirling tapestry of the dance. "I thought I ought to circulate, you know, since you were so busy with your uncle and *important* people."

The general blinked, taken aback by the unprovoked sharpness of his aide's tone. Nikki was counterattacking when there'd been no attack, Radescu had only said. . . . "Ah, yes, there's no doubt something over a hundred people here I really ought to talk to for one reason or another," he said, filing Tzigara's tone in memory but ignoring it in his response because he hadn't the faintest notion of its cause. Nikki really ought to wear full makeup the way Radescu himself had done ever since he understood the effectiveness of Uncle Grigor's poker face. Antonescu might not have become Chief Tribune, despite all his gifts, had he not learned to rule his expression. Heavy makeup was the edge which concealed the tiny hints from blood and muscle that only the most accomplished politician could wholly control.

And Man, as Aristotle had said, was the political animal.

"Rather like being on the edge of a rhododendron thicket," Radescu continued, looking away from his aide to give Nikki room to compose himself, for pity's sake. Uncle Grigor had worked his way a few meters along the margin of the circular hall so that he was almost hidden by a trio of slender women whose beehive coiffurs made them of a height with the tall Chief Tribune. "Very colorful, of course, but one can't *see* very much through it, can one?

"Which reminds me," he added rising onto the toes of his gilded boots despite the indignity of it—and finding that he could see no farther across the ballroom anyway, "do you know where the mercenary adjutant is, Major Steuben?"

"Why would I know *that*? He could be anywhere!"

Makeup wouldn't keep Nikki's voice from being shrill as a powersaw when the boy got excited, Alexander Radescu thought; and thought other things, about the way Nikki's medals were now disarranged, rowels and wreathes and dangling chains caught and skewed among themselves. The back of Radescu's neck was prickling, and the hairs along his arms. He *hoped* it wasn't hormonal, hoped that he had better control of his emotions than that. But dear Lord! He didn't care about Nikki's sexual orientation, but *surely* he had better sense than to get involved with a killer like Steuben . . . didn't he?

Ignoring the whispers in his mind, Radescu eyed the gorgeous show on the ballroom floor and said, "This is *why* the war's being fought, you know, Nikki? The—all the men having to wear uniforms, all the women having to be *seen* with men in uniforms." Except for Uncle Grigor, who distanced himself and his fellow Tribunes from the war by starkly traditional robes. Everyone else— of the aristocracy—gained from the war the chance to cavort in splendid uniforms, while Grigor Antonescu settled for real control of the Oltenian State. . . .

"They don't fight the war—*we* don't fight the war, even the ones of us with regular commissions," Radescu continued, turning to face Nikki again and beginning to straighten the boy's medals, a task that kept his eyes from Tzigara's face. "But it couldn't be fought without our support."

The whole surface of his skin was feeling cold as if the nerves themselves had been chilled, though sweat from the hot, swirling atmosphere still tingled at his joints and the small of his back. The two blue john urns stood tall and aloof just as they had done for centuries, but between them—

"I think maybe the Molts would have something to say about ending the war," said Nikki Tzigara. "I mean, you have your *opinions*, Alexi, but we can't make peace if—"

"*Nikki!*" Radescu shouted, for suddenly there was an ancient Molt warrior directly behind the young aide. The Molt's hide was the color of an algae-covered stone, soaked for decades in peat water, and his right brow horn was twisted in a way unique in the general's experience. The powergun he held was a full-sized weapon, too heavy for the Molt's stringy muscles to butt it against his shoulder the way one of the Slammers would have done.

The warrior had no need for technique at this range, of course.

Nikki had begun to turn, his mouth still open and saying "—the Molts don't—" when the warrior fired.

The first of his twenty-round magazine.

The human nearest to Ferad flew apart in an explosive cavitation effect, two-thirds of the mass of his thorax having been converted to super-hot steam by the bolt it absorbed from the powergun almost in contact with it. The remainder of the corpse was flung backward by the ball of vaporized matter which coated everything within a five-meter radius, Ferad and the urns included. The flailing yellow sleeves were still

attached to the rest of the body, but the
scarlet bodice which they had complemented
was scooped away to the iridescent white of
the membrane covering the inner surface of
the victim's spine and ribs.

The taller human in pearl and gold who
had been standing behind the first had
locked eyes with Ferad. He was an easy
target, fallen in a tangle of dancers and
only partially covered by the corpse of the
companion which had knocked him down
. . . but the theme elder's finger paused and
twitched only after the muzzle had swung
to cover a paunchy man in green and brown
and the silvery cape of an immature Molt.
Ferad did not need to be fussy about his
targets and could not afford the time it would
take to pick and choose anyway; but in the
case of the human screaming something on
the floor, he chose *not* to kill. Perhaps it was
the eyes, or something behind them.

The thickly-packed humans were trying
to surge away from the gun like the waves
of compression and rarefaction in a gas.
Only those closest to Ferad knew what was
happening—the bolts of energy hammered
the air and struck with the sound of bombs
underwater, but the sounds were not sharp
enough to identify them to untrained ears
in the noisy ballroom.

The orchestra on the far side of the hall
continued to play some incomprehensible
human melody, its members aware of the
disturbance but stolidly unwilling to em-

phasize it by falling silent. Ferad shot into fleeing backs trapped by the press.

Sopasian had suggested a bomb in his calm voice that hid a cancer of emotions beneath—envy and scorn, but mostly envy. It was a reasonable suggestion, since a bomb would have killed more than the powergun could in targets as soft and frequent as these. The surface-absorbed two-centimeter bolts had no penetration, though the amount of energy they released could separate limbs from bodies—and the medals on the first victim's chest were still raining down all across the hall.

But Sopasian missed the point of this attack. They couldn't kill *all* the humans, not even if every Molt on the planet had Ferad's skill or Sopasian's. What Ferad brought to the gala was a personal death, not a sudden blast followed by dust and the screams of the injured. This attack went on and on in the safest place in the world, the victims would have said a moment before.

Cyan light spurted from a gunbarrel so hot that the scales on Ferad's left arm were lifting to trap a blanket of insulating air. The polished wood and stones inlaid into the groined ceiling reflected the shots as they echoed with the screams.

Ferad's peripheral vision was better than that of a human, an adaptation crucial to a Molt teleporting into the confusion of a battle or hunt who had to receive a great deal of data about his immediate surroundings in the first instant. The flash of white drew

Ferad to the left, the powergun's barrel shimmering its own arc through the air before him.

None of them were armed. The ballroom was like a nursery tunnel, females and infants and all of them helpless as the veriest newborn—but it had to be done.

One of the Tribunes stood in glistening white, facing Ferad though the three shrieking females in between were scrabbling away. The theme elder fired, clearing a path for his next bolt by taking a female at the point where her bare skin met the ruffles at the base of her spine. Her corpse scissored backwards, its upper portion scarcely connected to the splaying legs, and the other two females—now in gowns only half pastel—were thrust from either side to close the gap.

The trio had been caught not by the general confusion but by the grip of the Tribune's arms, protective coloration and, in the event, a shield.

Ferad, wishing for the first time in decades that he had the muscles of a young adult, squeezed off another bolt that parted the white-gowned male from his females, only one of them screaming now and the gown covered with the residues from the flash-heated steam. Had Ferad been younger, he could have leaped on the Tribune, thrusting the heavy powergun against his target and finishing in an instant the business it had taken two shots to prepare. But a young, athletic warrior could never have gotten here, and the Tribune was now sprawled on the floor, his back against the wainscoting and only his palms and spread fingers between his face and the white iridium disk of the powergun muzzle.

The Molt's gun did not fire. Ferad had already spent the last round in his magazine.

The theme leader dropped his useless weapon on the floor, where wood and wax crackled away from the barrel. The hours he had spent in locating the urns here in Belvedere, in gripping them with his mind, were gone from memory. The antechamber of the tunnel system which had been the center of his existence for a hundred and forty years was a dazzling beacon though a thousand kilometers separated it from the theme elder.

For the instant only.

The ballroom and the carnage almost as dreadful to Ferad as to the humans surviving trembled for a moment, superimposed on the stone and lamps and shouting warriors of the nursery cave.

Two humans made a final impression on him: the male knocked down by the first bolt, now trying to rise; and another in the khaki of the mercenaries, so much more dangerous than the forces of the settlers themselves. This mercenary must have wedged his way through a countercurrent of bodies in screaming panic. His hand was raised, a pistol in it, and there was a blue-green flash from the muzzle that Ferad did not quite see.

In his millisecond of limbo, the theme elder wondered what success his rival Sopasian was having.

"There's a Molt—" said Lieutenant Hawker as the tone in his left earpiece gave him a distance and vector, *bloody* close, but the target designation was figured from the jeep and not where he himself stood a couple paces away.

The trooper sent to collect Hawker's gun snatched the weapon away, nervous to be reaching into the crossed cones of fire of the tribarrels to either flank. "*Drop* it, he said, cophead!" the headquarters trooper snarled, just as somebody shouted to Hammer from the other combat car, "Sir, we've got'n incoming!"

For operations against the Molts, all the Slammers' line armor—the tanks and combat cars—had been fitted with ionization detectors similar to those on the team's jeep. For reasons of space and the need for training to operate more sophisticated gear, however, the detectors which equipped the big blowers were relatively rudimentary. The troops of A Company, Hammer's personal guard, were picked as much for technical skills as they were for ruthlessness and lethality—qualities which were not in short supply in the line companies either. The man calling, "Thirty-five left, eight meters— Colonel, he's coming right beside your car!" was getting more precision from his hardware than Hawker would have thought possible.

The big lieutenant stepped over the body of the Oltenian officer, setting the limbs a-twitch again when the sole of his boot brushed a thigh. The trooper with Hawker's gun holstered his own pistol so that he could level the automatic weapon as he turned toward Hammer and the combat car.

"Loot!" called Profile Bourne, familiar enough with Hawker to know that the lieutenant's disquiet was not simply because a warrior was about to attack. The White Mice could handle *that*, the Lord knew, they weren't poofs who needed a picture to figure which end to piss with.

The trooper who had advanced to take Bourne's gun as his companion did Hawker's was now poised between the sergeant and Hammer, impaled on the horns of a dilemma. Bourne held his weapon muzzle-high, the barrel vertical and threatening to no one who had not seen how quickly he moved. The left hand, however, was thrust out like a traffic warden's—a barrier in defiance of the pistol which the man from A Company still pointed.

The fellow in the combat car had the vector right and the distance, but there was *something* wrong with what he'd said.

Hawker dropped into his seat in the jeep and laid the infant Molt beside him as Hammer's own combat car slid a few meters upslope, swinging so that the two manned guns still covered the expected target with-

out threatening the dismounted troops besides. The flashing holograms of Hawker's
display shifted simultaneously with a sub-
tlety that no tone signal could have conveyed.

"Drop it or you're *dead*, trooper!" the man
in front of Profile shouted, but even as he
spoke, his pistol and his eyes were shifting
to the danger behind him, the tribarrels
that might be aligned with his spine.

"Colonel, it's right under you!" shouted
the man on the combat car's detector.

Hammer's great car spurted sideways like
fluff blown from a seed pod and the digits
on Hawker's display shifted as quickly.

"Colonel!" the lieutenant bellowed, trying
to make himself heard over the fans of the
big blowers roaring in the machine equivalent of muscles bunched for flight. His unit
link was to Henderson's infantry company,
and tonguing Central wouldn't have given
him the direct line to Hammer that he
needed now.

"It's *in* your car!" Hawker shouted as he
leaped out of the jeep, snatching for the
submachinegun that had been taken from
him.

The Molt was so old that wrinkles showed
like dark striping on his face as the warrior
appeared in the fighting compartment between Hammer and the other gunner, both
of them craning their necks to scan the rocky
ground beside the car. If their body hairs
felt the sudden shift in electrostatic balance
as the autochthone appeared behind them,

that warning was buried in the subconscious of veterans faced with a known threat.

"Contact!" the A Company detection specialist shouted into the instruments on which his attention was focused, and his companion at the wing tribarrel triggered a shot into the empty soil by reflex. The Molt warrior's wiry arms held, raised, a blade of glittering blue steel; the junction between Hammer's helmet and body armor was bared as the Colonel stretched to find a target before him.

Hawker caught his gun, but the trooper holding it wouldn't have been in the White Mice if he were soft. He held the weapon with one hand and rabbit-punched the lieutenant with the other, an instinctive, pointless act since Hawker was wearing body armor; but the trooper *held* the gun as the Molt's sword swung downward, unseen by anyone but Hawker—

—and Sergeant Bourne. The Molt swordblade was a sandwich of malleable iron welded to either side of a core of high carbon steel, quick-quenched to a rich blue after forging. That razor sharp steel and the black iron which gave the blade resilience glowed momentarily cyan in reflecting the bolt flicking past them, brighter for that instant than the sun.

Hammer flattened behind the iridium bulkhead, his commo helmet howling with static induced by the bolt which had bubbled the plastic surface.

The trooper who should have disarmed

Profile Bourne was one of those whose eyes were drawn by the bolt to the warrior in the combat car. The autochthone's sword sparked on the lip of the fighting compartment and bounced out. The Molt himself twisted. His face had two eyesockets but only one eye, and the wrinkles were bulged from his features when his head absorbed the energy of the single shot.

The driver of Hammer's car had no view of the scene behind him. He drew a pistol and presented it awkwardly through his hatch, trying to aim at Bourne while still holding the car steady with one hand.

"No!" cried the trooper who had tried to disarm Bourne, windmilling his arms as he made sure he was between the sergeant and the guns threatening him.

Lieutenant Hawker and the trooper with whom he struggled now separated cautiously, Hawker releasing the submachine-gun and the man from A Company licking the scraped knuckles of his left hand. There was a pop in the lieutenant's helmet, static from a message he did not himself receive, and the sound level dropped abruptly as both combat cars grounded and cut their fans.

The Molt's sword had stuck point first in the soil. It rang there, a nervous keening that complemented the cries of the infant Molt, dumped without ceremony on the driver's seat when Hawker had gotten into the jeep. The big lieutenant walked back toward his vehicle and lifted the Molt with both hands to hide the fact that they were both trembling.

Colonel Alois Hammer reappeared, standing up with deliberation rather than caution. He held something in his left hand which he looked at, then flipped like a coin to fall spinning onto the ground near the sword. It was the sapphire condensing plate from a combat car's navigation display, a thick fifty-millimeter disk whose internal cross-hatching made it a spot of fluid brilliance in the sunlight.

"He was holding that," said the Colonel, pointing to the disk with the pistol in his right hand. He fired, igniting grass and fusing a patch of soil without quite hitting his target. "I didn't know they could do that," and the condensing plate shattered like a bomb, the scored lines providing a myriad fracture sites.

Hammer fired twice more into the mass of glittering particles that carpeted the ground.

"Now, kid, it could be a lot worse," muttered Enzo Hawker as he patted the shivering infant's back and wondered if that were true for the little Molt, for any of them. The sounds of distant battle were like hogs rooting among the mast, shellfire and diesels and the mighty soughing of the Slammers' ground-effect vehicles.

"Hey!" called Sergeant Bourne, holding his weapon vertical again and aloft at the length of its sling. "Still want *this*, Colonel?" His voice was high and hectoring, a reaction to having made a shot that he would never have dared attempt had he paused to think about what he was doing. A millimeter, two millimeters to the right, and the bolt would have expended itself on Hammer's face an instant before the sword finished the business.

"Disarm the man," Hammer ordered in a voice as far away as the breeze moving wispy clouds in the high stratosphere.

"Sure, all right," said Profile, and perhaps only Hawker realized that the brittle edge in his voice was terror and not a threat. The sergeant's left hand fumbled with the sling catch while his right hand held clear the submachinegun, though its barrel was by now cool enough to touch.

"Only one thing—" the enlisted man added.

"Profile, don't—" said Hawker, aware that three tribarrels were again aimed at his partner's chest.

"Only you better keep the Loot on his console," Bourne completed as he flung his weapon to the ground. "Until you hunt up somebody else who knows how to use the bloody gear, at least."

Three pistol bolts struck within a palm's scope, the first shattering the urn of blue john. The other two sparkled among the shivered fragments, reducing some of the flurospar to its ionized constituents. Other chips now ranged in color from gray to brilliant amethyst, depending on how close they had been to the momentary heat. Larger chunks, the upper third of the urn, cascaded over the gun the Molt had dropped and, dropping it, disappeared.

Ozone and nascent fluorine battled for ascendancy between themselves, but neither could prevail over the stench of death.

Someone had kicked Alexander Radescu in the temple as he flopped backwards to the floor. His memory of the past thirty seconds was a kaleidoscope rather than a connected series, but he was not sure that the blow had anything to do with his disorganization. The gun muzzle flickering like a strobe light while the white glow of the iridium remained as a steady portent of further death. . . .

Radescu's right hand lay across his gilded cap, so he could don it again without looking down. He stumbled on his first step toward Chief Tribune Antonescu, but he knew what was binding his right foot and knew also that he dared not actually view it.

Lifting his foot very carefully to clear what was no longer Nikki or anything human, the young general murmured, "I'm going to be fine if I don't think about it. I just don't want to think about it, that's all." His tone would have been suitable had he been refusing a glass of sherry or commenting on the hang of a uniform. He couldn't keep from remembering and imagining concrete realities, of course, but by acting very carefully he could keep them from being realities of *his* experience.

The screams had not stopped when the Molt warrior disappeared. Most of the crowd still did not know what had happened. Would the *Lord* that Alexander Radescu were as ignorant!

"I was afraid you'd been shot, my boy," said Grigor Antonescu, politic even at such a juncture, "by that—" he nodded toward the spilled crystals of blue john, cubic and octohedral, and the gun they lay across like a stone counterpane "—or the other."

Staring over his shoulder, Radescu saw Major Steuben picking his way toward them with a set expression and quick glances all around him, ready now for any target which presented itself. Hammer's bodyguard had been marginally too late for revenge, and not even *his* reflexes would have been quick enough to save Nikki. None of the rest mattered to Radescu, not the dead or the maimed, those catatonic with fear or the ones still screaming their throats raw.

But that was over, and the past could not be allowed to impede what the future required.

"This can't go on, Uncle Grigor," Radescu said with a twist of his neck, a dismissing gesture.

The Chief Tribune, whose face and robes were now as much red as white, said, "Security, you mean, Alexi? Yes, we should have had real guards, shouldn't we? Perhaps Hammer's men. . . ."

In his uncle's reasonable voice, Radescu heard himself—a mind that should have been in shock, but which had a core too tough to permit that in a crisis.

Members of the Honor Guard were running about, brilliant in their scarlet uniforms and almost as useless in a firefight as the unarmed militia 'officers' attending the ball. They were waving chrome and rhodium plated pistols as they spilled in through the doors at which they'd been posted to bar the uninvited. If they weren't lucky, there'd be more shots, more casualties. . . .

"Not security, not here at least," said General Radescu, gesturing curtly at one of the Honor Guards gagging at a tangle of bodies. "It's the war itself that has to be changed."

"We can't do that," Antonescu replied bitterly, "without changing the army."

"Changing its command, Uncle Grigor," said Alexander Radescu as his mind shuddered between Nikki's flailing body and the gunbarrel of the aged Molt. "Yes, that's exactly what we have to do first."

The young general flicked at spots on his jacket front, but he stopped when he saw they were smearing further across the pearl fabric.

"I need two gunmen who won't argue about orders," said Radescu to Colonel Hammer, standing where a granite pillar had been blasted to glittering gravel to prevent Molt warriors from materializing on top of them. The Oltenian general spoke loudly to be heard over the pervasive intake rush of the four command vehicles maneuvering themselves back to back to form the Field Operations Center. The verdigrised black head and cape of an ancient Molt were mounted on a stake welded to the bow of one of the cars.

The aide standing with Hammer smiled, but the mercenary colonel himself looked at Radescu with an expression soured both by the overall situation and specifically by the appearance of Alexander Radescu: young, dressed in a uniform whose gold and pearl fabrics were showing signs of blowing grit only minutes after the general disembarked from his aircraft—and full facial makeup, including lip tint and a butterfly-shaped beauty patch on his right cheekbone.

"There's a whole Oltenian army out there," said Hammer bitterly, waving in the direction of the local forces setting up in the near distance. "Maybe you can find two who know which end of a gun the bang comes out of. Maybe you can even find a couple willing to get off their butts and *move*. Curst if I've been able to find 'em, though."

Radescu had worn his reviewing uniform for its effect on the Oltenian command staff, but it was having the opposite result on the mercenaries. "The Tribunes are aware of that," he said with no outward sign of his anger at this stocky, worn, *deadly* man. Grime and battledress did not lower Hammer in the Oltenian's opinion, but the mercenary's deliberate sneering *coarseness* marked him as incurably common. "That's why they've sent me to the field: to take over and get the army moving again. My uncle—" he added, by no means inconsequently "—is Chief Tribune."

The Oltenian general reached into a breast pocket for his identification—a message tube which would project a hologram of Chief Tribune Antonescu with his arm around his nephew, announcing the appointment 'to all members of the armed forces of Oltenia and allied troops.' Hammer's aide forestalled him, however, by saying, "This is General Radescu, sir."

"Sure, I haven't forgotten," Colonel Hammer remarked with an even deeper scowl, "but he's not what *I* had in mind when I heard they were going to send somebody out to take charge."

He looked from his aide to Radescu and continued, "Oh, don't look so surprised, General. That's part of what you hired us for, wasn't it? Better communications and detection gear than you could supply on-planet?"

Radescu's tongue touched his vermilion lips and he said, "Yes, of course, Colonel," though it was not 'of course' and he was quite certain that Chief Tribune Antonescu would have been even more shocked at the way these outsiders had penetrated the inner councils of the State. Radescu had flown to the front without even an aide to accompany him because of the complete secrecy needed for the success of his mission. Though what the mercenaries knew of his plan was not important ... so long as they had not communicated what they knew to the Oltenian planetary forces.

Which brought the young general back to the real point at issue. "This time the help I need involves another part of the reason we hired you, though."

"General," said Hammer coldly, "I've lost equipment and I've lost men because local forces didn't support my troops when they advanced. We're going to carry out basic contract commitments from here on ... but I don't do any favors for Oltenian tarts. No, I don't have two men to spare."

"There's Hawker and Bourne," said the aide unexpectedly. He gave Radescu a sardonic smile as he continued. "Might be a way out of more problems than one."

A trio of Slammers were striding toward their leader from the assembled Operations Center, two men and a woman who looked too frail for her body armor and the equipment strapped over it. Hammer ignored them for the moment and said to his aide, "Look, Pritchard, we can't afford to lose our bond over something like this."

"Look, I have full—" Radescu interjected.

"We're turning them over to the local authority for processing," said Pritchard, as little impressed with the general in gold and pearl as his colonel was. "Via, Colonel, you don't want to call out a firing party for our own men, not for something like that."

Hammer nodded to the three officers who had halted a respectful two paces from him; then, to Radescu, he said as grimly as before, "General, I'm turning over to you Lieutenant Hawker and Sergeant-Commander Bourne, who have been sentenced to death for the murder of six members of the allied local forces. Whatever action you take regarding them will be regarded as appropriate."

He turned his head from Radescu to the waiting trio. "Captain?" he said on a note of query.

"Hammer to Radescu," the woman said with a nod. "It's being transmitted to the Bonding Authority representative."

"All right, General Radescu," Hammer continued, "you'll find the men in the adjutant's charge, Car four-five-niner. I wish you well of them. They were good men before they got involved with what passes for an army here on Oltenia."

Hammer and his aide both faced toward the trio of other mercenaries as if Radescu had already left them.

"But—" the Oltenian general asked, as unprepared for this development as for the scorn with which the offer was made. "*Why* did they, did they commit these murders?"

Hammer was deep in conversation with one of the other officers, but Pritchard glanced back over his shoulder at Radescu and said, "Why don't you ask *them*, General?" He smiled again without warmth as he turned his head and his attention again.

General Alexander Radescu pursed his lips, but he sucked back the comment he had started to make and quenched even the anger that had spawned it. He had made a request, and it had been granted. He was in no position to object that certain conventions had been ignored by the mercenaries.

"Thank you for your cooperation, Colonel," he said to the commo helmets bent away from him above backs clamshelled in porcelain armor. The woman, the communications officer, cocked an eye at the general only briefly. "I assure you that from here on you will have no call to complain about the cooperation the Oltenian forces offer you."

He strode away briskly, looking for a vehicle with skirt number 459. The set of his jaw was reflected alternately in the gilded toe-caps of his shoes.

"One moment, sir," said a graying man who might have been the adjutant—none of the Slammers seemed to wear rank insignia in the field, and officers wore the same uniforms as enlisted men.

Another of the mercenaries had, without being asked, walked to a room-sized goods container and rapped on the bars closing the front of it. "Profile!" he called. "Lieutenant Hawker! He's here to pick you guys up."

"We were informed, of course, sir," said the probable adjutant who looked the Oltenian up and down with an inward smile which was obvious despite its lack of physical manifestations. "Did you get lost in the encampment?"

"Something like that," said Radescu bitterly. "Perhaps you could find a vehicle to carry me and, and my new aides, to, ah, my headquarters?"

"We'll see about that, of course, sir," said the graying man, and the smile did tug a corner of his mouth.

The Slammers had sprayed the area of their intended base camp with herbicide. Whatever they used collapsed the cell walls of all indigenous vegetation almost completely so that in the lower, wetter areas, the sludge of dissolved plant residue was as much as knee deep. That didn't seem to bother the mercenaries, all of whom rode if they had more than twenty meters to traverse—but it had created a pattern of swamps for Radescu which he finally crossed despite its effect on his uniform. He would look a *buffoon* when he called the command staff together!

Then he relaxed. He dared not hold the meeting without two gunmen behind him, and if the mercenaries' public scorn were the price of those gunmen—so be it. Alexander Radescu had thought a long time before he requested this duty from his uncle. He was not going to second-guess himself now.

"Got your gear over here, Profile," said the mercenary who had opened the crude cell and stepped inside the similar—unbarred—unit beside it. He came out again, carrying a heavy suit of body armor on either arm.

The men who had just been freed took their equipment, eying Radescu. The young general stared back at them, expecting the sneering dismissal he had received from other mercenaries. What he got instead was an appraisal that went beneath the muck and his uniform, went deeper into Alexander Radescu than an outsider had ever gone before.

It was insufferable presumption on the part of these hirelings.

Lieutenant Hawker was a large, soft-looking man. There were no sharp angles to his face or frame, and his torso would have been egg-shaped in garments which fit closer than the floppy Slammers battledress. He swung the porcelain clamshell armor around himself unaided, however, an action that demonstrated exceptional strength and timing.

His eyes were blue, and the look in them made Radescu wonder how many of the six Oltenians Hawker had killed himself.

Profile, presumably Sergeant Bourne, was no taller than Colonel Hammer and was built along the lines of Radescu's own whippy thinness rather than being stocky like the mercenary commander. His bold smile displayed his upper incisors with the bluish tinge characteristic of tooth buds grown *in vitro*.

There was a scar on the sergeant's throat above his right temple, a bald patch of keloid that he had tried to train his remaining hair to cover, and a streak of fluorescent orange wrapping his bare right forearm. Radescu thought the last was a third scar until he saw that it terminated in a dragon's head laid into the skin of Bourne's palm, a hideous and hideously obtrusive decoration. . .and a sign of scarring as well, though not in the physical sense.

Bourne locked shut his body armor and said, "Well, this is the lot of it, Major?" to the graying adjutant.

That mercenary officer grimaced, but he said, "Give them their guns, Luckens."

The Slammer who had brought the armor had already ducked back from the storage container with a submachinegun in either hand and ammunition satchels in the crooks of both elbows, grinning almost as broadly as Sergeant Bourne.

The lieutenant who had just been freed had no expression at all on his face as he started to load his own weapon. His left hand slid a fresh magazine into the handgrip of his powergun, a tube containing not only the disks which would liberate bolts of energy but the liquid nitrogen which worked the action and cooled the chamber between shots. As his hands moved, Hawker's eyes watched the Oltenian general.

"I'll need to brief you men in private," Radescu said, managing to override the unexpected catch in his throat. "I'm General Radescu, and the two of you are assigned at my discretion." How private the briefing could be when Hammer listened to discussions in the Tribunal Palace was an open question . . . but again, it didn't matter what the *mercenary* command knew.

"Major Stanlas," said Hawker to the adjutant, only now rotating his face from the Oltenian, "do you see any problem with me borrowing back my jeep for the, ah, duration of the assignment?"

"General," said the adjutant, thumbing a switch in the oral notepad he pointed toward Radescu, "do you accept on behalf of your government the loan of a jeep with detection gear in it?" That gave Hammer somebody to bill if something went wrong. . . and they must already have a record of the level to which the Tribunes had authorized Radescu's authorization.

"Yes, yes, of course," the general snapped, noticing that Bourne had anticipated the question and answer by striding toward a saucer-shaped air cushion vehicle. It had been designed to hold four people, but this one had seats for only two because the back was filled with electronics modules.

"You may not be real comfortable riding on the hardware that way," Hawker said, "but it beats having a Molt pop out of the air behind you." He turned his head slowly, taking in the arc of nondescript landscape he could not have seen through the barred front of his cell. "Not," he added, "that we'll see action around here."

Radescu gave the big mercenary a brief, tight smile. "You don't think so, Lieutenant? I wouldn't have come to Colonel Hammer for someone to drive me and—" he appraised Hawker in a different fashion, then made a moue which flapped the wings of his beauty patch before he concluded "—bring me tea at night."

Hawker spat on the ground. He would probably have dropped the conversation even without Sergeant Bourne spinning the jeep to an abrupt halt between the two officers and calling cheerfully, "Hop in, everybody." His submachinegun was now carried across his chest on an inertia-locked sling which gave him access to the weapon the instant he took his right hand from the tiller by which he now guided the jeep.

The general settled himself, finding that the modules had been arranged as the back and sides of a rough armchair, with room enough for his hips in the upper cavity. The handles for carrying the modules made excellent grips for Radescu; but there was no cushion, only slick, hard composite, and he hoped Bourne would not play the sort of game with the outsider which he in fact expected.

"Get us a short distance beyond this position and stop," the Oltenian said, bracing himself for an ejection-seat start. He thought of ordering Hawker to trade places with him, but he was sure such a demand would also turn into an embarrassment for him. "I'll brief you there."

Instead of a jackrabbit start, the mercenary sergeant powered up the jeep in an acceleration curve so smooth that only the airstream was a problem to Radescu on his perch. The Oltenian snatched off his glistening, metalized cap and held it against his lap as he leaned forward into the wind.

Bourne was driving fast, but with an economy of movement on the tiller and such skill that the attitude of the jeep did not change even when it shot up the sloping inner face of the berm around the firebase and sailed above the steep outer contour in momentary free flight. He wasn't trying to dump Radescu off the back: Bourne took too much pride in his skill to drive badly as a joke.

"Colonel won't like the way you're speeding in his firebase," Lieutenant Hawker said mildly to the sergeant.

"What's he going to do?" Bourne demanded. "Sentence me to death?" But he slacked off the trigger throttle built into the grip of the tiller.

Between the encampments, Oltenian and mercenary, was a wooded ridge high enough to block shots fired from either position toward targets in the no man's land between. Radescu had understood the forces were integrated, but obviously the situation in the field had changed in a fashion which had not yet been reported to the Tribunes in Belvedere. Bourne threaded his way into a copse of broad-leafed trees on the ridge while Radescu held his seat firmly, aware that even at their present reduced speed he would be shot over the front of the vehicle if the driver clipped one of the boles around which he maneuvered so blithely.

It was without incident, however, that Bourne set the jeep down out of direct sight of either encampment. He turned and looked up at Radescu with a sardonic grin; and Hawker, still-faced, looked as well.

Radescu laughed harshly. "I was wondering," he said to the surprised expressions of the mercenaries, "whether I'm speaking to you from the height of a throne—or of a cross." He swung himself to the ground, a trifle awkwardly because the padding in his uniform trousers to exaggerate his buttocks had not been sufficient to prevent the hard ride from cutting blood circulation to his legs.

"That's fitting, in a way," the Oltenian said to the Slammers watching as his hands massaged his thighs, a thumb and forefinger still gripping the gilded brim of his hat, "because the Tribunes have granted me power of life and death over all members of the armed forces of the State—but they haven't taught me how to bring the dead to life."

Without speaking Lieutenant Hawker slipped from his own seat and stood with one heel back against the ground-effect mantle of the jeep. Bourne shifted only very slightly so that he faced Radescu directly; the head of the dragon on his palm rested on the grip of his submachinegun.

"I have been given *full* authority to take command and get the offensive against the

Molts on track again," Radescu continued, "and I have the responsibility as well as authority to deal with the situation. But the present command staff is going to resent me, gentlemen, and I do not believe I can expect to do my job unless I go into my initial meeting with you present."

"You think," said Hawker as something small and nervous shrilled down at the men from a treetop, "that the present officers will arrest you if we aren't there to protect you."

"There's two of us, General," added Profile Bourne whose index finger traced the trigger guard of his weapon, "and there's three divisions over there." He thumbed toward the encampment. "We can't handle that, friend. No matter how much we might like to."

"The army command, and the commander and chief of staff of each division will be present," said General Radescu, stretching his arms out behind his back because when the muscles were under tension they could not tremble visibly. "And they won't do anything overt, no, it's not what they'll say—"

The young Oltenian straightened abruptly, glaring at the Slammers. "But I don't *care* what they say, gentlemen, I didn't come here to preside over an army sinking into a morass of lethargy and failure. I will remove any officer who seems likely to give only lip service to my commands.

"And—" he paused, for effect but also because the next words proved unexpectedly hard to get out his throat "—and if I give the signal, gentlemen, I expect you to kill everyone else in the room without question or hesitation. I will give the signal—" he twirled the band of his hat on his index finger "—by dropping my hat."

Glittering like a fairy crown in a shaft of sunlight, Radescu's hat spun to the forest floor. The only sound in the copse for the next ten seconds was the shrieking of the animal in the foliage above them.

"Via," said Sergeant Bourne, in a voice too soft for its precise emotional loading to be certain.

"Sir," said Lieutenant Hawker, shifting his weight from the jeep so that both feet rested firmly on the ground, "does Colonel Hammer know what you intend? For us?"

Radescu nodded crisply, feeling much lighter now that he had stated what he had not, as it turned out, clearly articulated even in his own mind. He felt as though he were listening to the conversation from a vantage point outside his own body. "I have told no one of my specific plans," his mouth said, "not even Chief Tribune Antonescu, my uncle. But I believe Colonel Hammer did—would not be surprised by anything that happened. The point that caused him to grant my request was your, your special status, gentlemen."

"Via," Sergeant Bourne repeated.

Hawker walked over to the gilded cap and picked it up with his left hand, the hand which did not hold a submachinegun.

"Here, sir," he said as he handed the hat back to General Radescu. "You may be needing it soon."

"Hoo, *Lordy*!" said Sergeant Bourne to the captain who nervously ushered them into the staff room to wait. "Where's the girls, good son?" He pinched the Oltenian's cheek, greatly to the man's embarrassment. "Not that you're not cute yourself, dearie."

"This the way you—gentlemen—normally operate in the field?" Hawker asked as his palm caressed the smooth surface of a nymph in a wall fountain.

"Well, the water's recycled, of course," Radescu said in mild surprise as he considered the matter for the first time.

He looked around the big room, the tapestries—reproductions, of course—and ornately carven furniture, the statues in the wall niches set off by foliage and rivulets. The Slammers lieutenant looked as incongruous here, wearing his scarred armor and unadorned weapon, as a bear would in a cathedral: but it was Hawker, not the fittings, which struck Radescu as out of place. "This does no harm, Lieutenant, beyond adding a little to our transport requirements. A modicum of comfort during staff meetings doesn't prevent officers from performing in a responsible and, and courageous manner in action."

He was wondering whether there would be enough time to requisition an orderly to clean the muck from his boots. On balance, that was probably a bad idea since the pearl trousers were irredeemably ruined. Better to leave the ensemble as it was for the moment rather than to increase its absurdity. . . .

"Just how *do* you expect to get bloody Oltenian officers to act courageously, General-sir?" Bourne asked in a tone much more soberly questioning than the sarcasm of the words suggested. The three men were alone in the room now that the poof captain had banged the door nervously behind him, and Bourne watched Radescu over the decorated palm of his right hand.

"I'm going to lead from the front, Sergeant Bourne," the young general said quietly, noticing that the expression on the mercenary's face was very similar to that on the dead Molt staked to the bow of Hammer's command vehicle.

Radescu had seen no trophies of that sort in their drive through the State encampment. That could be a matter of taste—but equally, it might mean that Oltenian forces had failed to kill any of the aliens.

Of the autochthones. Oltenia was, after all, the Molts' world alone until the human settlement three centuries before.

"I . . . ," said Radescu, choosing to speak aloud on a subject different from that on which his mind would whisper to him if his mouth remained silent. "Ah. . . . Tell me, if you will, how the—charges came to be leveled against you, the two of you."

"Why we blew away those heroes of the Oltenian state, Lieutenant," restated Bourne with a bitter smile.

The big Slammers lieutenant sat down on the coping of the fountain. The seat of his trousers must have been in the water, but he did not appear to notice. "Sure, General," he said in the accentless Oltenia-Rumanian which all the Slammers had been sleep-taught when their colonel took the present contract. "I'll tell you about what happened."

Hawker closed his eyes and rubbed his brow with the knuckles of his right hand. In a heart-stopping flash, Radescu realized that the mercenary was removing his fingers from the grip of his weapon before he called up memories of the past.

"We cleared a bottleneck for a battalion of locals," Hawker said.

"Your boys, General," Sergeant Bourne interjected.

"Killed a few ourselves, pointed some others out with gunfire," the lieutenant continued. "No point in knowing where a Molt's going to appear a minute ahead of time if it took us ten to relay the data. These're a pretty good short-range data link." He patted the gray plastic receiver of his sub-machinegun.

"You were able to have that much effect yourselves?" Radescu said, seating himself at the head of the long conference table. The richly-grained wood hid the ruin of his boots and uniform; though when the time came, he really ought to rise to greet the officers he had summoned. "To clear a corridor, I mean?"

"Got our bag limit that day," said Bourne, wiping his lips with the dragon on his palm. "By the *Lord* we did."

"We took the Molts by surprise," Hawker explained. "There really aren't that many of them, the warriors, and we cleared out the ones who knew the territory before they figured things out."

Hawker's right thumb stripped something from a belt dispenser to give his hands something to play with as he talked. The gesture relaxed Radescu somewhat until he realized that the mercenary was now juggling an eyeball-sized minigrenade.

"We ducked into a nursery tunnel then, to get clear of the snipers," Hawker said. "Figured that warriors could come at us there, but before we were in danger Profile'd hand'em one to keep."

"Where the chicken got the axe," said Bourne, running an index finger—his left—across his throat. Radescu thought the gesture was figurative. Then he noticed the knife blade, the length of the finger along which it lay and so sharp that light rippled on its edges as it did on the water dancing down the nymph's stone arms.

Bourne smiled and flicked his left hand close to some of the decorative foliage in the nearest wall niche. A leaf gave a startled quiver; half of it fluttered to the floor, severed cleanly. Satisfied, Bourne stropped both sides of the blade against his thigh to clean any trace of sap from the weapon.

"Thing about the Molts," he went on, leaning closer to Radescu, "is that how far they can pop through the air depends on how old they are." It was the sort of lecture the sergeant would have given a man fresh to the field . . . as Radescu was, but he and his ancestors in unbroken line had been living with the Molts for three hundred years. The Oltenian general listened with an air of careful interest, however; the disquisition indicated a level of positive feeling toward him on the mercenary's part; and for more reasons than his plan for the meeting, Radescu wanted Bourne to like him.

"The old males," the sergeant said, "there's no telling how far they can hop if there's a big enough piece of hard rock for 'em to get a *grip* of, like. With their minds, you know? But the females—not bad looking some of 'em either, in the right light—"

"Profile . . . ?"

"Yessir." Bourne's right hand nodded a gobbling gesture in front of his mouth as if the dragon's head were swallowing the words he had just spoken. "But the females can hop only maybe ten kays and it takes 'em longer to psych into doing it, even the old ones. And the little babies, they can't jump the length of my prick when they're newborn. So the adults keep 'em in holes in the rock so their minds can get the feel of the rock, like; touch the electrical charge when the rock shifts. And there they were when we got in, maybe a dozen a' the babes."

"And that was about when it dropped in

the pot, I s'pose, General," said Hawker as he stood up deliberately and faced the wall so that he would not have to look at the cosmetic-covered Oltenian face as he finished the story. "A, a local officer. . . I told him to get the little ones out of the tunnel; figured they'd be put in a holding tank somewhere. And he killed them."

Hawker's back muscles strained against his clamshell armor, hunching it. "There was one more I was holding, a little Molt I'd brought out myself."

He turned again, proceeding through stress to catharsis. "I blew that poof to Hell, General Radescu, before he could kill that baby too."

Alexander Radescu had seen the Slammers' powerguns demonstrated. The snap of their blue-green energy was too sudden to be fully appreciated by the senses, though the retinas danced for almost a minute thereafter with afterimages of the discharge's red-orange complement. A shot would be dazzling in a cavern of dark rock lighted by Molt torches and the lamps of the vehicles driven headlong within. The blood and stench of the sudden corpse, that too Radescu could visualize—had to be able to visualize or he would not stay functionally sane if this meeting this morning proceeded as he feared it might, planned that it might. . . .

"And you, Bourne," Radescu said, "you were condemned simply for being present?" It was more or less what he had expected, though he had presumed that the sergeant was the principal in the event and Lieutenant Hawker was guilty of no more than failure to control his murderous subordinate. It was the sort of clean sweep Chief Tribune Antonescu would have made. . . .

"Oh, one a' the poofs threw down on the Loot," Bourne said. He was smiling because he had returned to an awareness of the fact that he was alive: when Radescu had first seen the sergeant, Bourne was dead in his own mind; waiting as much for burial as the shot in the back of his neck that would immediately precede interment. "I took him out and, Via, figured better safe'n sorry."

He looked at the mercenary officer, and the set of his jaw was as fierce for the moment as any expression he had thrown Radescu. "I still think so, Loot. There a couple of times, I figured I'd been crazy to hand this over and let them put us in that box." His index finger tapped the submachinegun's receiver, then slipped within the trigger guard as if of its own volition. "And you know, we aren't out of it yet, are we?"

Bourne shifted his torso to confront Hawker, and the muzzle of the slung weapon pointed as well.

"Anybody ever swear you'd get out of the Slammers alive, Sergeant?" Lieutenant Hawker asked in a voice as slick and cold as the iridium barrel of the gun thrusting toward him.

Radescu tensed, but there was no apparent fear in Hawker's grim visage—and no more of challenge, either, than that of a

man facing a storm cloud in the knowledge
that the rain will come if it will.

"Ah, Via, Loot," Bourne said, the sling
slapping the submachinegun back against
his chest when he let it go, "I didn't want ta
grease the Colonel, cop. After all, he gave
this poor boy a job didn't he?"

Hawker laughed, and Bourne laughed; and
the door beside the sergeant opened as the
first of the command staff entered the meeting room, already three minutes after the
deadline in Radescu's summons.

The Oltenian general looked from the newcomer to the wall clock and back to the
newcomer, Iorga, the Second Division commander. When Radescu himself smiled, Sergeant Bourne was uneasily reminded of a
ferret he had once kept as a pet—and Hawker
caught a glimpse, too, beneath the beauty
patch and lip tint, of a mind as ruthless as
the blade of a scythe.

It took the command staff thirty-six minutes to assemble in the large trailer in the
center of the Oltenian encampment, though
none of the officers were more than a kilometer away at the summons and Radescu
had clearly stated that anyone who did not
arrive in fifteen minutes put his command
in jeopardy for that fact alone. It was not,
he thought, that they did not believe the
threat: it was simply that the men involved
would be *unable* to act that promptly even
if it were their lives that depended on it.

Which indeed was the case.

The quarters of the Army Commander, Marshal Erzul, adjoined the conference trailer; but it was to no one's surprise that Erzul arrived last of the officers summoned ... and it did not surprise Alexander Radescu that the marshal attempted to enter surrounded by his personal aides. The milling, disconsolate troop of underlings outside the doorway of the conference room was warning enough that Radescu hewed precisely to the language of the summons; but Erzul's action was not motivated by ignorance.

Radescu had motioned the six earlier arrivals to chairs while he himself sat on a corner of the conference table and chatted with them—recruiting figures, the Season's colors in the capital, the gala for the Widows of the War at which a Molt had appeared with a powergun, firing indiscriminately. "There were two stone urns, no more than that, and the Molt focused on them across over a thousand kays—" he was saying, when the door opened and the divisional officers leaped to their feet to salute Marshal Erzul.

Radescu cocked his head toward the marshal and his entourage, then turned away. He did not rise for Erzul who was not, despite his rank, Radescu's superior officer, and he twisted the gold-brimmed cap furiously in his hands. Around and back, like the glittering spirals of a fly jumped by a spider, both of them together buzzing on the end of the spider's anchor line; around and back.

The young general took a deep breath. By

looking at the two officers closest to where
he sat at the head of the table, he was able
to avoid seeing either of the Slammers poised
along the wall where they seemed muddy
shadows against the opulence and glitter of
the room's furnishings and other occupants.
He could not avoid his own imagination,
however, and the doubt as to whether there
would be any safe place in the room when
the guns began to spray. He closed his eyes
momentarily, not a blink but part of the
momentary tensioning of all his muscles
... but he *had* to learn whose orders they
would take, these men around him.

"Generals Oprescu and Iorga," Radescu
said loudly, fixing the commanders of the
First and Second Divisions with eyes as pure
as the blue enamel on his shoulder boards,
"will you kindly put out of the conference
room all those who seem to have entered
with the marshal? All save General Forsch,
that is, since the Tribunes have ordered him
to attend as well."

There was a frozen pause. Iorga looked
at Oprescu, Oprescu at his manicure as a
flush mounted from his throat to the cheeks
which he had not had time to prepare with
a proper base of white gel.

Erzul was a stocky, jowly bulldog to
Radescu's cat. As his aides twitched and
twittered, the marshal himself crashed a
step forward. "This is *my* command," he
thundered to the back of Radescu's head,
his eyes drawn unwillingly to the flickering

highlights of the cap in the general's hands, "and *I* decide where my aides will be!"

"The summons that brought you here, Marshal," Radescu announced in a voice which became increasingly thin in his own ears, though no one else in the room seemed to hear the difference, "informed you that the Tribunes had placed me in charge of all personnel of the First Army, yourself included."

"The Tribunes," sneered Erzul as everyone else in the room stayed frozen and Sergeant Bourne's eyes focused on something a thousand leagues away. "Your *uncle*."

"Yes," said the young general as he rose to his muddy feet, fanning himself gently with the cap in his hand, "my uncle."

General Iorga made a little gesture with the backs of his hands and fingers as if he were a house servant trying to frighten a wasp out of the room with a napkin. "Go on," he said to the captain closest to him in a voice with a tinge of hysteria and desperation. "Go *on* then, you shouldn't *be* here!"

All of the divisional officers, not just the pair to whom Radescu had directed his order, sprang forward as if to physically thrust their juniors out of the conference room. General Forsch, Erzul's lanky, nervous, chief of staff, slid behind the marshal as if for concealment and in fear that the sudden onslaught would force him out the door with subordinate aides.

Neither of the mercenaries changed the expression—lack of expression—on his face.

Lieutenant Hawker stretched his left arm to the side and began flexing the fingers of that hand like a man trying to work out a muscle cramp.

"Marshal Erzul," said Radescu as he suppressed a hysterical urge to pat the blood-suffused cheek of the former army commander, "your resignation on grounds of health is regretfully accepted. Your services to the State will be noted in my report to Chief Tribune Antonescu." He paused. "To my uncle."

Radescu expected the older man to hit him, but instead Erzul's anger collapsed, leaving behind an expression that justified the accusation of ill-health. The marshal's flush drained away abruptly so that only the grimy sallowness of pigment remained to color his skin. "I—" he said. "General, don't—"

General Iorga stepped between the two officers, the former army commander and the man who had replaced him. "Go on!" he cried to the marshal. Iorga's hands fluttered on the catches of his holster.

In a final burst of frustration, Marshal Erzul snatched off his cap, formal with ropes of gold and silver, and hurled it blindly across the room. It thudded into the wall near Hawker, who neither smiled nor moved as the hat spun end over end to the floor. Erzul turned and charged the door like a soccer player driving for the goal regardless of who might be in his way.

In this case, Erzul's own chief of staff was

the only man who could not step clear in time. General Forsch grunted as his superior elbowed him in the pit of the stomach and then thrust past him through the outside door.

Under other circumstances, Forsch might have followed. Now, however, he watched the marshal's back and the door banging hard against its jamb—the automatic opening and closing mechanisms had been disconnected to permit aides to perform those functions in due deference to their superiors. The divisional officers were scurrying for their places around the table, and Radescu was finally preparing to discuss the main order of business—the war with the Molts.

"It's easy to bully old men who've spent their lives in the service of Man and the Tribunate, isn't it, Master Radescu?" said Forsch in a voice as clear and cutting as a well-played violin. "Do you think the Molts will be so obliging to your whim?"

Radescu slid into the chair at the head of the table, looking back over his shoulder at Forsch. The chief of staff stood with his chin thrust out and slightly lifted, rather as though he were baring his long, angular throat to a slaughterer's knife. Radescu had not realized the man even *had* a personality of his own: everything Antonescu's nephew had been told suggested that Forsch was no more than Erzul's shadow—a gaunt, panicky avatar of the marshal.

"No, General," said Radescu in a voice that did not tremble the way his hands would have done save for the polished tabletop against which he pressed them. "I don't think the Molts are going to be obliging at all. Why don't you sit down and we'll discuss the problem like loyal officers of Oltenia?"

He tapped with the brim of his cap on the chair to his immediate right. Forsch held himself rigid for a moment, his body still awaiting death or humiliation while his brain with difficulty processed the information freeing him from that expected end. Moving like a marionette with a string or two broken, the chief of staff—now Radescu's chief of staff, much to the surprise of both men—seated himself as directed.

"Hawker," said General Radescu as if the mercenary were his batman, "take this until we're ready to leave. I won't need it inside here."

Lieutenant Hawker stepped obsequiously from his place at the wall and took the gilded cap Radescu held out without looking away from his fellow Oltenian generals. The Slammer even bowed as he backed away again. . . but when he reached the fountain in its niche, he flipped the cap deliberately from his hand. The Oltenians, focused on one another, did not or did not seem to notice.

Profile Bourne relaxed and began rubbing his right arm with his left forefinger, tracing the length of the glowing orange dragon. Not that it would have mattered, but Radescu's cap was not on the floor.

It lay atop the hat which Erzul had thrown in anger.

"This war can only be a war of attrition," said pudgy General Oprescu with a care that came naturally to a man who needed to avoid dislocating his make-up. Radescu, watching the divisional commander, understood very well how the preternatural calm of the other man's face could cloak thoughts as violent as any which had danced through Marshal Erzul's features moments before. Radescu's face had been that calm, and he was willing to go to lengths beyond anything the Marshal had suspected. Perhaps Oprescu also had a core of rigid capability within. . .but it was very well hidden if that were the case.

"We can only hurt the Molts when they attack *us*," Oprescu continued as he examined his manicure. "Naturally, they inflict more damage on such occasions than we do . . .but likewise, their population base is much lower than ours."

"I believe the estimate," said the pale-eyed General Vuco, who had been a reasonably effective intelligence officer before promotion to Second Division chief of staff, "is seventy-three to one. That is, we can ultimately wipe the Molts from the face of Oltenia so long as we suffer no more than seventy-three casualties for each of the scaly-headed demons that we bag."

"The *problem* is," Oprescu went on, "that the seventy-three casualties aren't limited to the bunion-heads in the lower ranks, not when a Molt can pop out of the air in the middle of an officers' barracks that chances to be too close to a lump of granite."

Radescu's heart stopped for an instant and his eyes, unbidden, flicked sideways to Sergeant Bourne. The mercenary non-com grinned back at him, as relaxed as the trigger-spring of his submachinegun. It struck the young Oltenian that there was a flaw in his plan of engaging gunmen to do what he could not have accomplished with guns alone: you have control over a gun as you do not over a man ... not over men like those, the soft-featured lieutenant who was willing to kill for a matter of principle, and the scarred sergeant who needed far less reason than that. In Radescu's mind echoed the sergeant's gibe in the jeep: "What's he going to do? Sentence me to death?"

But Bourne smiled now and the moment passed with General Forsch saying as he gripped his biceps with bony fingers, "Of course the Molts have a—feeling for the casualty ratio, too; and while they're not as formally—organized as we—" he blinked around the conference table, finally fixing Radescu with a look like that of a small animal caught at night in the headlights. "Ahem. Not as structured as we are. Nonetheless, when they feel that the fighting is to their disadvantage, they stop fighting— save for random attacks far behind the 'lines,' attacks in which they almost never suffer losses."

"Then," said Alexander Radescu, wishing that his voice were deep and powerful—though surely it could not be as tinny as it sounded in his own hypercritical ears—"we have to shift our strategy. Instead of advancing slowly—" 'ponderously' was the word his mind suppressed a moment before his tongue spoke it; the lavish interior of the conference room had taken on a somewhat different aspect for Radescu since the mercenary lieutenant sneered at it "—into areas which the Molts infest, we shall make quick thrusts to capture the areas which make them vulnerable: the nursery caves."

"We can*not* advance quickly," said General Vuco, who was more able than the others to treat Radescu as a young interloper rather than as the man with demonstrated control over the career of everyone else in the room, "so long as everyone in the assault must expect attack from behind at every instant. To—" he made a gesture with his left hand as if flinging chaff to the wind "—charge forward regardless, well, that was attempted in the early days of the conflict. Panache did not protect the units involved from total destruction, from massacre.

"Of course," Vuco added, directing his eyes toward a corner of the ceiling, "I'm perfectly willing to die for the State, even by what amounts to an order of suicide."

He dropped his gaze, intending to focus on the play of water in the alcove across the table from him. Instead, the Oltenian's eyes met those of Lieutenant Hawker. Vuco snapped upright, out of his pose of bored indolence. His mouth opened to speak, but no words came out.

"The mercenaries we hire, Hammer's troops," said Radescu, suppressing an urge to nod toward Hawker in appreciation, "manage well enough—or did," he added, glaring at his elders and new subordinates, "until our failure to support them led to what I and the Tribunate agreed were needless and excessive casualties, casualties not covered by the normal war risks of their hiring contract."

Now for the first time, most of the senior officers looked up as though Hawker and Bourne were specimens on display. Vuco instead rubbed his eyes fiercely as if he were trying to wipe an image from their surface. Hawker accepted the attention stolidly, but the sergeant reacted with an insouciance Radescu decided was typical, making a surprisingly graceful genuflection —a form of courtesy unfamiliar on Oltenia and shockingly inappropriate from a man as ruggedly lethal as Profile Bourne.

"All very well," said General Forsch in the direction of the Slammers but answering Radescu's implied question, "if we had the detection capability that the mercenaries do. *They* have time, a minute or more, to prepare for an attack, even when they're moving."

Radescu's eyes traversed the arc of the divisional officers and General Forsch. His mind was too busy with his present words and the action which would develop from those words in the immediate future, however, for him really to be seeing the men around him. "Nonetheless," he heard his voice say, "General Forsch will determine a target suitable for sudden assault by Oltenian forces."

It was the intention he had formed before he accepted his uncle's charge, an intention vocalized here in the conference room for the first time.

"Troops for the exercise will come from Second Division. Generals Iorga, Vuco, your staff will coordinate with mine to determine the precise number and composition of the units to be involved in the exercise."

Radescu blinked. It was almost as if he had just opened his eyes, because the staring officers sprang suddenly back into his awareness. "Are there any questions, gentlemen?"

General Forsch leaned forward, almost close enough for his long neck to snake out to Radescu's hand like a weasel snapping. "Youth will be served, I suppose," he said. "But, my leader, you have no idea of what it is like to battle the Molts on their own ground."

"I will before long, though," said Alexander Radescu as he rose in dismissal. "I'll be accompanying the force in person."

The sound of his subordinates sucking in breath in surprise was lost in the roar of blood through the young general's ears.

The most brilliant strategy, the most courageous intent, come alike to naught if the troops are marshalled at one point and their transport at another. The command group had scuttled out of the conference room with orders to plan an assault which none of them believed could be carried through successfully.

Radescu waited until he heard the door bang shut behind the last of his generals, Forsch; then, elbows on the table, he cradled his chin in his palms while his fingers covered his eyes. He did not like failure and, as he came nearer to the problem, he did not see any other likely result to his attempts.

It occurred to the young general that his subconscious might have planned the whole operation as a means of achieving not victory but solely an honorable excuse for him not to explain defeat to his uncle. The chances were very slim indeed that Alexander Radescu would survive a total disaster.

His pants legs were not only filthy, they stank. How his generals must be laughing at him!

"Sir. . . ?" intruded a voice whose owner he had forgotten.

"Ah, Lieutenant Hawker," said the Oltenian general, his personality donning its public mien as he looked up at the big mercenary. "Forgive me for not dismissing you sooner. I'll contact your colonel with thanks and—"

"General," Sergeant Bourne interrupted as he strode to the nearest chair and reversed it so that its back was toward the

conference table, "those birds're right so
far: if you just bull straight in like you're
talking, your ass is grass and the Molts'll
well and truly mow it. You need support—
and that's what you hired us Slammers for,
isn't it?"

Bourne sat down, the weight of his gear
suddenly evident from the crash it made
when it bumped the chair. The sergeant's
legs splayed to either side of the seat back
which rose like an outer, ornately-carven,
breastplate in front of his porcelain armor.
The mercenary's method of seating himself
was not an affectation, Radescu realized:
the man's belt gear and the bulges of electronics built into the shoulders of his back-
plate would prevent him from sitting in a
chair in the normal fashion.

"I thank you for your concern, Sergeant,"
Radescu said—had he ever before known
the name of an enlisted man? He really
couldn't be sure. "Colonel Hammer is no
longer willing to divide his own forces and
trust the Oltenian army to carry out its
own portion of the operation. When I have
proved my troops are capable of—active
endeavor—on their own, then I believe we
can come to an accommodation, he and I.

"For now," Radescu added brusquely as
he rose, "I have business that does not concern mercenaries. If you'll be so good—"

"Sir, the Colonel *has* offered you troops,"
said Lieutenant Hawker as loudly as necessary to silence Radescu's voice without shrill-
ness. "Us. All Profile means is you ought to

use us, the best curst detection team in the Slammers. And he's right—you *ought* to use us, instead of throwing yourself away."

Radescu sat down again, heavily. The Slammers lieutenant was so much larger than the general that only by tricking his mind could Radescu keep from being cowed physically. "He didn't second you to me for that," he said, "for detection. You—you know that."

Bourne snorted and said, "Bloody *cop* we do!"

At his side, with a hand now on the noncom's shoulder, Hawker replied, "the Colonel doesn't talk to me, sir. But if you think he doesn't keep up with what's happening with the people who hired him, hired *us*, there you're curst well wrong. Don't ever figure a man like Colonel Hammer isn't one step ahead of you—though he may not be ready to commit openly."

"Not," Bourne completed grimly, "when he's ready to call in the Bonding Authority and void the contract for employer's nonperformance."

"My Lord," said Radescu. He looked at the pair of mercenaries without the personal emotion—hope or fear or even disgust— he had always felt before. The implications of what Hawker had just said stripped all emotional loadings from the general's immediate surroundings. Hawker and Bourne could have been a pair of trees, gnarled and gray-barked; hard-used and very, very hard themselves. . . .

"My Lord," the Oltenian repeated, the words scarcely moving his lips. Then his gaze sharpened and he demanded, "You mean it was, was a game? You wouldn't have . . . ?"

"Try me, General," said Profile Bourne. He did not look at Radescu but at his open palm; and the dragon there bore an expression similar to that of the mercenary.

"It's not a game, killing people," said the lieutenant. "We got into the box where you found us by doing just what we told you we did. And believe me, sir, nobody ever complained about the support Profile and me gave when it came down to cases." The fingers of his right hand smoothed the receiver of the submachinegun where the greenish wear on the plastic showed the owner's touch was familiar.

"It's just I guess we can figure one thing out, now," the sergeant remarked, looking up with the loose, friendly look of a man lifting himself out of a bath in drugs. "We'd heard our sentence four days ago, not that there was a whole lotta doubt. I mean, we'd done it. The colonel watched us."

He gave Radescu the grin of a little boy caught in a peccadillo, sure of a spanking but winkingly hopeful that it might still be avoided. "We don't stand much on ceremony in the Slammers," Bourne went on. "For sure not on something like a shot in the neck. So the Loot'n me couldn't figure what the colonel was waiting for.

"I guess," the sergeant concluded with a

very different sort of smile again, "he was waiting for you."

Hawker pulled a chair well away from the table, lifting it off the floor so that it did not scrape. The mercenary handled the chair so lightly that Radescu could scarcely believe that it was made of the same dense, heavily-carven wood as the one in which the Oltenian sat.

"You see, sir," the lieutenant said as he lowered himself carefully onto the seat, hunching forward a little to be able to do so, "we can't cover more than a platoon, the two of us—but a platoon's enough, for what you need."

"Any more'n that, they get screwed up," added Bourne. "Even if *we* get the range and bearing right, they don't. Just gives the Molts more targets to shoot at. That's not what we're here for."

"What *are* you here for?" Radescu asked, reaching out to touch Bourne's right palm to the other's great surprise. The skin was dry and callused, not at all unlike the scaly head of a reptile. "What your colonel may want, I can see. But the danger to you personally—it isn't as though you'd be protected by, by your own, the tanks and the organization that strikes down Molts when they appear."

He withdrew his hand, looking at both the Slammers and marvelling at how stolid they appeared. Surely their like could have no emotion? "I'm an Oltenian," Radescu continued. "This is my planet, my State.

Even so, everybody in the room just now—"
his fingers waggled toward the door through
which his fellow generals had exited "—thinks
I'm mad to put myself in such danger. You
two aren't lumps like our own peasants.
You made it clear that I couldn't even *order*
you without your willingness to obey. Would
Hammer punish you if you returned to him
without having volunteered to accompany
me?"

"Guess we're clear on that one, wouldn't
you say, Loot?" remarked Sergeant Bourne
as he glanced at Hawker. Though the non-
com was physically even smaller than Radescu, he did not sink into the ambience of
the big lieutenant the way the Oltenian felt
he did himself. Profile Bourne was a knife,
double-edged and wickedly sharp; size had
nothing to do with the aura he projected.

For the first time, Radescu considered the
faces of his divisional officers as they watched
him in the light of the emotions he tried
to hide when he looked at the pair of mercenaries. It could be that the Oltenians saw
in him a core of something which he knew
in his heart of hearts was not really there.

Hawker's body armor shrugged massively.
"Look, sir," he said without fully meeting
the Oltenian's eyes, "if we liked to lose,
then we wouldn't be in the Slammers. I
don't apologize for anything that happened
before—" now he did focus his gaze, glacial
in a bovine face, on Radescu "—but it
wasn't what we were hired to do. Help win
a war against the Molts."

Bourne tilted forward to grasp Radescu's hand briefly before the sergeant levered himself back to his feet. "And you know, General," the mercenary said as he rose, "until I met you, I didn't think the poofs had a prayer a' doin' that."

The encampment should in theory have been safe enough, with no chunk of crystalline rock weighing more than a kilogram located within a meter of the ground surface. Nobody really believed that a three-divisional area had been swept so perfectly, however, especially without the help which Hammer had refused to give this time.

The center of the encampment, the combined Army and the Second Division Headquarters had been set up in a marsh and was probably quite secure. The nervousness of the troops mustered both for the operation and for immediate security was due less to intellectual fear of the Molts than to the formless concern which any activity raised in troops used to being sniped at from point-blank ambush with no time to respond.

Alexander Radescu felt sticky and uncomfortable in his new battledress, though its fabric and cut should have been less stiff than the formal uniforms he ordinarily wore. He could not bring himself to don body armor, knowing that it would cramp and distract him through the next hours when his best hope of survival lay in keeping flexible and totally alert.

Hawker and Bourne wore their own back-and-breast armor, heavier but far more resistant than the Oltenian version which Radescu had refused. They were used to the constriction, after all, and would probably have been more subconsciously hindered by its absence than by the weight.

Radescu would have been even more comfortable without the automatic shotgun he now cradled, a short-barrelled weapon which sprayed tiny razor-edged airfoils that spread into a three-meter circle ten meters from the muzzle. The gun was perfectly effective within the ranges at which Molt warriors were likely to appear; but it was the general's dislike of *personal* involvement in something as ignoble as killing, rather than his doubts about how accurately he could shoot, which put him off the weapon.

Still, he had to carry the shotgun for protective coloration. The mercenaries' jeep would stand out from the Oltenian units anyway, and the sole unarmed member of a combat patrol would be an even more certain choice for a Molt with the leisure to pick his target.

"Cop!" snarled Lieutenant Hawker from the side-seat of the jeep as he surveyed the numbers his apparatus projected glowing into the air before him. The mercenary's commo helmet was linked to epaulette speakers issued to the entire Oltenian contingent for this operation. Radescu heard the words both on his own borrowed helmet and, marginally later, directly from the lieutenant's mouth. "Discard Beacon Eighty-Seven. Team Seven, that's three duds so far outa this lot, and you've had *all* of 'em. Are you sure you know how to switch the bloody things on?"

"The numbers of the beacons being tested appear—on your screen, then?" General Radescu asked the mercenary sergeant beside him, wiggling his fingers toward the floating yellow numbers. Obviously, there was no screen; but he was uncertain how to describe in any other way what he saw.

"Naw, that's the playback from Central," replied Profile Bourne. He nodded his head toward the distant ridge beyond which sheltered Colonel Hammer and his armored regiment. "Doesn't matter if *we* pick up the signal or not, but How Batt'ry can't bust up rocks for us if they don't get the beacon."

"Yes, well . . . ," said General Radescu as he looked at the men and equipment around him. The Oltenian contingent was forty men mounted on ten light trucks—each with a load of explosives and radio beacons, plus a pintle-mounted automatic weapon which at the flip of a switch fired either solid shot for long-range targets or beehives of airfoil flechettes like the hand weapons.

The trucks were somewhat larger than the Slammers' jeep on which Radescu himself would be mounted. More significantly, the Oltenian vehicles rode on wheels spun from spring-wire rather than on air cushions. Ground effect vehicles of sufficient ruggedness and payload for scouting through brush required drive-systems of a better power-to-weight ratio than Oltenia could supply. The mercenaries' jeeps and one-man skimmers had the benefit of cryogenic accumulators, recharged at need—every hundred kilometers or so—from the fusion powerplants of the heavier combat cars and tanks.

The jeep which Sergeant Bourne drove and the energy weapon slung against his chest were thus both of a higher technology level than their Oltenian equivalents—but in neither case was the difference significant to the present mission. The range and quickness of the electronics which detected Molts before they appeared physically, and the needle-threading accuracy which terminal guidance gave the Slammers' rocket howitzers, were absolute necessities if the present operation were to succeed, however; and Colonel Hammer was supplying both.

Despite his public dismissal of Radescu, Hammer was giving him and the State of Oltenia one chance to seize back the initiative in this *accursed* war with the planet's dominant autochthones.

"We're ready, sir," said Lieutenant Hawker with his helmet mike shut off to make the report more personal than a radio message to the general two meters away. "The hardware is."

Radescu nodded. Bourne had already slipped onto his seat on the left side of the jeep. Radescu had eaten a light, perfectly bland, meal of protein supplement an hour earlier. The food now lay like an anvil in his belly while his digestive system writhed in an attempt to crush it.

"Captain Elejash," the young general said, his signal broadcast to every member of the assault party, "are your men ready?" He lifted himself carefully onto his electronic throne on the back of the jeep, pleased to note that the motion decreased his nausea instead of causing him to vomit in the sight of several thousand putative subordinates.

"Yes sir," replied the commander of the Oltenian platoon, a rancher before the war as were most of his men. They were a hard-bitten crew, many of them as old as the general himself, and very different in appearance from the pasty-faced young factory workers who made up the ordinary rank and file of the army. Forsch and Iorga had gone at least that far toward making the operation a success.

"General Radescu, the support battalion is ready," said an unbidden voice over the wailing background which Radescu had learned to associate with recompressed ultra-low frequency transmissions from Army HQ.

Alexander Radescu looked imperiously around him at the faces and heavy equipment and distant, wooded hills, all of which blurred in his fear-frozen mind to gray shadows.

"All right," he said in his cool, aristocratic voice. "Then let's go."

And before the last word had reached the general's throat mike, Profile Bourne was easing the jeep forward at a rapidly accelerating pace.

How smoothly it rides, thought General Radescu as the ground effect jeep sailed up a hillside pocked by the burrows of small grazing animals and Lieutenant Hawker opened fire from the front seat with shocking unexpectedness.

The ionization detectors had given no warning because the Molt was already sited, a picket waiting near the Oltenian base on a likely course of advance. Hawker's face shield was locked in place, and through its electronic additions to the normal sensory spectrum—passive infra-red or motion enhancement—the mercenary had spotted his target as it rose to attack.

Cyan flashes squirted from Hawker's gun at a cyclic rate so high that their afterimage combined to form a solid orange bar on Radescu's dazzled retinas. The vehicles were in line abreast at ten-meter intervals with the Slammers' jeep in the center. A multistemmed bush to the jeep's right front hissed and shrivelled as it drank the energy bolts; then it and recognizable portions of an adolescent Molt were blasted apart by a violent secondary explosion. The autochthone had carried either a satchel charge or an unusually-powerful shoulder-launched missile. The red flash of its detonation, though harmless to the assault platoon, caused the driver of the nearest truck to stall his engine. He knew that if Hawker had been seconds slower, the blast would have enveloped the Oltenian vehicle.

"Eight red thirty degrees," said Hawker as unemotionally as though his gun's barrel was not pinging and discoloring the finish of the forward transom on which he rested it to cool. Numbers and symbols, not the ones the mercenary was relaying to the assault force, hung as images of yellow and violet in the air before him. "Four yellow zero degrees."

Most of the pintle-mounted weapons snarled bursts toward the range and bearing each gunner had computed from the Slammer's rough direction. First Hawker gave the number of the truck he chose as a base for that deflection; then red, orange or yellow for fifty, seventy-five or hundred meter arcs around that truck; and finally the bearing itself. Molts beyond a hundred meters were rarely dangerous to a moving target, even with the most modern weapons. When possible, the mercenary would point out such warriors with a burst from his own gun or even call in artillery; but there was no need to complicate a system of directions which had to work fast if it were to work at all.

"Cease fire," Hawker ordered as the jeep slid through a line of palmate leaves springing from the hillcrest and Radescu covered his face with one hand, "*Cease* fire, Six, they were going away!"

More pickets, Radescu thought as the echoes of gunfire died away and the line of vehicles rocked down the next slope without immediate incident. The blips of plasma which the mercenaries' detection equipment had caught this time were those resulting from Molts disappearing, not coalescing to attack. The pickets would be returning to their council, their headquarters, with warning of the direction and nature of the attack.

There was the sharp crash of an explosion nearby. The crew of Truck Six had tossed a charge overboard, onto a patch of crystalline rock which their own sensors had identified. Dirt showered the jeep and Radescu, while dual blasts sounded from opposite ends of the patrol line, deadened somewhat by distance. The shaped-charge packets were weighted to land cavity-down—most of the time. Even so, they did not have enough stand-off for the pencil of super-heated gas to reach maximum velocity and effectiveness before it struck the rock it was to shatter.

The bombs which the patrol set off could not break up even surface outcrops so effectively that no Molt could home on them. However, the charges did, with luck, lessen and change the piezoelectrical signature by relieving stresses on the crystalline structure. The oldest, most experienced, Molts could still pick their way to the location, sorting through the sea of currents and electrical charges for bits of previous reality which their brains could process like those of paleontologists creating a species from bone fragments.

Even these older warriors were slowed

and limited as to the range from which they could project themselves to such damaged homing points, however. Younger Molts, equally deadly with their guns and buzzbombs, were effectively debarred from popping into ambush directly behind the advancing patrol.

Powerguns—and the Molts carried them, though Oltenian regulars did not—had an effective anti-personnel range, even in atmosphere, of line of sight. There was no practical way to prevent Molt snipers from firing into distant human arrays, then skipping back to safety. No way at all, except by killing every male Molt on Oltenia.

Or by ending the war, which everyone high in the government thought was also impossible. Everyone but Alexander Radescu.

"Six red one-eighty!" shouted Lieutenant Hawker, emotionless no longer as his instruments warned him of the Molt blurring out of the air through which Truck Six had just driven. The attacker was in Hawker's own blind spot, even if he had dared take his eyes from the read-outs now that the attack had come in earnest. "Ten yellow ninety!"

The jeep dropped a hand's breadth on irregular ground as the general twisted to look over his shoulder. The sinking feeling in his guts was more pronounced than the actual drop when he realized that all the pintle-mounted guns in the patrol had been swung forward at the first contact. The guns on even-numbered trucks were to have cov-

ered the rear at all times, but nervousness
and enthusiasm had combined to give the
autochthones a perfect opening. Now gunners were tugging at the grips of their long-
barreled weapons, more handicapped by
cramped footing than by the guns' inertia.

Black smoke from the shaped charge dis-
sipated above the scar in the sod and flattened grass. Squarely in the center of the
blast circle—so much for the effectiveness
of the charges—a shadow thickened to solid
form.

The Molt's gray scales had a blue tinge
and what Radescu would have called a metallic luster had not the iridium barrel of
the creature's powergun showed what luster truly was. The general did not even realize he had fired until the butt of the shotgun
slammed him in the ribs: he had loose-
gripped the unfamiliar weapon, and its
heavy recoil punished the error brutally.

Radescu's shot twinkled like a soap bubble as the cloud of airfoils caught the sunlight twenty meters above their target. The
Molt's figure was perfectly clear for a moment as it hulked behind the reflection of
its gun; then the autochthone began to shrink
and dissolve in a manner that made Radescu
think it had teleported itself to another location before firing.

No.

There was a scarlet cloud in the air beyond
the Molt as the trucks and jeep bounded
away, blood and flesh and chips of yellow
bone. An Oltenian soldier with a weapon like

Radescu's and a skill the general had never been expected to learn had fired three times. The autochthone crumpled before the machineguns could even be rotated back in its direction.

Half a dozen shaped charges went off almost simultaneously, and there was heavy firing from the right. A powergun bolt sizzled across the ragged line of vehicles, an event so sudden that Radescu, as he turned back, could not be certain from which end it had been fired. Hawker was calling out vectors in the tight, high voice of a sportscaster. The young general hoped his fellows could understand the mercenary's directions; he was baffled by the unfamiliar data himself.

Sergeant Bourne banked the jeep around a copse of trees in a turn so sharp that the left side of the skirt dragged, spilling air in its brief hesitation. "Five red zero!" Hawker was calling, and the blur that focused down into a Molt was directly in front of the Slammers vehicle. Bourne spun the tiller with his left hand and crossed his chest with his right, firing a burst of cyan bolts which the vehicle's own motion slewed across the creature's torso. The Molt fell onto its missile launcher, dead before its psychic jump was complete enough for the creature to be aware of its new surroundings.

Radescu's gun tracked the Molt as the jeep skidded past. He did not fire—it was obviously dead—but his bruised side throbbed as if the butt were pounding him again.

There was a whistle from the sky behind,

bird cries which expanded into a roar so overpowering that earth fountained in apparent silence behind nearby trucks as they dropped shaped charges at the same time. The sound was so intense that Radescu felt it as a pressure on the back of his neck, then on his forehead and eyeballs. He wanted very badly to jump to the ground and cower there: the universe was so large and hostile. . . .

Instead, the young general gripped the handle of one of the modules which formed his seat and stood up as straight as he could without losing his hold. He was bent like someone trying to ride a bucking animal— but the defiance was real.

A craggy, wooded hilltop three hundred meters ahead of the vehicles dimpled, dirt and fragments of foliage lifting into the air. There were no explosions audible. Radescu, slammed back into his seat when the jeep rose to meet him, thought the shell blasts were lost in the waterfall rush from overhead. That blanket of sound cut off with the suddenness of a thrown switch, its echoes a whisper to ears stunned by the roar itself.

Only then did the sextet of shells explode, their blasts muffled by the depth to which they had penetrated the rocky core of the hill. The slope bulged, then collapsed like cake dough falling. Larger trees sagged sideways, their roots crushed when the substrate was pulverized beneath them. No stones or fragments of shell casing were spewed out by the deep explosions, but a pall of dust rose to hide the immediate landscape—including the pair of Molts, killed by concussion just as they started to aim at the oncoming vehicles.

"Via!" swore Alexander Radescu. He had arranged the fire order himself two days earlier, six penetrator shells to land on a major intrusion of volcanic rock identified by satellite on the patrol's path. The plan had worked perfectly in demolishing what would otherwise have been a bastion for the autochthones—

But it had frightened him into a broil of fury and terror, because he had no personal experience with the tools he was using. Planning the fire order had been much like a game of chess played on holographic maps in the rich comfort of Army HQ. It had never occurred to Radescu that a salvo of twenty-centimeter shells would be louder than thunder as they ripped overhead, or that the ground would ripple at the hammerblows of impact even before the bursting charges went off.

Commanding soldiers is not the same as leading them.

"General, we—" Sergeant Bourne started to say, turning in his seat though it was through Radescu's commo helmet that the words came.

"Teams One through Five, break left," the general said, overriding his driver's voice by keying his own throat mike. "Six through Ten—and Command—" the last an afterthought "—break right, avoid the shelled area."

There was confusion in the patrol line as trucks turned and braked for the unanticipated obstacle—which Radescu knew he should have anticipated. The churned soil and toppled vegetation would have bogged the trucks inextricably; and, while the terrain itself might have been passable for the air-cushion jeep, the dust shrouding it would have concealed fallen trunks and boulders lifted from the shuddering earth.

Bourne's head turned again as he cramped the tiller. His face shield had become an opaque mirror, reflecting Radescu in convex perfection. The Oltenian had forgotten that the Slammers' array of night vision devices included personal sonar which would, when necessary, map a lightless area with the fidelity of eyesight—though without, of course, color vision. The sergeant had been perfectly willing to drive into the spreading cloud, despite the fact that it would have blinded the hologram display of Hawker's detectors. That wasn't the sort of problem Profile Bourne was paid to worry about.

"We're blowing Truck Two in place," said a voice which Radescu recognized with difficulty as that of Captain Elejash. Almost at once, there was a very loud explosion from the left side of the line.

Looking over his shoulder, Radescu could see a black column of smoke extending jaggedly skyward from a point hidden by the undergrowth and the curve of the land. The jeep slowed because the trucks which had been to its right and now led it turned more awkwardly than the ground effect vehicle, slowing and rocking on the uneven ground. The smell of their diesel exhaust mingled with the dry, cutting odor of the dust shaken from the hillside.

Hawker was silent, though the yellow digits hanging in the air before him proved that his instruments were still working. They simply had no Molts to detect.

"Truck Two overturned," resumed Elejash breathlessly. "We've split up the crew and are proceeding."

After blowing up the disabled vehicle, thought Radescu approvingly, to prevent the Molts from turning the gun and particularly the explosives against their makers. The trucks had better cross-country performance than he had feared—wet weather might have been a different story—but it was inevitable that at least one of the heavily-laden vehicles would come to grief. Truck Two had been lost without enemy action. Its driver had simply tried to change direction at what was already the highest practical speed on broken ground.

"Sir," said Sergeant Bourne, keying his helmet mike with his tongue-tip as he goosed the throttle to leap a shallow ravine that the Oltenian vehicles had to wallow through, "how'd you convince 'em to pick up the truck's crew?"

It was the first time Bourne had called him 'sir' rather than the ironic 'general'.

"I said I'd shoot—order shot—anyone who

abandoned his comrades," Radescu replied grimly, "and I hoped nobody thought I was joking."

He paused. "Speed is—important," he continued after a moment spent scanning the tree-studded horizon. The separated halves of the patrol line were in sight of one another again, cutting toward the center. Boulders shaken by shellfire from the reverse slope of the hill still quivered at the end of trails that wormed through the vegetation. They would need follow-up salvos, but for the moment the Molts seemed unable to use their opportunities. . . . "But we have a war to win, not just a mission to accomplish. And I won't win it with an army of men who know they'll be abandoned any time there's trouble."

Numbers on Hawker's hologram display flashed back and forth from yellow to the violet that was its complement, warning at last of a resumption of Molt attacks. The mercenary lieutenant said, "Purple One," on a command channel which Radescu heard in his left ear and the other Oltenians did not hear at all.

"What?" he demanded, thinking Hawker must have made a mistake that would give a clear shot to the teleporting autochthone.

"Mark," said Hawker, in response to an answer even the general had not heard.

Bourne, fishtailing to avoid Truck Five—itself pressed by Truck Four, the vehicles had lost their spacing as they reformed in line abreast—said, "They're landing way behind us, sir. Loot's just called artillery on 'em while they're still confused." Then he added, "We told you this was the way. Not a bloody battalion, not a division—one platoon and catch 'em with their pants down."

They were in a belt of broad-leafed vegetation, soft-trunked trees sprouted in the rich, well-watered soil of a valley floor. There was relatively little undergrowth because the foliage ten meters overhead met in a nearly solid mat. The other vehicles of the patrol were grunting impressions, patterns occasionally glimpsed through random gaps in the trees. Amazingly, Truck Two appeared to have been the only vehicle lost in the operation thus far, though the flurry of intense fighting had almost certainly caused human casualties.

But teleporting Molts were vulnerable before they were dangerous, and Radescu had been impressed by the way bursts of airfoils had swept patches of ground bare. He had felt like a step-child, leading men armed with indigenous weapons against an enemy with powerguns bought from traders whose view of the universe was structured by profit, not fantasies of human destiny. Though the energy weapons had advantages in range and effectiveness against vehicles—plus the fact that the lightly built autochthones could not easily have absorbed the heavy recoil of Oltenian weapons—none of those factors handicapped the members of the patrol in their present job.

As trees snapped by and Bourne lifted the

jeep a centimeter to keep his speed down but still have maximum maneuvering thrust available, the right earpiece of Radescu's helmet said in a machine voice, "Central to Party. Halt your forces."

They were that close, then, thought the Oltenian general. Without bothering to acknowledge—the satellite net that was Hammer's basic commo system on Oltenia would pick up the relayed order—Radescu said, "All units halt at once. All units halt." If he had tried to key the command channel alone to acknowledge, he might have had trouble with the unfamiliar mercenary helmet. Better to save time and do what was necessary instead of slavishly trying to obey the forms. If only he could get his officers to realize that simple truth. . . .

Sergeant Bourne had the principle of lower-rank initiative well in mind. Without waiting for the general to relay the order from Central, Bourne angled his fans forward and lifted the bow of the jeep to increase its air resistance. The tail skirt dragged through the loam but only slightly, not enough to whip the vehicle to a bone-jarring halt the way a less expert driver might have done in his haste.

Hawker's display was alive with flashes of yellow and violet, but he still did not call vectors to the Oltenian troops. A branch high above the jeep parted with an electric crackle as a bolt from a powergun spent itself in converting pulpy wood into steam and charred fragments.

The leaf canopy had become more ragged as the ground started to rise, so that Radescu could now see the escarpment of the ridge whose further face held their goal. The tilted strata before them were marked with bare patches from which the thin soil had slumped with its vegetation, though the trucks could— General Forsch had assured his commander—negotiate a route to the crest.

If it were undefended.

The world-shaking vibration of shells overhead was Radescu's attempt to meet his chief of staff's proviso.

Somebody should have ordered the members of the patrol to get down, but there was no opportunity now given the all-pervasive racket that would have overwhelmed even the bone-conduction speakers set into the Slammers' mastoids. The hiss-*thump* of powerguns as overeager Molts fired without proper targets also was lost, but the rare flicker of bolts in the foliage was lightning to the sky's own thunder. The thick soil of the valley floor was a warranty that no warrior was going to appear at arm's length of the deafened, cowering patrol, and the Molts' disinclination to cover significant distances on foot made it unlikely that any of them would race into the forest to get at the humans they knew were lurking there.

The initial shellbursts were lost in the rush of later salvoes. The first fire order had been intended to destroy a beacon on which the Molts would otherwise have focused. The present shellfire was turning the escarpment ahead into a killing ground.

Profile Bourne tapped the general's knee for attention, then gestured with the open, savage cup of his tattooed right hand toward the images which now hung over the jeep's bow. The modules projected a three-dimensional monochrome of the escarpment, including the heavy forest at its foot and the more scattered vegetation of the gentle reverse slope.

The Oltenian wondered fleetingly where the imaging sensor could be: all of the patrol's vehicles hid behind the barrier of trees, which concealed the escarpment as surely as it did the trucks. The angle was too flat for satellite coverage, and aircraft reconnaissance was a waste of hardware—with the crews if the aircraft were manned—in a military landscape dominated by light-swift powerguns. Perhaps it was a computer model using current satellite photography enhanced from a data base—of Hammer's, since the State of Oltenia had nothing of its own comparable.

The image of the rock face shattered. Instead of crumbling into a slide of gravel and boulders the way the hillock had done earlier when struck by penetrators, the escarpment held its new, fluid form as does a constantly replenished waterfall.

The rain feeding this spray was of bomblets from the firecracker rounds being hurled by all eighteen tubes of the Slammers' artillery. It was a prodigiously expensive undertaking—mechanized warfare is far more sparing of men than of material—but it was the blow from which Radescu prayed the Molts in this region would be unable to recover.

Each shell split in the air into hundreds of bomblets which in turn burst on the next thing they touched—rock, leaf, or the face of a Molt sighting down the barrel of his powergun. The sea of miniature blasts created a mist of glass-fiber shrapnel devouring life in all its forms above the microscopic —but without significantly changing the piezoelectrical constant of the rock on which the autochthones homed.

Hawker's detectors continued to flash notice of further Molts springing into the cauldron from which none of them would return to warn the warriors who followed them to doom.

Lieutenant Hawker was as still as the jeep, though that trembled with the shell-spawned vibration of the earth on which it now rested. Sergeant Bourne watched not the image of the fire-rippled escarpment but the detector display. His grin was alive with understanding, and he tapped together the scarred knuckles of his hands. Every violet numeral was a Molt about to die.

Short bursts were an inevitable hazard, impinging on Radescu's senses not by their sound—even the wash of the main bombardment was lost in the ballistic roar of the shells themselves—but by the fact that shafts of sunlight began to illuminate the forest floor. Stray bomblets stripped away the foliage they touched, but the low-mass shrapnel was not dangerous more than a meter or two from the center of each blast.

The Oltenian was nonetheless startled to see that the backs of his hands glittered in the sudden sunlight with glass fibers scarcely thicker than the hairs from among which they sprang. He had been too lost in the image of shellfire devouring the Molts to notice that it had put its mark on him as well.

The ionization detectors had been quiescent for almost a minute when the face of the escarpment slumped, no longer awash with firecracker rounds. Through the pulsing silence as the shellfire ceased came the rumble of collapsing rock—the final salvo had been of penetrator shells, now that the Molts had either recognized the killing ground for what it was—or had run out of victims to send into the useless slaughter.

Like a bright light, the thunder of shellfire left its own afterimage on the senses of the men who had been subjected to it. Radescu's voice was a shadow of itself in his own ears with all its high frequencies stripped away as he said, "Platoon, forward. Each crew find its own path to the crest and await further orders."

Lord who aids the needy! thought the general as the jeep rocked onto its air cushion again. He was alive, and he had apparently won this first round of his campaign to end the war.

The second round: the command group of the army had been his opponent in the first,

and he had won that too. Both victories due
to the pair of mercenaries before him; and
to the harsh, unexpectedly complex, colonel
who commanded them.

With no need to match his speed to that
of the trucks, Bourne sent his jeep through
the remaining half-kilometer of forest with
a verve that frightened Radescu—who had
thought the initial salvo of shells passing
overhead had drained him of any such emotion for months.

A few trees had grown all the way up to
the original face of harder rock, but for the
most part hard-stemmed scrub with less
need for water and nutrient had replaced
the more substantial vegetation near the
escarpment. Everything, including the thin
soil, had been swept away by the salvoes of
antipersonnel bomblets. The paths down
which tons of rock shattered by the penetrators slid were scarcely distinguishable
from the stretches to either side which were
untouched by the heavy shells.

The surface of an airless plantetoid could
not have been more barren; and there, at
least, Radescu's nostrils would not have
wrinkled at the smell of death.

Bourne took his right hand off his gunbutt
long enough to pull rearward a dashboard
lever while his left squeezed the hand throttle on the tiller wide open. The lever must
have affected the angle of the fans within
the plenum chamber, because the vehicle
began to slide straight up the slope, stern

lifted almost to a level with the bow like
that of a funicular car.

The original angle of the escarpment had
been in the neighborhood of one to one. The
salvo of penetrators had shaken portions of
the overhang down into a ramp at the foot
of the slope, easing the ascent at the same
time it changed the electrical signature. The
sergeant's bow-on assault was still a surprise, to the Oltenian and to the Slammers
lieutenant, judging from Hawker's quick
glance toward his fellow. The rear fans, those
directly beneath Radescu and the electronics modules, spun with the angry sound of
bullets ricocheting as they drove the vehicle upward.

Both mercenaries had locked their faceshields down less for visibility than for protection against pebbles still skipping from
the hill's crumbled facade. Dust and grit,
though blanketed somewhat by the over-
burden of topsoil from the further slope,
boiled in the vortices beneath the skirt of
the jeep.

The trucks of the patrol's Oltenian element crawled rather than loped in their
ascent, but they were managing adequately.
Their tires were spun from a single-crystal
alloy of iron and chrome, and they gripped
projections almost as well as the fingers of
a human climber. Such monocrystal fila-
ments were, with beef, the main export props
of the economy of human Oltenia.

The Molts provided traders with the lustrous, jewel-scaled pelts of indigenous her-

bivores and with opportunities to mine pockets of high-purity ores. The senses which permitted the autochthones to teleport were far more sensitive and exact than were the best mechanical geosurveying devices in the human universe. Even so, Molt trade off-planet was only a tiny fraction of that of members of the Oltenian state.

The needs of the autochthones were very simple, however. As the jeep topped the rise, bouncing fully a meter in the air by its momentum, a bolt from a powergun burst the trunk of one of the nearby trees mutilated in the hammering by firecracker rounds.

Bourne swore savagely in a language Radescu did not know, then cried, "Loot?" as he whipped the jeep in a double-S that brought it to a halt, partly behind another of the stripped boles which were the closest approach to cover on the blasted landscape.

"Take him," said the lieutenant as he rolled out of his seat before the jeep had fully grounded. As an afterthought, while he cleared his own weapon in the vehicle's shelter, he added, "Via, General, get *down*!"

The shot had come from across a valley three kilometers wide and as sere as the forest behind the patrol was lush. When slabs of granite tilted to form shallow wrinkles, layers of porous aquifer had been dammed and rerouted with startling effects for the vegetation on opposite sides of the impermeable divide. This valley had nothing like the dense canopy which had sheltered the vehicles while they waited for the firecracker rounds to do their work. Direct rainfall, the sole source of water for the vegetation here, had paradoxically stripped away much of the soil which might otherwise have been available because there was no barrier of foliage and strong root systems to break the rush of periodic torrents.

The native grass which fattened terran beefalo as efficiently as imported fodder provided a straggly, russet background to the occasional spike-leafed tree. Hiding places in the knobs and notches of the valley's further slope offered interlocking fields of fire across the entire area, and frequent outcrops among the grass below warned that Molts had free access to the valley floor as well.

The present shot had come from the far escarpment, however: it chopped shorter the trunk it hit at a flat angle. As he tumbled off his seat, obedient to the mercenary lieutenant, Radescu took with him a memory of the terrain three thousand meters away—an undifferentiated blur of gray and pale ochre—a background which could conceal a thousand gunmen as easily as one.

"We can't possibly find him!" the Oltenian whispered to Hawker as Sergeant Bourne scanned for potential targets with only his eyes and weapon above the jeep's front skirt. "We'll have to wait for the artillery to get him."

The shelling had resumed, but it was of a different scale and tenor. Black splotches like oil-soaked cotton bloomed around momentary red cores as Oltenian artillery pummeled the far side of the valley. Hammer's three fully-automated batteries of rocket howitzers were not involved in this bombardment. Their accuracy was needless—even indigenous artillery couldn't miss by three kilometers. The greater effectiveness of the mercenaries' shells would not change the fact that no practicable volume of fire could really affect the vast area involved. The shellbursts, though violent, left no significant mark once the puff of combustion products dispersed in the light breeze.

The State could not *afford* to use Hammer's hogs needlessly: the shells were imported over long Transit distances. Quite apart from their high cost in money terms, the length of time for replenishment might be disastrous in an emergency if stocks on Oltenia had been needlessly squandered.

Even as he spoke, General Radescu realized the absurdity of waiting for the shells speckling an area of twenty square kilometers to silence a single marksman. He grimaced, wishing he wore the makeup which would ordinarily have covered his flush of embarrassment.

"We got pretty good at countersniper work here on Oltenia," the lieutenant said mildly. The shellfire was not passing directly overhead, and in any case the trajectories were much higher than when the patrol cowered just short of the impact area of the heavy salvoes. "If this one just tries once more, Profile'll spot the heat signature and nail 'im." Hawker scowled. "Wish those bloody poofs'd get up here before the bastard decides to blow our detection gear all to hell. That first shot was too *cursed* close."

Alexander Radescu got to his feet, feeling like a puppet-master guiding the cunningly-structured marionette of his body. He walked away from the jeep and the slender treetrunk which was probably as much an aiming point as protection for the crucial electronics. He stumbled because his eyes were dilated with fear and everything seemed to have merged into a blur of glaucous yellow.

"Sir!" someone cried. Then, in his head phones, "*Sir! Get back here!*"

Poofs could only draw fire, could they? Well, perhaps not even that. Radescu's ribcage hurt where the gun had kicked him the only time he fired a shot. As he lifted the weapon again, his vision steadied to throw boulders and hummocks across the valley into a clear relief that Radescu thought was impossible for unaided vision at that distance. His muscles were still shuddering with adrenalin, though, and the shotgun's muzzle wobbled in an arc between bare sky and the valley floor.

That didn't matter. The short-range projectiles could not reach the far slope, much less hit a specific target there. Radescu squeezed off and the recoil rotated his torso twenty degrees. A bitch of a weapon, but it hadn't really *hurt* this time because he had nestled the stock into him properly before he fired. The Molts were not marksmen either; there was no real danger in what he was doing, no *reason* for fear, only physiological responses to instinct—

The muzzle blast of his second shot surprised him; his trigger finger was operating without conscious control. Earth, ten meters downslope, gouted and glazed in the cyan flash of the sniper's return bolt. As grit flung by the release of energy flicked across Radescu's cheeks and forehead, another powergun bolt splashed a pit in the soil so close to Radescu's boots that the leather of them turned white and crinkled.

The crackling snarl of the bolt reaching for his life almost deafened the Oltenian to the snap of Bourne's submachinegun returning fire with a single round. Radescu was still braced against a finishing shot from the heavy powergun across the valley so that he did not move even as the sergeant scrambled back into the jeep and shouted, "Come *on*, let's get this mother down a *hole!*"

The jeep shuddered off its skirts again before even Lieutenant Hawker managed to jump aboard. Radescu, awakening to find himself an unexpected ten meters away, ran back to the vehicle.

"D'ye get him?" Hawker was asking, neither Slammer using the radio. There were things Central didn't have to know.

"Did I shoot at him?" the sergeant boasted, pausing a moment for Radescu to clamber onto his seat again. "Cop, yeah, Loot—he's got a third hole in line with his eyeballs." As the jeep boosted downslope, gravity adding to the thrust of the fans, Bourne added, "Spoiled the bloody trophy, didn't I?"

Radescu knew that even a light bolt could be lethal at line of sight, and he accepted that magnification through the helmet face-plate could have brought the warrior's image within the appearance of arm's length. Nonetheless, a micron's unsteadiness at the gun muzzle and the bolt would miss a man-sized target three kays away. The general could not believe that anyone, no matter how expert, could rightfully be as sure of his accuracy as the Slammers gunman was.

But there were no further shots from across the valley as the jeep slid over earth harrowed by the barrage of firecracker rounds and tucked itself into the mouth of the nursery tunnel which was the patrol's objective.

The multiple channels of the commo helmets were filled with message traffic, none of it intended for Radescu. If he had been familiar with the Slammers code names, he could have followed the progress of the support operation—an armored battalion rein-forced by a company of combat engineers—which should have gotten under way as soon as the patrol first made contact with the enemy. For now, it was enough to know that Hammer would give direct warning if anything went badly wrong: not because Radescu commanded the indigenous forces, but because he accompanied Hawker and Bourne, two of Hammer's own.

"Duck," said the helmet with unexpected

clarity, Bourne on the intercom, and the general obeyed just as the vehicle switched direction and the arms of the tunnel entrance embraced them.

Though the nursery tunnels were carved through living rock—many of them with hand tools by Molts millenia in the past— the entrances were always onto gentle slopes so that no precocious infant projected himself over a sharp drop. That meant the approach was normally through soil, stabilized traditionally by arches of small ashlars, or (since humans landed) concrete or glazed earth portals.

Here the tunnel was stone-arched and, though the external portion of the structure had been sandblasted by the firecracker rounds, blocks only a meter within the opening bore the patina of great age. Radescu expected the jeep's headlights to flood the tunnel, supplementing the illumination which seeped in past them. Instead Profile Bourne halted and flipped a toggle on the dashboard.

There was a *thud!* within the plenum chamber, and opaque white smoke began to boil out around the skirts. It had the heavy odor of night-blooming flowers, cloying but not choking to the men who had to breath it. Driven by the fans, the smoke was rapidly filling the tunnel in both directions by the time it rose so high that Radescu, his head raised to the arched roof, was himself engulfed by it.

The last thing he saw were the flashing

holograms of Hawker's display, warning of Molt activity in the near distance. Before or behind them in the tunnel in this case, because the rock shielded evidence of ionization in any other direction.

Something touched the side of Radescu's helmet. He barely suppressed a scream before his faceplate slid down like a knife carving a swath of visibility through the palpable darkness. He could see again, though his surroundings were all in shades of saffron and the depth of rounded objects was somewhat more vague than normally was the case. Lieutenant Hawker was lowering the hand with which he had just manipulated the controls of the Oltenian's helmet for him.

"Molts can't see in the smoke," Hawker said. "Want to come with me—" the muzzle of his gun gestured down the tunnel—"or stay here with the sarge?"

"I ought—" Radescu began, intending to say 'to join my men.' But the Oltenian portion of the patrol under Captain Elejash had its orders—set up on the crest, await support, and let the vehicles draw fire if the Molts were foolish enough to provide data for the Slammers' gunnery computers. Each location from which a satellite registered a bolt being fired went into the data base as a point to be hit not now—the snipers would have teleported away—but at a future date when a Molt prepared to fire from the same known position. In fact, the casualties during the patrol's assault seemed to have left

the surviving Molts terrified of shellfire, even
the desultory bombardment by Oltenian
guns. "Yes, I'm with you," the general added
instead.

The nursery tunnel would normally have
been wide enough to pass the jeep much
deeper within it, but the shock of the penetrators detonating had spalled slabs of rock
from the walls, nearly choking the tunnel a
few meters ahead.

"Dunno if it's safe," the mercenary said,
feeling a facet of the new surface between
his left finger and thumb.

"It's bedrock," Radescu responded non-
chalantly. He had a fear of heights but no
touch of claustrophobia. "It may be blocked,
but nothing further should fall."

Hawker shrugged and resumed his careful advance.

The tunnel was marked by several sharp
changes of direction in its first twenty meters, natural since its whole purpose was to
train immature Molts to sense and teleport
to locations to which they had no physical
access. There were glowstrips and some light
trickling through the airshafts in the tunnel
roof, but the angled walls prevented the
infants from seeing any distance down the
gallery.

Radescu's gun wavered between being
pointed straight ahead in the instinctive fear
that a Molt warrior would bolt around a
corner at him, and being slanted up at 45°
in the intellectual awareness that to do otherwise needlessly endangered Lieutenant

Hawker, a step ahead and only partially to the side. Noticing that, the Oltenian pushed past the Slammer so as not to have that particular problem on his mind.

When Radescu brushed closer to the wall, he noticed that its surface seemed to brighten. That was the only evidence that he was 'seeing' by means of high-frequency sound, projected stereoscopically from either side of the commo helmet and, after it was reflected back, converted to visible light within microns-thick layers of the face shield.

It was the apparent normalcy of his vision that made so amazing the blindness of the pair of Molts which Radescu encountered in the large chamber around the fourth sharp angle. One of them was crawling toward him on hands and knees, while the other waddled in a half crouch with his arms spread as though playing blind-man's-bluff.

The shotgun rose—Radescu had instincts that amazed him in their *vulgarity*—but the general instead of firing cried, "Wait! Both of you! I want to talk about peace!"

The crawling Molt leaped upright, an arm going back to the hilt of a slung weapon, while the other adult caught up an infant. Both adults were very aged males, wizened though the yellowish tinge which was an artifact of the helmet's mechanism disconcerted eyes expecting the greenish-black scales of great age. The one who was crouching had a brow horn twisted like that of the old warrior in Belvedere. . . .

Hawker was a presence to his left but the Oltenian general concentrated wholly on the chamber before him, sweat springing out on his neck and on the underside of his jaw. There were not merely two Molts in the chamber but over a score, the rest infants in their neat beds of woven grass scattered across the floor of the room—where the adults, their lamps useless, could find them now only by touch.

"Keir, *stop!*" shouted the Molt who had not reached for a weapon. He was speaking in Rumanian, the only language common among the varied autochthonal themes as well as between Molts and humans. In this case, however, the Molts almost certainly spoke the same dialect, so the choice of language was almost certainly a plea for further forbearance on the part of the guns which, though unseen, must be there. "If they shoot, the young—"

The other Molt lunged forward—but toward a sidewall, not toward the humans. He held a stabbing spear, a traditional weapon with two blades joined by a short wooden handgrip in the center. One blade slashed upward in a wicked disemboweling stroke that rang on the stone like a sack of coins falling.

"We won't hurt your infants—" Radescu said as the spearcarrier rotated toward the sound with his weapon raised. Hawker fired and the Molt sagged in on himself, spitted on a trio of amber tracks: smoke concealed the normal cyan flash of the powergun, but shockwaves from the superheated air made their own mark on the brush of high-frequency sound.

The adult with the twisted horn disappeared, holding the infant he had snatched up as Radescu first spoke.

Alexander Radescu tried to lean his gun against the wall. It fell to the floor instead, but he ignored it to step to the nearest of the infant Molts. The little creature was surprisingly dense: it seemed to weigh a good five kilos in Radescu's arms, twisting againt the fabric of his jacket to find a nipple. Its scales were warm and flexible; only against pressure end-on did they have edges which Radescu could feel.

"We'll carry them outside," said the Oltenian. "I'll carry them. . . . We'll keep them in—" his face broke into a broad smile, hidden behind his face shield "—in the conference room; maybe they'll like the fountains."

"Hostages?" asked Hawker evenly, as faceless as the general, turning in a slow sweep of the chamber to ensure that no further Molts appeared to resume the rescue mission.

The infant Radescu held began to mew. He wondered how many of the females and prepubescent males had been fleeing from the ridge in short hops when the bomblets swept down across them. "No, Lieutenant," Radescu said, noting the ripples of saffron gauze in his vision, heat waves drifting from the iridium barrel of Hawker's powergun. "As proof of my good faith. I've proved other things today."

He strode back toward the exit from the

tunnel, realizing that his burden would prevent any hostile action by the Molts.

"Now I'll prove that," he added, as much to himself as to the mercenary keeping watch behind him in the lightless chamber.

The image of Grigor Antonescu in the tank of the commo set was more faithful than face-to-face reality would have been. The colors of the Chief Tribune's skin and the muted pattern of his formal robes glowed with the purity of transmitted light instead of being overlaid by the white glaze of surface reflection as they would have been had General Radescu spoken to him across the desk in his office.

"Good evening, Uncle," Radescu said. "I appreciate your—discussing matters with me in this way." Relays clicked elsewhere in the command car, startling him because he had been told he would be alone in the vehicle. Not that Hammer would not be scowling over every word, every nuance. . . .

"I'm not sure," replied the Tribune carefully, "that facilities supplied by the mercenaries are a suitable avenue for a conversation about State policy, however."

His hand reached forward and appeared to touch the inner surface of the tank in which Radescu viewed him. In fact, the older man's fingers must have been running across the outside of the similar unit in which he viewed his nephew's image. "Impressive, though. I'll admit that," he added.

The Tribune had the slim good looks common to men on his side of Radescu's family. He no longer affected the full makeup his nephew used regularly, because decades of imperious calm had given him an expression almost as artful. The general aped that stillness as he went on. "The key to our present small success has been the mercenaries; similarly, they are the key to the great success I propose for the near future."

"Wiping out an entire theme?" asked Antonescu over fingers tented so that the tips formed a V-notch like the rear sight of a gun.

"Peace with all the themes, Uncle," Radescu said, and no amount of concentration could keep a cheek muscle from twitching and making the wings of his butterfly beauty patch flutter. "An end to this war, a return to peaceful relations with the Molts—which off-planet traders have easily retained. There's no need for men and Molts to fight like this. Oltenia has three centuries of experience to prove there's no need."

Cooling fans began to whirr in a ceiling duct. Something similar must have happened near the console which Antonescu had been loaned by Hammer's supply contingent in Belvedere, because the Chief Tribune looked up in momentary startlement— the first emotion he had shown during the call. "There are those, Alexi," he said to the tank again, "who argue that with both populations expanding, there is no longer enough room on Oltenia for both races. The toll on human farm stock is too high, now that most Molts live to warrior age—thanks to improvements in health care misguidedly offered the autochthones by humans in the past."

"Molt attacks on livestock during puberty rites are inevitable," Radescu agreed, "as more land is devoted to ranching and the number of indigenous game animals is reduced." He felt genuinely calm, the way he had when he committed himself in the conference room with Marshal Erzul. There was only one route to real success, so he need have no regrets at what he was doing. "We can't stop the attacks. So we'll formalize them, treat them as a levy shared by the State and by the Molts collectively."

"They don't have the organization to accomplish that," Antonescu said with a contemptuous snap of his fingers. "Even if you think our citizens would stand for the cost themselves."

"What are the costs of having powerguns emptied into crowded ballrooms?" the younger man shot back with the passionless precision of a circuit breaker tripping. "What is the cost of this army—in *money* terms, never mind casualties?"

Antonescu shrugged. Surely he could not really be that calm. . . . He said, "Some things are easier in war, my boy. Emotions can be directed more easily, centralized decisionmaking doesn't arouse the—negative comment that it might under other circumstances."

"The Molts," said the young general in

conscious return to an earlier subject, "have been forced by the war to organize in much the same way that we have rallied behind the Tribunate."

By an effort of will, he held his uncle's eyes as he spoke the words he had rehearsed a dozen times to a mirror. "There could be no long-term—no middle-term—solution to Molt-human relations without that, I agree. But with firm control by the leaders of both races over the actions of their more extreme members, there *can* be peace—and a chance on this planet to accomplish things which aren't within the capacity of *any* solely human settlement, even Earth herself."

The Chief Tribune smiled in the warm, genuinely affectionate, manner which had made him the only relative—parents included—for whom Alexander Radescu had cared in early childhood. Radescu relived a dual memory, himself in a crib looking at his Uncle Grigor—and the infant Molt squirming against him for sustenance and affection.

Antonescu said, "Your enthusiasm, my boy, was certainly one of the reasons we gave the army into your charge when traditional solutions had failed. And of course—" the smile lapsed into something with a harder edge, but only for a moment "—because you're my favorite nephew, yes.

"But primarily," the Chief Tribune continued, "because you are a very intelligent young man, Alexi, and you have a record of doing what you say you'll do . . . which will bring you far, one day, yes."

He leaned forward, just as he had in Radescu's infancy, his long jaw and flat features a stone caricature of a human face. "But how can you offer to end a war that the Molts began—however fortunate their act may have been for some human ends?"

"I'm going to kick them," the general said with a cool smile of his own, "until they ask *me* for terms. And the terms I'll offer them will be fair to both races." He blinked, shocked to realize that he had been speaking as if Chief Tribune Antonescu were one of the coterie of officers he had brought to heel in the conference room. "With your permission, of course, sir. And that of your colleagues."

Antonescu laughed and stood up. Radescu was surprised to see that the Chief Tribune remained focused in the center of the tank as he walked around the chair in which he had been sitting. "Enthusiasm, Alexi, yes, we expect that," he said. "Well, you do your part and leave the remainder to us. You've done very well so far.

"But I think you realize," the older man went on with his hands clasped on the back of a chair of off-planet pattern, "that I've stretched very far already to give you this opportunity." Antonescu's voice was calm, but his face held just a hint of human concern which shrank his nephew's soul down to infancy again. "If matters don't—succeed, according to your plans and the needs of the State, then there won't be further options for you. Not even for you, Alexi."

"I understand, Uncle," said Alexander Radescu, who understood very well what failure at this level would require him, as an Oltenian aristocrat, to do in expiation. "I have no use for failures either."

As he reached for the power switch at the base of the vision tank, he wondered who besides Hammer would be listening in on the discussion—and what *they* thought of his chances of success.

The bolt was a flicker in the air, scarcely visible until it struck an Oltenian armored car. The steel plating burned with a clang and a white fireball a moment before a fuel tank ruptured to add the sluggish red flames of kerosene to the spectacle. The vehicle had been hull down and invisible from the ridge toward which the next assault would be directed; but the shot had been fired from the rear, perhaps kilometers distant.

Three men in Oltenian fatigues jumped from the body of the vehicle while a fourth soldier screamed curses in a variety of languages and squirmed from the driver's hatch, cramped by the Slammer body armor which he wore. The turrets on several of the neighboring armored cars began to crank around hastily, though the sniper was probably beyond range of the machineguns even with solid shot. There was no chance of hitting the Molt by randomly spraying the landscape anyway; Radescu's tongue poised to pass an angry order down when some subordinate forestalled him and the turrets reversed again.

"Nothing to be done about that," Radescu said to the pair of men closest to him. He nodded in the direction of a few of the hundred or so armored vehicles he could see from where he stood. Had he wished for it, satellite coverage through the hologram projector in the combat car would have shown him thousands more. "With a target the size of this one, the odd sniper's going to hit something even if he's beyond range of any possible counterfire."

A second bolt slashed along the side of an armored personnel carrier a hundred meters from the first victim. There was no secondary explosion this time—in fact, because of the angle at which it struck, the powergun might not have penetrated the vehicle's fighting compartment. Its infantrymen boiled out anyway, many of them leaving behind the weapons they had already stuck through gunports in the APC's sides. Bright sunlight glanced incongruously from their bulky infrared goggles, passive night vision equipment which was the closest thing in the Oltenian arsenal to the wide assortment of active and passive devices built into the Slammers' helmets.

Thank the Lord for small favors: in the years before squabbling broke out in open war between men and Molts, the autochthones had an unrestricted choice of imports through off-planet traders. They had bought huge stocks of powerguns and explosives, weapons which made an individual warrior the bane of hundreds of his sluggish human opponents. Since theirs would be the decision of when and where to engage, however, they had seen no need of equipment like the mercenaries' helmets— equipment which expanded the conditions under which one could fight.

"Don't bet your ass there's no chance a' counterfire," growled Profile Bourne; and as he was speaking, the main gun of one of Hammer's tanks blasted back in the direction from which the sniper's bolts had come.

The flash and the *thump!* of air closing back along the trail blasted through it by a twenty-centimeter powergun startled more Oltenians than had the sniper fire itself.

General Forsch had started to walk toward Radescu from one of the command trailers with a message he did not care to entrust either to radio or to the lips of a subordinate. When the tank fired, the gangling chief of staff threw himself flat onto ground which the barrage of two days previous had combed into dust as fine as baby powder. Forsch looked up with the anger of a torture victim at his young commander.

Radescu, seeing the yellow-gray blotches on the uniform which had been spotless until that moment, hurried over to Forsch and offered a hand to help him rise. Radescu had deliberately donned the same stained battledress he had worn during the previous assault, but he could empathize nonetheless with how his subordinate was feeling.

"The meteorologists say there should be a period of still air," the chief of staff muttered, snatching his hand back from Radescu's offer of help when he saw how dirty his palms were.

"Our personnel say that it may last for only a few minutes," Forsch continued, dusting his hands together with intense chopping motions on which he focused his eyes. "The—*technician* from the mercenaries—" he glanced up at Hawker and Bourne, following Radescu to either side "—says go with it." His face twisted. "Just 'Go with it.'"

The sky was the flawless ultramarine of summer twilight. "Thank you, General Forsch," Radescu said as he looked upward, his back to the lowering sun. Profile had been right: whether or not the tank blast had killed the sniper, its suddenness had at least driven the Molt away from the narrow circuit of rocks through which he had intended to teleport and confuse counterfire. A single twenty centimeter bolt could shatter a boulder the size of a house, and the consequent rain of molten glass and rock fragments would panic anyone within a hundred meters of the impact area.

Radescu tongued the helmet's control wand up and to the left, the priority channel that would carry his next words to every man in the attacking force and log him into the fire control systems of the Oltenian and mercenary gun batteries. "Execute Phase One," he said, three words which subsumed hundreds of computer hours and even lengthier, though less efficient, calculations by battery commanders, supply officers, and scores of additional human specialties.

True darkness would have been a nice bonus, but the hour or so around twilight was the only real likelihood of still air—and that was more important than the cloak Nature herself would draw over activities.

"All right," Alexander Radescu said, seeing General Forsch but remembering his uncle. The trailers of the Oltenian operations center straggled behind Forsch because of the slope. A trio of Slammers combat cars with detectors like those of the jeep guarded the trailers against Molt infiltrators. Hull down on the ridge line, the seventeen tanks of Hammer's H Company waited to support the assault with direct fire. A company of combat cars, vulnerable (as the tanks were not) to bolts from the autochthones' shoulder weapons, would move up as soon as the attack was joined.

Apart from the combat car in which the commander himself would ride, every vehicle in the actual assault would be Oltenian; but all the drivers were Hammer's men.

Forsch saluted, turned, and walked back toward the trailers with his spine as stiff as a ramrod. There was an angry crackle nearby as a three-barrelled powergun on one of the combat cars ripped a bubble of ionization before it could become a functioning Molt. There were more shots audible and those only a fraction of the encounters which distance muffled, Radescu knew. A satchel charge detonated—with luck when a bolt

struck it, otherwise when a Molt hurled it
into a vehicle of humans whose luck had
run out.

The autochthones were stepping up their
harrassing attacks, though their main effort
was almost certainly reserved for the moment that humans crowded into the killing
ground of the open, rock-floored valley. Bolts
fired from positions kilometers to either side
would enfilade the attacking vehicles, while
satchel charges and buzzbombs launched
point-blank ripped even Hammer's panzers.
Human counterfire itself would be devastat-
ing to the vehicles as confusion and prox-
imity caused members of the assault force
to blast one another in an attempt to hit
the fleeing Molts.

It might still happen that way.

"Might best be mounting up," said Lieutenant Hawker, whose level of concern was
shown only by the pressure-mottled knuckles of the hand which gripped his submachinegun. Bourne was snapping his head
around like a dog trying to catch flies. He
knew the link from the combat car to the
lieutenant's helmet would beep a warning
if a Molt were teleporting to a point nearby,
but he was too keyed up to accept the stress
of inaction. "Three minutes isn't very long."

"Long enough to get your clock cleaned,"
the sergeant rejoined as he turned grate-
fully to the heavy vehicle he would drive in
this assault.

The first shells were already screaming
down on the barren valley and the slope

across it. The salvo was time-on-target: calculated so that ideally every shell would burst simultaneously, despite being fired from different ranges and at varying velocities. It was a technique generally used to increase the shock effect of the opening salvo of a bombardment. This time its purpose was to give the Molts as little warning as possible between their realization of Radescu's plan and its accomplishment. The young general sprinted for the combat car, remembering that its electronics would give him a view from one of the tanks already overlooking the valley.

Colonel Hammer and his headquarters vehicles were twenty kilometers to the rear, part of the security detachment guarding the three batteries of rocket howitzers. The mercenary units had been severely depleted by providing drivers for so many Oltenian vehicles, and a single Molt with a powergun could wreak untold havoc among the belts of live ammunition being fed to the hogs.

There was in any case no short-term reason that high officers should risk themselves in what would be an enlisted man's fight. Radescu had positioned his own headquarters in a place of danger so that his generals could rightfully claim a part in the victory he prayed he would accomplish. He was joining the assault himself because he believed, as he had said to Hawker and Bourne when he met them, in the value of leading from the front.

And also because he *was* Alexander Radescu.

There were footpegs set into the flank of the combat car, but Hawker used only the midmost one as a brace from which to vault into the open fighting compartment. The big mercenary then reached down, grasped Radescu by the wrist rather than by the hand he had thought he was offering, and snatched him aboard as well. Hawker's athleticism, even hampered by the weight and restriction of his body armor, was phenomenal.

The detection gear which had been transferred to the combat car for this operation took up the space in which the forward of the three gunners would normally have stood. The pintle-mounted tribarrels were still in place, but they would not be used during the assault. The Slammers' submachineguns and the shotgun which the general again carried would suffice for close-in defense without endangering other vehicles.

The thick iridium sides of the mercenary vehicle made it usable in the expected environment which would have swept the jeep and any men aboard it to instant destruction. Radescu touched his helmet as he settled himself in the corner of the fighting compartment opposite Hawker: firing from the combat car meant raising one's head above the sidewalls.

The big vehicle quivered as Bourne, hidden forward in the driver's compartment, fed more power to the idling fans. Hawker brought up an image of the valley over the crest, his hands brushing touchplates on the package of additional instruments even before Radescu requested it. Very possibly the lieutenant acted on his own hook, uninterested in Radescu's wishes pro or con. . . .

The hologram was of necessity monochrome, in this case a deep red-orange which fit well enough with what Radescu remembered of the contours of rock covered by sere grass. The shell-bursts hanging and spreading over the terrain were the same sullen, fiery color as the ground, however, and that was disconcerting. It made Radescu's chest tighten as he imagined plunging into a furnace to be consumed in his entirety.

The tanks began to shoot across the valley with a less startling effect than the single countersniper blast. These bolts were directed away from the assault force, and they added only marginally to the ambient sound. The bombardment did not seem too loud to Radescu after the baptism he had received from shells plunging down point-blank the previous day. The sky's constant thrum was fed by nearly a thousand guntubes, some of them even heavier—though slower firing—than the Slammers' howitzers, and the effect was all-pervasive even though it had not called itself to the general's attention.

Dazzling reflections from the 200 mm bolts played across even the interior of the combat car, washing Hawker's grim smile with the blue-green cast of death. The bolts did not show up directly on the display, but air heated by their passage roiled the upper reaches of the smoke into horizontal vortices. Across the valley the shots hammered computer-memorized positions from which Molts had sniped in the past. Rock sprayed high in the release of enormous crystalline stresses, and bubbles of heated air expanded the covering of smoke into twisted images larger than the tanks which had caused them.

"Base to Command," said the helmet in the voice of General Forsch, overlaid by a fifty-cycle hum which resulted from its transmission through the mercenaries' commo system. There were spits of static as well, every time a tank main gun released its packet of energy across the spectrum. "Phase One coverage has reached planned levels."

"Terminate Phase One," said Radescu. Across from him, Lieutenant Hawker patted a switch and the image of the valley collapsed. He did not touch other controls, so presumably the detection apparatus had been live all the time. The smile he flashed at Radescu when he saw the general's eyes on him was brief and preoccupied, but genuine enough.

"Phase One terminated," Forsch crackled back almost at once.

There was no effect directly obvious to the assault force, but that was to be expected: the flight time of shells from some of the guns contributing to the barrage was upwards of thirty seconds. "Prepare to execute Phase Two," said Radescu on the command channel as clearly as the hormones jumping in his bloodstream would permit. Everything around him was a fragment of a montage, each existing on a timeline separate from the rest.

"Give'em ten seconds more," Profile broke in on the intercom. "Some bastard always takes one last pull on the firing lanyard to keep from having to unload the chamber."

"Execute Phase Two," ordered Radescu, his tongue continuing its set course as surely as an avalanche staggers downhill, the driver's words no more than a wisp of snow fencing overwhelmed in the rush of fixed intent.

Whatever Bourne may have thought about the order, he executed it with a precision smoother than any machine. The combat car surged forward, lagging momentarily behind the Oltenian APCs to either flank because the traction of their tires gave them greater initial acceleration than could the air cushion. Seconds later, when the whole line crested the ridge, the Slammers vehicle had pulled ahead by the half length that Bourne thought was safest.

In the stillness that replaced the howl of shells, small arms sizzled audibly among the grumble of diesels as soldiers responded to teleporting Molts—or to their own nervousness. A full charge of shot clanged into the combat car's port side, although Hawker's instruments showed that the gunman in the personnel carrier could not have had a real target.

Radescu raised himself to look over the bulkhead, though the sensible part of his mind realized that the added risk was considerable and unnecessary. To function in a world gone mad, a man goes mad himself: to be ruled by a sensible appreciation of danger in a situation where danger was both enormous and unavoidable would drive the victim into cowering funk—countersurvival in a combat zone where his own action might be required to save him. Bracing himself against the receiver of the tribarrel locked in place beside him, Alexander Radescu caught a brief glimpse of the results of his plan—before he plunged into them.

The sweep of the broad valley the assault must cross boiled with the contents of the thousands of smoke shells poured over it by the massed batteries. The brilliant white of rounds from Hammer's guns lay flatter and could be seen still spreading, absorbing and underlying the gray-blue chemical haze gushing from Oltenian shells. The coverage was not—could not be—complete, even within the two-kilometer front of the attack. Nonetheless, its cumulative effect robbed snipers of their targets at any distance from the vehicles.

Molts teleporting to positions readied to meet the attack found that even on the flanking slopes where the warriors were not blanketed by smoke, their gunsights showed featureless shades of gray instead of Oltenian vehicles. The wisest immediately flickered back to cover on the reverse slope. Younger, less perceptive autochthones began firing into the haze—an exercise as vain as hunting birds while blindfolded.

A pillar of crimson flame stabbed upward through the smoke as the result of one such wild shot; but Hammer's tanks and the combat cars joining them on the ridge combed out the frustrated Molts like burrs from a dog's hide. Had the snipers picked a target, fired once, and shifted position as planned, they would have been almost invulnerable to countermeasures. Warriors who angrily tried to empty their guns into an amorphous blur lasted five shots or fewer before a tank gun or a burst of automatic fire turned them into a surge of organic gases in the midst of a fireball of liquid rock.

All colors narrowed to shades of yellow as the combat car drove into the thickening smoke and Radescu switched on the sonic vision apparatus of his borrowed helmet. What had been an opaque fog opened into a 60° wedge of the landscape, reaching back twenty or thirty meters. It would not have done for top speed running, but the visibility was more than adequate for an assault line rolling across open terrain at forty KPH.

A tree stump, ragged and waist high, coalesced from the fog as the helmet's ultrasonic generators neared it. Bourne edged left to avoid it, the combat car swaying like a leaf in the breeze, while the Slammer driving the Oltenian vehicle to the right swerved more awkwardly in the other direction.

Alexander Radescu had been loaned a helmet from mercenary stores, but there was no question of equipping enough local troops to drive all the vehicles in the assault. The alternative had been to scatter a large proportion of the Slammers among packets of Oltenian regulars. That Hammer had found the alternative acceptable was praise for Radescu which the Oltenian had only hoped to receive.

A Molt with a buzzbomb on his shoulder, ready to launch, appeared beside the tree stump.

The smoke did nothing to prevent warriors from teleporting into the valley to attack. The autochthones had expected a barrage of high explosives and armor piercing rounds, which would have had some effect but only a limited one. This valley was the center of a theme's territory; in a jump of a kilometer or two over ground so familiar, a young adult could position himself on a chunk of granite no larger than his head.

What the smoke shells *did* do was to prevent the autochthones from seeing anything after they projected themselves into the fog. Radescu cried out, raising his shotgun. The Molt was turned half away from them, hunching forward, hearing the diesel engine of the nearest APC but unable to see even that.

The combat car's acceleration and slight change of attitude threw the Oltenian general back against the hard angles of the gun

mount beside him. Bourne had brought up
power and changed fan aspect in a pair of
perfectly matched curves which showed just
how relatively abruptly an air cushion vehicle could accelerate on a downslope, when
gravity was on its side and the rolling fric-
tion of wheels slowed the conventional vehicles to either flank.

The Molt must have heard the rush of air
at the last, because he whirled like a dancer
toward the combat car with a look of utter
horror as the bow slope rushed down on
him. Radescu fired past the car's forward
tribarrel, his shot missing high and to the
left, as the autochthone loosed his shoulder-
launched missile at the vehicle.

The buzzbomb struck the combat car beside the driver's hatch and sprang skyward,
its rocket motor a hot spot in the smoke to
infrared goggles and a ghostly pattern of
vortices in the Slammers' ultrasound. The
combat car which weighed thirty-two tonnes
quivered only minutely as it spread the Molt
between the ground and the steel skirt of
the plenum chamber.

There was a violent outbreak of firing
from the vehicles just behind the combat
car. Passive infrared was useless for a driver
because terrain obstacles did not radiate
enough heat to bring them out against the
ambient background. For soldiers whose only
duty was to cut down Molts before the warriors could find targets of their own in the
smoke, passive infrared was perfect.

The gunners in the armored car turrets

and the infantrymen huddled behind vision blocks in the sides of their armored
personnel carriers could see nothing—until
Molt warriors teleported into the valley.

The autochthones' body temperature made
them stand out like flares blazing in a sea
of neutral gray. The automatic fire of the
turret guns was not very accurate; but the
ranges were short, the shot-cones deadly,
and there were over fifteen thousand twitching trigger fingers packed into a constricted
area. Warriors shimmered out of the smoke,
hesitated in their unexpected blindness, and
were swept away in bloody tatters by the
rattling crossfire. Charges of miniature airfoils sang from one vehicle to another, scarring the light armor and chipping away
paint like a desultory sandblasting. The projectiles could not seriously harm the vehicles, however, and the armor was sufficient
to preserve the crews and infantry comple-
ments as well.

The Molt Profile had just driven over was
a wide blotch to the goggles of the Oltenians
in the flanking APCs. Their guns stormed
from either side, stirring the slick warmth
and ricocheting from the rocky ground.

Lieutenant Hawker touched Radescu with
his left hand, the one which did not hold
the submachinegun. The combat car yawed
as Profile braked it from the murderous rush
he had just achieved, but the veteran lieutenant held steady without need to cling to
a support as the Oltenian did.

"Arming distance," Hawker said over the

intercom now that he had Radescu's attention. "The buzzbomb didn't go off because it was fired too close in. It's a safety so you don't blow yourself up, that's all. Profile wasn't taking any risks."

"Yee-*ha*!" shouted the driver, clearly audible over the windrush.

Alexander Radescu was later surprised at how little he remembered of the assault—and that in flashes as brief and abrupt as the powergun bolt that lanced past him from behind, close enough to heat the left earpiece of his commo helmet before it sprayed dirt from the ground rising in front of the combat car. Bypassed sniper or mercenary gunner forgetting his orders not to fire into the smoke? No way to tell and no matter: all fire is hostile fire when it snaps by your head.

The slope that was their objective on the other side of the valley had been shrouded as thickly as the rest of the ground which the assault needed to cross. The hogs had kicked in final salvoes of firecracker rounds to catch Molts who thought the fog protected them. That explosive whisking, added to the greater time that the curtain had been in place, meant that the smoke had begun to part and thin here where the ground rose.

A crag, faceted like the bow of a great sea vessel, appeared so abruptly in Radescu's vision that the Oltenian instinctively flipped up his face shield. The wedge of granite had a definite purple cast noticeable through the smoke of sun-infused white and gray streaming slowly down into the valley basin, heavier than the air it displaced.

It had been inevitable that the assault lines would straggle. Perhaps it was inevitable also that Profile Bourne would use his experience with his vehicle and its better power-to-weight ratio to race to the objective alone—despite clear orders, from Hawker as well as Radescu, to keep it reined in. There was no other vehicle close to them as the sergeant climbed to the left of the slab with his fans howling out maximum thrust and the ionization detector began flashing its violet and yellow warning, visible as the rock was through a thin neutral mask.

Alexander Radescu looked up and to the right, guided by instinct in the direction that the electronic tocsin was causing Hawker to turn with his submachinegun. The air solidified into a Molt with scales of as rich a color as the rock he stood on—spitting distance from the car laboring uphill, an easy cast for a satchel charge or a burst of fire into the open-topped compartment.

The Molt did not carry a weapon, and his right horn was twisted.

"*No!*" Radescu shouted, forgetting his intercom link as he lunged across the fighting compartment to grasp his companion's gun. His fingers locked at the juncture of the barrel and receiver, cold iridium and plastic which insulated too well to have any temperature apart from that which the general's hand gave the outer layer of molecules. "Not this one!"

"Steady," said Enzo Hawker, bracing the Oltenian with the free hand which could have plucked the man away, just as Radescu's slight body would have been no sufficient hindrance had the gunner wished to carry through and fire at the Molt. "Watch your side of the car."

The broad ravine into which Bourne plunged them was a watercut ramp to the crest. It held smoke dense enough to be instantly blinding. The autochthone had already disappeared, teleporting away with a smile which was probably an accident of physiognomy.

"I'm sorry, I—" Radescu said as he straightened, remembering this time to use his intercom. Hawker was as solid as the iridium bulkheads themselves, while the general's own mind leaped with fear and embarrassment and a sense of victory which intellectually he knew he had not yet won. "Shouldn't have touched you, Lieutenant, I was—" He raised his eyes to meet the other man's and saw nothing, even a hand's length apart, because the mercenary's face shield was a perfect mirror from the outside. "I didn't think."

"Just steady," Hawker said quietly. "You've been thinking fine."

Shells were hitting the ground, a considerable distance away but heavily enough that pebbles slid in miniature avalanches as the ravine walls quivered. As soon as the vehicles rolled into the valley, the artillery had shifted its points of aim to rocky areas within a few kilometers of the target of the assault.

These would be staging points for the Molt refugees, the females and the prepubescent males driven from what should have been the inviolable core of the theme holdings. They could stay ahead of human pursuit and would in a matter of a few hops scatter beyond the area which shells could saturate. But since the starting point was known, there was a finite number of initial landing areas available to the Molt noncombatants. Those were the targets for as many fragmentation and high-explosive rounds as the army could pump out.

Alexander Radescu had his own reasons, eminently logical ones, to want peace. He had to give the autochthones a reason whose logic the most high-spirited, glory-longing warrior would accept as overwhelming.

Dead comrades would not achieve that alone: a warrior *could* not accept the chance of dying as a sufficient reason to modify his actions, any more than could a mercenary soldier like Hawker, like Bourne in the forward hatch. Maimed females and children howling as they tried to stuff intestines back into their body cavities were necessary, as surely as the Molt in the ballroom of the Tribunal Palace in Belvedere had been, stooping behind the weight of his powergun—every shot turning a gay costume into burning, bloody rags.

"It's not worth it," the young general said, sickened by the coolness with which he had deliberated slaughter.

Only when Hawker said, "Hey?" did the Oltenian realize he had spoken not only aloud but loudly. He shrugged to the mercenary and their vehicle, sideslipping down the reverse slope, would have put an end to the conversation even had Radescu wished to continue it.

The smoke blanket here was tattered into no more than a memory of what the assault force had first driven into, though it—like a sheet of glass viewed endwise—was still opaque to a sniper trying to draw a bead any distance through it. There was a body sprawled forty meters from the combat car, an adult male killed by one of the shrapnel rounds which interspersed the smoke shells covering the ridge.

"Red two-ninety!" cried Lieutenant Hawker, "*Radescu*! Red two seventy!" and the general whirled to fire over the bulkhead at the Molt appearing almost beside the combat car, too close for Hawker himself to shoot.

The muzzle blast of the shotgun was a surprise, but this time the properly-shouldered stock thrust and did not slam the young general. Neither did the charge hit the autochthone, a male with a powergun, though a bush a meter from him was stripped in a sharp-edged scallop.

The Molt threw his arms up and ran as the car sailed past him. Radescu fired again, missing even worse because he had not figured the vehicle's speed into his attempt to lead the runner; and as the Slammer lieutenant aimed over the back deck, the autochthone dissolved away in a further teleport. Only then did Radescu realize that the Molt had not only been too frightened to shoot, he had dropped his powergun as he fled.

The cave entrance for which Bourne steered was much larger than the one they had captured on the other side of the ridge—larger, in fact, than anything of the sort which Radescu had previously seen. The size was accentuated by the hasty attempts the Molts had made to build a physical barrier across the huge, pillared archway. There was a layer of stones ranging from head-sized down to pebbles in the entrance, the foundation course of a crude wall. Around the stones were more bodies, half a dozen of them—probably adult males, but too close to the epicenter of the firecracker round that burst overhead for the bomblets to have left enough of the corpses for certain identification.

A puff of breeze opened a rent in the smoke through which the evening sky streamed like a comet's violet hair.

"Hang on," said the sergeant on the intercom. He had driven past the archway and now, as he spoke, spun the combat car on its axis to approach from the downhill side.

Radescu, clinging to the gun mount awkwardly because of the personal weapon in his hand, cried, "There's a barrier there, Sergeant—rocks!"

"Hang the cop on!" Bourne replied glee-fully, and the combat car, brought to the end of the tether of its downhill inertia, accelerated toward the entrance at a rate that sailed it over the pitiable stones through which a less ebullient driver would have plowed.

There was light in the cavernous chamber beyond, a portable area lamp of Oltenian manufacture, held up at arm's length by a Molt with a twisted horn.

As cool as he had been when he prepared to execute his own command group within minutes of meeting them, General Radescu said, "Neither of you shoot," on the intercom. Then, tonguing the command channel though he was not sure of signal propagation from inside the crystalline rock, he added, "Command to all units. Phase Two is complete. Terminate all offensive activity, shoot only in self-defense."

Bourne had not expected to halt immediately within the entrance, nor had the general specifically ordered him to do so. The sergeant would not have been condemned for murder, however, if he had felt the need to wait for orders before he took action he considered sensible. Now he used the steel skirts of the plenum chamber as physical brakes against the floor of polished rock, screeching and sparking in an orange-white storm instead of depending on the thrust of the fans to halt the heavy vehicle. The dazzling afterimages of saturated blue seemed for a moment brighter than the lamp which the autochthone had continued to hold steady while the car slewed around him in a semicircle.

When the skirts rested solidly on the pavement, Radescu realized that the ground itself was not firm. Earth shocks from the distant impact zones made dust motes dance around the globe of light, and the bulkhead quivered as Radescu dismounted.

Lag time, General Radescu hoped as he stepped toward the wizened Molt, shells fired before his order to desist. Behind him, the combat car pinged and sizzled as metal found a new stasis. There was also the clicking sound of Lieutenant Hawker releasing the transport lock of a tribarrel, freeing the weapon for immediate use.

"I hope you're here to talk of peace," said the Oltenian, reaching out to take the lamp which seemed too heavy for the frail autochthone.

"No," said Ferad who relinquished the lamp willingly, though he would have held it as long as need required—the way he had supported the powergun until he had emptied the magazine. "I am here this time to *make* peace."

The placid landscape had a slightly gritty texture, but Alexander Radescu was not sure whether that was a real residue from the smoke shells or if it was just another result of his own tiredness.

Losing would have taken just as much effort as the triumph he had in fact achieved.

Lieutenant Hawker murmured a reply to his commo helmet, then leaned toward Radescu and whispered, "Seven minutes."

The Oltenian general nodded, then turned to Forsch and the divisional generals assembled behind him, each with a small contingent of troops in dress uniforms. "The Tribunes are expected to arrive in seven minutes," Radescu called, loudly enough for even the enlisted men to hear him.

Radescu had gone to some lengths to give this event the look of a review, not an occupation. Weapons had been inspected for external gloss. Dress uniforms—blue with orange piping for the other ranks, scarlet for officers through field grade, and pearl with gold for the generals—would not remind the watching autochthones of the smoke-shrouded, shot-rippling assault by which the Oltenian Army had entered a theme stronghold.

The Molts would not forget, the survivors watching from distant hills with the representatives of the other themes. There was no need to rub their broad noses in it, that was all.

"General Radescu," said a voice. "Sir?"

Radescu turned, surprised but so much a man living on his nerves that no event seemed significantly more probable than did any other. "Yes?" he said. "General Forsch?"

Profile Bourne watched the chief of staff with the expression of disdain and despair which had summed up his attitude toward all the local forces—until the Oltenian line had made the assault beside him. Even those men were poofs again when they donned their carnival uniforms.

The sergeant's hands were linked on his breastplate, but that put them adequately near to his slung submachinegun. The reason the two Slammers had given for continuing to guard Radescu was a valid one: a single disaffected Molt could destroy all chances of peace by publicly assassinating Alexander Radescu. The general had not been impelled to ask whether or not that was the *real* reason.

Forsch was nervous, looking back at the divisional generals two paces behind him for support. Iorga nodded to him with tight-lipped enthusiasm.

"Sir," the lanky chief of staff continued, though he seemed to be examining his expression in the mirrors of Radescu's gilded boots, "I—we want to say that. . . ."

The hills whispered with the rush of an oncoming aircraft. That, and perhaps the sculptured placidity of Radescu's face, brought Forsch back to full functioning. "You may have sensed," he said, meeting his commander's eyes, "a certain hostility when you announced your appointment to us."

"I surprised you, of course," Radescu murmured to make Forsch easier about whatever he intended to say. The great cargo plane comandeered to bring the Tribunes to sign the accords was visible a kilometer away, its wing rotors already beginning to tilt into hover mode for the set-down. "All of you performed to the highest expectations of the State."

"Yes," the chief of staff said, less agreement than an acceptance of the gesture which Radescu had made. "Well. In any case, sir—and I speak for all of us—" more nods from the officers behind him "—we were wrong. You *were* the man to lead us. And we'll follow you, the whole army will follow you, wherever you choose to lead us if the peace talks break down."

Lord and his martyrs, thought Alexander Radescu, surveying the faces of men up to twice his age, they really would. They would follow him because he had gotten something done, even though some of the generals must have realized by now that he'd have shot them out of hand if they stood in the way of his intent. Lord and martyrs!

"I—" Radescu began; then he reached out and took Forsch's right hand in his and laid the other on the tall officer's shoulder. "General—men—the peace talks won't fail." It was hard to view the quick negotiations between Ferad and himself as anything so formal that they could have been 'broken off,' but it was the same implicit dependence on bureaucratic niceties which had turned the war into a morass on the human side. "But I appreciate your words as, as much as I appreciated the skill and courage, the *great* courage, the whole army displayed in making this moment possible."

The Molts' problem had been the reverse

of the self-inflicted wound from which the Oltenian Army had bled. The autochthones were too independent ever to deal the crushing blows that their ability to concentrate suddenly would have permitted them. Each side slashed at one another but struggled with itself, too ineffective either to win or to cease. And the same solution would extricate both from the bloody swamp: leaders who could see a way clear and who were willing to drive all before them.

"She's coming in," said Profile Bourne, not himself part of the formalities but willing to remind those who were of their duties. General Forsch wrung his superior's hand and slipped back to his place a pace to the rear, while the aircraft settled with a whining roar that echoed between the hills.

Debris and bodies had been cleared from the broad archway, and for the occasion the flagstone pavement had even been polished by a crew which ordinarily cared for the living quarters of general officers. Radescu had toyed only briefly with the thought of resodding the shell-scars and wheel tracks. The valley's rocky barrenness was the reason it had become a Molt center, and nothing the human attack had done changed its appearance significantly. It was perhaps well to remind the Tribunate that this was *not* merely a human event, that the autochthones watching from vantage points kilometers distant were a part of it and of the system the treaty would put into effect for the remainder of the planet's history.

The aircraft's turbines thrummed in a rapidly-descending rhythm when the oleo struts flexed and rose again as the wheels accepted the load. Dust billowed from among the russet grassblades, bringing General Radescu a flashback of a hillside descending in a welter of Molt bodies as the penetrators lifted it from within. He had been so frightened during that bombardment. . . .

The rear hatchway of the big cargo plane was levering itself down into an exit ramp. "Attention!" Radescu called, hearing his order repeated down the brief ranks as he himself braced. Most of the army was encamped five kilometers away in a location through which the troops had staged to the final assault. There they nervously awaited the outcome of this ceremony, reassured more by the sections of Hammer's men with detection gear scattered among them than they were by Radescu's promises as he rode off.

He'd done that much, at least, built trust between the indigenous and mercenary portions of his army on the way to doing the same between the intelligent species which shared the planet. It occurred to Alexander Radescu as he watched a pair of light trucks drive down the ramp, the first one draped with bunting for the ceremony, that wars could not be won: they could only be ended without having been lost. The skirmishes his troops had won were important for the way they conduced to the ends of peace.

The chairs draped in cloth-of-gold made

an imposing-enough background for the Tribunes, but no one seemed to have calculated what uneven ground and the truck's high center of gravity would do to men attempting to sit on such chairs formally. Radescu suppressed a smile, remembering the way he had jounced on the back of the jeep.

That experience and others of recent days did not prevent him from being able to don a dress uniform and the makeup which had always been part of the persona he showed the world; but a week of blood and terror had won him certain pieces of self-knowledge which were, in their way, as important to him as anything he had accomplished in a military sense.

The driver of the lead truck tried to make a sweeping turn in order to bring the rear of his vehicle level with the red carpet which had been cut in sections from the flooring of the living-trailers of high officers. An overly-abrupt steering correction brought an audible curse from one of the men in the back of the vehicle, men who looked amazingly frail to Alexander Radescu after a week of troops in battledress.

Hawker and Bourne had kept a settled silence thus far during the makeshift procession until the six guards in scarlet—none of them were below the rank of major— jumped from the second truck to help the Tribunes down the steps welded to the back of the first. At the Honor Guards' appearance, Enzo Hawker snorted audibly and

Radescu felt an impulse to echo the Slammer's disdain.

And yet those men were very similar to Radescu himself in background; not quite so well connected, but officers of the Tribunal Honor Guard for the same reason that Alexander Radescu was a general. That he *was* a man who could lead an army while they, with their rhodium-plated pistols, could not have guarded a school crossing, was an individual matter.

Grigor Antonescu, First among Equals, wore a pure white robe of office, while the collars of his two companions were black. Radescu saluted.

Instead of returning the formality the Chief Tribune took his nephew's hand in his own and raised it high in a gesture of triumph and acclamation. "Well done, my boy," the older man said loudly. "*Well* done."

More surprised by his uncle's open praise than he was by the brief scowls with which the other members of the Tribunate, Wraslov and Deliu, responded to it, the young general said, "Ah, Excellency, we all had confidence in the abilities of our men." Nodding to the side, toward the still-faced Bourne, he added in afterthought, "and in our allies, of course, in Colonel Hammer."

The presence of the troops braced to attention behind him vibrated in Radescu's mind like a taut bowstring. "Excellencies," he said, guiding down his uncle's hand and releasing it, "the actual meeting will be within the, the cavern, actually a tunnel complex as extensive as any Molt artifact on the planet, as it chances. The antechamber seemed a particularly suitable location for the signing since it—reminds the representatives of other themes that our troops are here without Molt sufferance."

Chief Tribune Antonescu patted at the front of his robe, frowning minutely when he realized that the marks he left in the fine dust were more disfiguring than the smooth layer which the ride from the plane had deposited over him. "The Molts are inside then, already?" he asked in a voice which, like his static face, gave away nothing save the fact that something was hidden.

"No, Excellency," said Radescu, finding that his slight, ingenuous smile had become a mask which he knew he must maintain, "they're—in sight, I suppose, the representatives."

He gestured with his spread fingers toward a few of the crags where, if he had squinted, he might have been able to see male autochthones waiting as the Oltenian Army waited in camp. "The young and females whom we captured are still at the lower levels within, under parole so to speak, those who might be able to teleport away now that we've stopped shelling."

For a moment, the general lost control of the smile he had been keeping neutral, and the Tribunes were shocked by the face of a man who recalled tumbled bodies and who now grinned that he might not weep. "But the theme elders who'll be signing—they'll arrive in the chamber when we set off a smoke grenade to summon them." The grin flashed back like a spring-knife. "Red smoke, not gray."

The pair of mercenaries, near enough to overhear, smiled as well, but the reference escaped the newcomers who had not been part of the assault.

"Then let's go within," said Antonescu, "and we *won't* have the Molts present until you and I—until we all—" taking his nephew's hand again, the Chief Tribune began to walk along the carefully-laid carpet "—have had a chance to discuss this among ourselves."

Radescu raised an eyebrow as he stepped into line beside his uncle, but the facial gesture was a restrained one, even slighter than necessary to avoid cracking his makeup. Antonescu, a master both of restraint and interpretation of minute signals, said, "Only for a moment, Alexi."

"I was afraid for a moment," the general said in a carefully modulated voice as he walked along, "a symptom of my youthful arrogance, I'm afraid—" echoing in nervousness his uncle's words and his own "—that you didn't realize that the agreement stands or falls as a piece—that it can't be modified."

He thought as he spoke that he was being overly blunt with the man who was both his protector and a necessary part of final success, but Tribune Antonescu only replied, "Yes, we were in no doubt of that, my boy. Not from the first."

The six Honor Guards fell in behind the Tribunes in what Radescu found himself thinking of as courtly, not military, precision. The two mercenaries drifted along to either side of the procession. The general risked a glance around to see that while Hawker walked to the left and eyed the head of the valley with its scatterings of autochthones, many of them picked out by iridium highlights, Profile Bourne glowered at the gaily-caparisoned troops on review to the right.

Radescu had heard the Slammers discussing whether or not they should wear dress uniforms of their own. He agreed with their final assessment: tailored khakis would only accentuate the scarred functionality of the helmets and body armor they would wear regardless.

"The whole army," Radescu said, hoping to direct his uncle's attention to the troops who had sweated as hard for this display as they had in preparation for the assault, "performed in a way to honor the State."

Surely as the plane circled to land, the Tribunes had seen the burned-out vehicles littering the course of the assault—particularly near the crest of this ridge, up whose gentle reverse slope the entourage now walked. Radescu's plan had made the attack possible and a success: nothing could have made it easy. The general's eyes prickled with emotion as he thought of these men and their comrades plunging into darkness to meet their terrifyingly-agile opponents.

"As written," muttered the Tribune, Deliu, who walked behind Radescu, "this treaty permits the Molts to import anything they want without State control—specifically including weapons. Hard to imagine anyone but the most arrant traitor suggesting that the Molts should be allowed powerguns after the way they used one in Belvedere last month."

"Not the place for that, Mikhail," Antonescu said over his shoulder, the very flatness of his remark more damning than an undertone of anger.

Radescu did not miss a step as he paced along in front of men picked not for their smartness on review but because of the way each had distinguished himself in the assault which made this ceremony possible. His mind, however, clicked into another mode at the paired statements which were neither a question nor an answer—yet were both.

Aloud, drowning the other voices in his mind, the general said, "Quite apart from the question of whether Ferad would have agreed to it, Excellency, the prohibition would have been useless—and the past few days have made me extremely intolerant of pointless behavior."

"I didn't care to discuss such matters here where the Molts may be listening through directional microphones," said Antonescu in a louder voice as he passed Captain Elejash and the platoon which had made the preliminary assault.

"Since I've told the leader of the Molts precisely what I'm going to tell you," Alexander Radescu continued with a cool hauteur which he was too fiercely angry to disguise, "you need not be concerned on that score. Oltenia has no effective means of preventing off-planet merchants from dealing directly with the Molts—even now, in the middle of open warfare. Since they, the theme elders as surely as the young bucks, couldn't feel secure in peace without the sort of equipment renewed fighting would require, then I saw no reason to make them even *more* insecure by pretending to embargo it."

Now at midday the threshold of the autochthones' cave complex was bathed in light, but that only emphasized the wall of darkness just within. The high-vaulted antechamber was ancient enough to be set with sconces for rushlights, though the battery-powered floods now secured in them to wash the ceiling were of an efficiency equal to anything on the planet. There was no need to match the brilliance outdoors, however, so it was only as their eyes adapted that the men took in the rich, vaguely-purple ambience which white light stroked from polished granite.

The table in the center of the room was of thin, stamped metal which the cloth drapery did little to disguise. Ferad had offered a lustrous pelt of an autochthonal herbivore, but on reflection it had seemed to both that the feathery scales would prove an impossible surface on which to sign the treaty.

"We couldn't be more pleased with the way you broke the Molts in so short a time, my boy," said Grigor Antonescu as the rock enclosed the party. There were three semi-circular doorways spaced about the inner face of the antechamber, barricaded now—not in a misguided attempt to keep the Molts hostage further within the cave system, but simply to prevent Oltenian soldiers from wandering into places where they might cause problems. "But there are some matters of judgment in which you are, in all deference to your abilities, too young to make the decisions."

He spoke, thought Alexander Radescu, as if the sharp exchange in the sunlight had not occurred. Deliu's interference was not to be allowed to affect the calm tenor of the tutorial the Chief Tribune had prepared to give his nephew.

Avoiding the real meat of the opening statement, Radescu replied, "I won a couple skirmishes against an unprepared enemy, Uncle. Scarcely a matter of breaking the Molts, or even the one theme primarily involved."

"There were sizable contingents from all across Oltenia," put in the eldest of the Tribunes, Constantin Wraslov, who even in Radescu's earliest recollection had looked too skeletal to be long for the world. His tone lacked the deliberate venom of Deliu's, but it had the querelousness common to even the most neutral of Wraslov's pronouncements. "We've seen the report on the examination of the corpses after the battle."

Radescu looked at the Tribune, surprised at the dispassion with which his mind pictured the old man as one of the victims being examined by the Intelligence Section: the body pulped by a sheet of rock giving way on top of it . . . flayed by microshrapnel from a dozen nearby bomblets. . . halved by a point-blank, chest-high burst from an armored car's gun. . . . "Yes," the general said with the dynamic calm of a fine blade flexing under the pressure of a thrust, "all the themes had representatives here. That made it possible for Ferad to inflate what was really a minor occurrence into enough of an event to panic the other themes into making peace. Ferad himself knows better—as, of course, do I."

"The infants are their weak point," said Tribune Deliu, adding with a grudging approval, "and you fingered that well enough, boy, I grant you." There was no affection in the look he gave Radescu, however; and when the gilt brim of the general's hat threw a band of light across Deliu's eyes, the Tribune's glare could have been that of a furious boar.

"Yes, you've shown us how to exterminate the autochthones," Wraslov agreed gleefully, rubbing his hands and looking around the big chamber with the enthusiasm of an archeologist who had just penetrated a tomb. "Before, we tried to clear areas so that they

couldn't attack *us*, you know, because it
seemed they could always escape."

From where he stood, Radescu could not
see the aged Tribune's face. The Honor
Guard had aligned itself as a short chord
across the portion of the curving wall toward
which Wraslov was turned. The worried
looks that flashed across the bland expressions of the six red-clad officers were a suggestion of what those men thought they saw
in the Tribune's eyes.

"Excellencies, we *can't* . . . ," Radescu began, breaking off when he realized that he
didn't know where to take the words from
there. His body felt so dissociated from his
mind that his knees started to tremble and
he was not sure that he could continue to
stand up.

He was not alone in feeling the tension in
the chamber. Chief Tribune Antonescu, for
all his outward calm, had an inner heat
which might have been no more than a
well-bred distaste for the scene which he
saw developing.

In fact, the only men in the antechamber
who *did* seem relaxed were the two Slammers, and theirs was the calm of soldiers
carrying out a familiar task. Hawker and
Bourne had their backs to the stone to one
side of the entranceway, too close together
for a Molt to attempt to teleport between
them but still giving their gun hands adequate clearance. They scanned the room,
their faceshields transparent but already
locked in place in case the lights went out
and vision aids were required.

Hawker's hands were still. Profile Bourne rubbed the grip of his submachinegun, not with his fingers but with the palm of his right hand. The orange dragon caressed the plastic in a fashion that gave Radescu a thrill of erotic horror before he snatched his eyes away.

His uncle had not pressed when a sense of the futility of words had choked the young general's first attempt at argument. Antonescu still waited with a placid exterior and a core of disdain for the emotional diatribe which he expected to hear. Wraslov was lost in his contemplation of corpses, past and future; but Tribune Deliu was watching the general with a grin of present anticipation.

He would not, thought Alexander Radescu, embarass Uncle Grigor and give that stupid *animal* Deliu a moment of triumph. For some reason, that seemed more important than the fact that the plan he'd expected to weld together the races of Oltenia had just disintegrated like a sand castle in the surf. Perhaps it was because he had control over himself; and now, as he tumbled from his pinnacle of arrogant certainty, he realized that he had no control over anything else after all.

"The arguments against exterminating the Molts," Radescu said in the tone of cool disinterest with which he would have enumerated to a friend the failings of an ex-lover, "the negative arguments that is—" He paused and raised an eyebrow in question. "Since I presume the positive argument of Oltenia leading the galaxy through its combination of human and autochthonal talents has already been discounted? Yes?"

"We don't *need* to hear your arguments," rasped Deliu, "since we've already decided on the basis of common sense."

"Thought is a beneficial process for human beings, Excellence," said Radescu in a voice as clear and hard as diamond windchimes. "You should try it yourself on occasion."

One of the Honor Guards ten meters across the chamber gasped, but Chief Tribune Antonescu waved the underling to panicked silence without even bothering to look at the man. "Deliu," said the Chief Tribune, "I promised my nephew a discussion, and that he shall have. His merits to the State alone have earned him that."

Antonescu's careful terminology and the edge in his voice were extraordinarily blunt reminders of the difference in the current government between Tribunes and the Chief Tribune. He nodded toward the general. "Alexi," he prompted.

Which left the real situation exactly where Radescu had feared it was, the dream of Man/Molt partnership dissolved in a welter of blood, but there is a pleasure to small triumphs in the midst of disaster. Was this happening to Ferad among *his* fellows as well . . . ?

Aloud, Radescu continued, "If we could destroy every nursery chamber, and if every infant Molt were within such a chamber, neither of which statements is true—" he did not bother to emphasize his disclaimer, knowing that rhetorical tricks would lessen at least in his own mind the icy purity of what he was saying "—then it would still be two, more realistically three, decades, before the operation would by itself deplete the ranks of effective Molt warriors. Prepubescents, even adolescents with a range of a few kays per hop, have been met on the battlefield only in cases like this one where we have gone to *them*."

"Yes, yes," said Tribune Wraslov, turning to nod at Radescu. The young general felt as if he stood at the shimmering interface between reality and expectation. On the side that was reality, the skeletal tribune agreed with what Radescu had said and gave his thin equivalent of a smile. But surely his assumption that Wraslov was being sarcastic must be correct? It was obvious that everything Radescu had said was a bitter attack on what the Tribunate seemed to have decided.

"And what conclusions do you draw from your analysis, Alexi?" asked Grigor Antonescu, very much the pleased uncle . . . though he beamed, like a moon, coolly.

"That at best, Uncle, we're talking about another generation of war," Radescu replied, walking toward the chintz-covered table because his legs worked normally again and he needed the opportunity to try them out. The whole conversation had the feel of something he might have overheard twenty years before—two aristocrats talking about a planned marriage of peripheral interest to both their households. It *couldn't* be a discussion which would determine the future of Oltenia for the foreseeable future!

And he, Alexander Radescu, wasn't really taking part in it. He could not have shut down his emotions so thoroughly and be proceeding dispassionately in his mind to end game, not if it were Alexi and Uncle Grigor talking here in a Molt cavern. . . .

"Another generation of ballrooms filled with bodies," Radescu continued as his index finger traced the chintz into hills and valleys like those outside, baptized already in blood.

"We've destroyed those urns, of course," snapped Tribune Deliu to the general's back.

"Buildings collapsing because the foundations were on bedrock and a Molt flitted in to set a bomb there," Radescu said calmly to the table. "There've been a few of those already, and there'll be more."

His copy of the treaty document, hand-lettered on parchment, crinkled in his breast pocket when he straightened. Ferad would bring the other copy himself, on archival-quality paper imported from Earth—and how long would the Molt leader wait for the red smoke before he realized that there would be no peace after all, not in his lifetime or the lifetime of anyone now on the planet . . . ?

"Yes, but we'll be killing many of them,

very many," said Tribune Wraslov, whose eyes had a glazed appearance that removed him as far from the present as Radescu felt he himself had been removed. The two of them were only reflections, their lips moving without stirring anything around them. Only Chief Tribune Antonescu was real. . . .

"A generation of men walking the streets of Belvedere, of every city and village on Oltenia," the general continued because he could not stop without having made every possible effort to prevent what would otherwise occur, "who have been trained to shoot infants—"

"Shoot *Molts*," Deliu interrupted.

"Shoot *infants* as harmless and helpless as anything human they're going to find when they go home on leave," Radescu said, feeling his voice tremble as his control began to break. Something terrible would happen if he ever lost control. *"That's* what we'll have if the war goes on!"

"We will have a Tribunate with complete control of the State," said Chief Tribune Antonescu in a voice that penetrated the ears of every listener like a swordblade being slammed home in its sheath. "That's what we'll continue to have for so long as the war goes on."

The six men of the Honor Guard were tense ciphers at the curving wall, nervously watching State policy being made in a scene like an argument over cards. But men were men when personal emotions ran high, thought Alexander Radescu, and nothing

could have been more personal than what
he had just been told.

How naive of him to assume that Uncle
Grigor would divorce personal benefit from
matters of State. A political appointee like
General Radescu should have known better.

The Chief Tribune walked over to his
nephew and put a hand on his shoulder. He
no longer towered over little Alexi; they
were eye to eye with any difference in height
to the younger man.... "Do you understand what I'm telling you, my boy?" he
asked with the real warmth which almost
none of his closest associates had heard in
Antonescu's voice. "Surely you understand?"

"I understand that it's wrong," said the
general. Loudly, almost shouting as he pulled
away from the Chief Tribune, he added, "I
understand that it's *evil*, Uncle Grigor!"

"Then understand *this*," roared Antonescu,
who had not raised his voice when informed
of his son's suicide thirty years before. "You
have the authority we choose to give you.
To carry out decisions of the Tribunate—and
no more!"

"Yes, yes," murmured Wraslov, and Deliu
blinked avid, swine-bright eyes beside him.

"You will summon the Molt leader, as
planned," the Chief Tribune said in frigid
certainty. "We will stand to the side, so
that the Molts can be killed as they appear.
These mercenaries are capable of that, I
presume?"

"Oh yes," General Radescu said with a
nonchalance born of a question with an easy

answer in the midst of so much that had no answer at all that he cared to accept. It was only after he spoke that he even bothered to look at Bourne and Hawker, gray figures who could so easily be dismissed as age-tattered statues . . . until the sergeant gave Radescu a wink almost veiled beneath the highlights on his faceshield.

"I think we'd best leave it to the professionals, then," the Chief Tribune said, dismissing with a nod the motions the hands of the Honor Guard were making toward their gleaming, black-finished pistol holsters.

"Yes, of course" the general agreed, as his mind superimposed every image of Ferad that it held in memory—and one image more, the wizened Molt staggering backwards with his chest shot away and the treaty ablaze in his hand.

Antonescu was walking toward the great archway with his nephew, though of course he could not leave the antechamber without warning the Molts of what was prepared. The other Tribunes were drifting for safety toward the young officers of the Honor Guard, out of the line of fire through autochthones appearing beside the flimsy table. "The trouble with you, my boy," said the Chief Tribune, laying his hand again on his nephew's shoulder, "is that you're very clever, but you're young—and you don't understand the use of power."

"Sir?" said General Forsch, waiting just outside in the sunshine. Beside him was Captain Elejash, looking uncomfortable in his scarlet uniform and holding the smoke grenade in big, capable hands.

Radescu shook his head sharply, then turned to look at his uncle and the plea in the older man's eyes that his protégé accept reality without an unpleasant scene.

"Don't I understand power, Uncle Grigor?" the general said, raising his right hand to his brow. "Well, perhaps you're right." The only thing his eyes could see as he looked back into the antechamber was the gape of the dragon that Bourne's palm stroked across the grip of his weapon.

Alexander Radescu tossed his cap toward the table in a scintillating arc.

The Honor Guard was crumpling before the cyan flashes which killed them were more than a stroboscopic effect to the men in the chamber. One Guard managed to open his holster flap, but his chest was lit by smoky flames which seemed to spring from the scarlet dye rather than the black craters the powergun had punched in the uniform.

Radescu could forget that afterwards, could forget the way Deliu's bladder and bowels stained his white robes as the bolts hit him and the look of ecstasy on Wraslov's face as his eyeballs reflected the blue-green glare from the muzzle of Hawker's submachine gun.

What he would never forget, however, was the wetness on his face, his fingertips coming down from his cheek red with the splattered blood of his Uncle Grigor.

*   *   *

When the weapons detector chimed, the man behind the console shouted, "The little one's holding!" and three shotguns pointed instinctively at Hawker and Bourne in the anteroom of the Chief Executive's Residence.

"Hey, it's Profile," said one of the quartet of guards, lifting the muzzle of his weapon in embarrassment. Down the hall, the bell responder in the guard commander's office shut off when that worthy bolted toward the anteroom.

"What's this cop?" Bourne snapped in outrage, not so angry, however, as to take a blustering step toward the leveled shotguns. "We offloaded our bloody hardware 'fore we came over!"

"Don't care if he's the Lord himself come to take me to heaven," rejoined a guard with his gun still centered. He was dressed in issue battledress, but the yellow bandana worn as a headcovering and the paired pistols in crossdraw holsters gave him a piratical air. "If he's packin', he stays where he is."

"Excuse me, Sergeant Bourne," said the guard at the detector console as the guard commander—Elejash, now Colonel Elejash—burst into the anteroom with yet another shotgun, "but if you'd check your left forearm, the underside . . . ?"

"That's all right, Culcer," said Elejash, lifting his own weapon and stepping across the line of fire from his men to their targets. "You did right, but we're to admit this pair as is."

"Via," said Profile Bourne, blushing for the first time in his partner's memory.

He twitched his left hand, and the spring clip on his wrist flipped the knife into his waiting grip. "Lord and martyrs, man, you're right," the sergeant said to the shimmering blade in a voice of wonder. "I forgot it."

Enzo Hawker laughed, both in amusement and from a need to release the rigid lock into which he had set his muscles at the unexpected challenge. The Oltenian guards, all of them men he and Bourne had helped train, joined with various levels of heartiness.

"That's all right, Sergeant," Elejash said as Bourne strode over to the console and offered his knife pommel-first to the guard seated there.

"Like hell it is," Bourne muttered, laying the little weapon on the console when the guard refused to take it. "I couldn't even bitch if they'd blown me away, could I?"

Elejash looked at Hawker and the big mercenary, shrugging, said, "Well, we weren't expecting any special treatment, but I think I'd have been disappointed in you fellows if you'd shot us now, yeah."

"Briefly disappointed," said the guard at the console.

"Well," muttered Profile Bourne, starting to regain his composure—mistakes about weapons weren't the sort of thing the sergeant accepted in anyone, least of all himself, "it wouldn't be the first time I'd missed Embarcation Muster—but usually I was drunk 'r in jail."

"You can go on in," said the guard commander. "The Chief Executive told me to expect you."

"Or both," Bourne added to the nearer pair of guards. All the Oltenians wore personal touches on their uniforms, and the fatigues of the man at the console were patterned with a loose gray mesh in which he could have passed at a distance for a Molt warrior.

"Hey, how in blazes did he know that?" Bourne asked Colonel Elejash. "We didn't—you know, want to intrude when things were still settling out. This was pretty much spur a' the moment, with us gonna lift ship in a couple hours."

The guard commander shrugged, a gesture similar enough to that of the mercenary lieutenant earlier to be an unconscious copy. Others of the Slammers had helped to train the new Executive Guard, but Hawker and Bourne had had a particular impact because of their earlier association. "Why don't you ask him?" the Oltenian said, making a gesture that began as a wave toward the inner door and ended by opening it.

"The Slammers are here, sir," Elejash called through the doorway.

"Two of us, anyhow," said Bourne as he squared his shoulders and, swaggering to cover his nervousness—it wasn't the sort of thing he was used to, but the Loot was right to say they *had* to do it—he led the way into the circular Reception Chamber.

Across from the door, against the wall

behind the desk and Chief Executive Radescu rising from his seat, was an urn of large blue and indigo crystals in a white matrix.

"Enzo, Profile," Radescu said, holding out his hands to either man. He was wearing trousers and a loose tunic, both of civilian cut and only in their color—pearl gray, with gold piping on the pants legs—suggestive of anything else. "I'd—well, I didn't want to order you in here, but I was really hoping to see you again before lift-off."

"Well, you were busy," the lieutenant said uncomfortably as he shook the hand offered him, "and we, we had training duties ourselves." Funny; they'd *made* him what he was, but Radescu was fully a planetary ruler now in Hawker's mind. . .while he and Profile were better'n fair soldiers in the best outfit in the galaxy.

"What do you think of them?" Radescu asked brightly, drawing the mercenaries to the trio of chairs beside his desk—prepared for them, apparently, for the Oltenian leader seated himself in the middle one and guided the others down to either side. "What do you think of them, then? The new Guards?"

"They'll do," said Profile Bourne, wriggling his back against a chair he found uncomfortable because it was more deeply upholstered than he was used to.

"We told a couple of them," Hawker amplified, "that the Slammers were always hiring if they felt like getting off-planet."

"Via, though, they still don't *look* like soldiers," the sergeant said, miming with his left hand the bandana of the guard with the evident willingness to have blown him away.

"Conversely," said Alexander Radescu, "you know that there's a job here for you if you decide to stay. I'll clear it with Colonel Ham—"

"Sure, Profile," interrupted the big lieutenant, "and when's the last time you wore a fatigue shirt with a right sleeve on it? *Talk* to me about issue uniforms!"

Sometimes the best way to give a negative answer to a question, an offer, was to talk about something else instead. Well, Radescu thought, he could appreciate the courtesy, though he would much have preferred the other response.

To the Slammers, the Chief Executive said, "There's been a tradition here on Oltenia that officers could modify their outfits according to personal taste—when they weren't on field service, that is. I decided that the same standards should apply to the Exec—to my personal guard. A—" he spread and closed his fingers as his mind sorted words and found some that were close enough "—mark of the honor in which I hold them."

He laughed aloud, knowing as he heard the sound that there was very little humor in it. "After all," he said, "they keep me alive."

Sergeant Bourne had been eyeing the room, spacious and looking the more so for its almost complete lack of furnishings: the trio of chairs which seemed out of place; the large desk with an integral seat; and the blue john urn toward which Profile now nodded and asked, "That there what I think it is?"

"Yes, the surviving one of the pair," agreed the Chief Executive, following the sergeant's eyes. Neither mercenary had ever been in this building when it was the Tribunal Palace, but that story would have gotten around. "I'd been told it was destroyed also, but it appears that my uncle had instead removed it to storage in a warehouse. It permits Ferad to visit me at need." He smiled. "Or at whim. We've gotten to be friends, in a way, in the month since the shooting stopped."

Radescu got up and stepped toward the circular wall, his arm describing a 90° arc of the plain surface. "That's going to be covered with a twenty-centimeter sheet of black granite," the leader—the dictator—of Oltenia said. "It's been quarried by machinery, but the polish is being put to it by Molts—by hand. From every theme, and all of them who want to help. Ferad tells me that mothers are bringing infants as small—"

He coughed, clearing away the construction of memory from his throat "—as small as the one I took out of the nursery chamber myself. They're putting the little ones' hands on the stone and sliding them along it, so that in the future, they'll be able to find this room as they can anything on the planet."

Sergeant Bourne guffawed, but anything he might have intended to say was swallowed when Radescu continued bitterly,

"That means, I suppose, that my human enemies will find a way to hire a Molt warrior to assassinate me. No doubt my spirit will lie more easily for having helped achieve that degree of cooperation between the two intelligent races on the planet."

"Problems, General?" Bourne asked, levering himself out of the chair with an expression which did not seem so much changed from what he had worn a moment before but rather was a refinement of it. As when a fresh casting is struck to remove the sand clinging to its surface, thus the lines of the sergeant's face sprang into full relief when the thought of action rang in the little man's mind.

"I meant it about the job," replied the young Oltenian evenly, meeting the mercenary's eyes.

"We've been moving around a lot," said Hawker, with the same calm and the same underlying determination as had been in Radescu's voice when he repeated the offer. "Being with the Regiment, it more or less keeps an edge on without it getting—you know, outa control."

Profile Bourne looked quizzically at his lieutenant, not at all unwilling himself, at this point, to have heard more about what Radescu wanted—and needed. Hawker, knowing that and determined to forestall the discussion, went on, "If we left Hammer and tried to settle down here, either we'd dump it all, all we'd been—doing, you know, you aren't talking about a couple detection specialists now, are you?"

He took a deep breath, raising his hand to hold the floor for the moment he had to pause before continuing, "We'd lose it, or we'd—" his eyes flicked toward Sergeant Bourne in a gesture so minute that Radescu could not be certain that it had been intentional "—go the other way, turn into something you couldn't have around anyplace you'd—be wearing civilian clothes, put it that way."

Alexander Radescu nodded brusquely and turned again to face the wall that would be replaced by a surface of polished granite. He did not speak.

To his back, Lieutenant Hawker said in a tone that reminded Bourne of the way the Loot had stroked the little Molt, "You're having trouble with the—Chief Tribune's relatives, then? Sort of thought you might. . . ."

"Them?" said Alexander Radescu with sardonic brightness as he turned again to the Slammers. "Oh, no, not at all. For one thing, they're my relatives too, you know. They think they're sitting well—which they are, since they're the only pool of people I can trust, besides the army. And anyway, nobody on either side of the family was close enough to Uncle Grigor to think of, of avenging him.

"Nobody but me."

Radescu began to pace, his left hand swinging to touch the wall at intervals as he circled it. Bourne rotated to watch him, but Lieutenant Hawker remained seated, his eyes apparently on the backs of his hands. "Things are settling in quite well, people forgetting the war—and the Molts putting it behind them as well, from what Ferad says and the other reports, the *lack* of incidents."

"There's been shooting," Sergeant Bourne interjected.

He talked to Oltenians, now, to members of the Guard and to the soldiers *they* talked to. It gave him more awareness of the planet on which he served than he could ever before remember having. Planets, to one of Hammer's Slammers, were generally a circumscribed round of fellows, 'recreation establishments,' and gunsight pictures. For the past month, Profile Bourne had found fellows among the local forces.

"There's always *been* incidents," Radescu snapped. His cheeks were puffier than they had been in the field, thought Lieutenant Hawker as he glanced sidelong. . . . "There's going to be shootings in mining camp bars and ranch dormitories as long as there's men, much less men and Molts. But it's no worse than, oh, ten years ago—I can get the exact figures. Having the Slammers around for an additional month to settle what *anybody* started, that was useful; but basically, three years of war haven't undone three centuries of peace, or as close to peace as Nature seems ready to allow anyone."

"Well," said Bourne, still standing, figuring that they'd done what, Via, courtesy demanded in making the call. He didn't look real great, the general didn't, but at least he wasn't a tarted-up clown the way he had been that first day, through the bars of the holding cell. . . . "Glad things are workin' out, and you know that if you need the Slammers again—"

"It's the Tzigara family," said Radescu, speaking through the sergeant's leave-taking as if oblivious to it. "Isn't that amusing?"

Lieutenant Hawker met the Chief Executive's painted smile with calm eyes and no expression of his own, waiting to hear what would be dragged out by the fact that when he and Bourne upped ship there would be no one for Radescu to speak to. That was what they had come for, though Profile didn't know it. That, and the one thing Hawker needed to say to pay their debt to the man who, after all, had saved their lives. . . .

"You never met Nikki, did you?" Radescu continued in a bantering tone. "He was my aide, k-killed at the, in the ballroom . . . that night."

He cleared his throat, forced unwillingly to pause, but neither of the Slammers showed any sign of wanting to break in on the monologue. "He had a cousin, and I don't think I even knew that, in the, you know, in the Honor Guard. And it couldn't have made any difference, I don't mean *that*, but the family blames me now for both deaths."

"He was one a' the ones we blew away in the cave, you mean?" the sergeant asked, not particularly concerned but hoping that if the question were clarified he would be able to understand what in blazes the general was driving at.

"You did what I ordered you to do, what *had* to be done!" Alexander Radescu replied in a tone more fitting for condemnation than approval. But it was the world which he wanted to condemn, not the pair of mercenaries . . . and not even himself, though that was increasingly easy to do, when he lay awake at three in the morning. "There's been one attempt to kill me already, poison, and I've had word of others planned. . . ."

Radescu tented his fingers in front of him and seemed to carry out a brief series of isometrics, pressing the hands together and letting them spring back. "Sometimes I think that I won't be safe so long as there's a single one of the Tzigaras alive," he said. Then, with his eyes still determinedly focused on his fingertips, he added, "I'd be— very pleased if you gentlemen changed your minds, you know."

Lieutenant Hawker rose from the chair without using his arms to lift him, despite the depth and give of the upholstery. The lack of body armor made him feel lighter; and, though most of his waking hours were spent as he was now, without the heavy porcelain clamshell latched to him, being around Radescu made the Slammers lieutenant feel that he *ought* to be in armor. Habituated response, he supposed.

"I think we'd best be getting back to the regiment, sir," said Enzo Hawker, stretching out his hand to shake Radescu's.

"Of course," agreed the Chief Executive, clasping the mercenary's firmly. "Colonel

Hammer performed to the perfect satisfaction of his contract. What you two did was more."

"Don't worry 'bout missing us, general," said Profile as he took the hand offered him in turn. "You got boys out there—" he nodded to the anteroom "—can handle anything we would."

He laughed, pleasantly in intention, though the harshness of the sound made Radescu think of the fluorescent dragon on the palm wringing his. "Dudn't take a world a' smarts, dudn't even take a lotta training. Just to be willing, that's all." He laughed again and stepped toward the door.

Hawker touched the sergeant on the shoulder, halting and turning him. "Sir," the big lieutenant said as his subordinate watched and waited with a frown of confusion, "you're where you are now because you were willing to do what had to be done. Everybody else wanted an easy way out. Wanted to kill Molts instead of ending a war."

"Where I am now," Alexander Radescu repeated, quirking his lips into a smile of sorts.

"If you didn't have the balls to handle a tough job," said Hawker sharply, "you'd have seen the last of me 'n the sarge a long while back, mister."

Hawker and Radescu locked eyes while Bourne looked from one man to the other, puzzled but not worried, there was nothing here to worry about.

"I appreciate the vote of confidence," said

the Oltenian as he broke into a grin and reached out to shake the lieutenant's hand again.

"Oh, there's one thing more," Hawker added in a gentle voice as he willingly accepted the handclasp. "Profile, I'll bet the Chief Executive thinks we were firing long bursts there when we cleared the cave."

"What?" said Radescu in amazement, pausing with the mercenary's hand still in his.

"Oh, Via, no," Profile Bourne blurted, *his* surprise directed at the suggestion rather than the fact that the Loot had voiced it. "Blood 'n martyrs, General, single shots only. Lord, the polish that stone had, the ricochets'd fry us all like pork rinds if we'd just tried to hose things down." He stared at Radescu in the hopeful horror of a specialist who prays that he's been able to prevent a friend from doing something lethally dangerous through ignorance.

"That's right sir," said Enzo Hawker as he met the Chief Executive's wondering eyes. "You have to know exactly what you're doing before you decide to use guns."

Radescu nodded very slowly as the two guns for hire walked out of his office.

INTERLUDE:
The Interrogation Team

*T*HE MAN THE PATROL BROUGHT IN was about forty, bearded, and dressed in loose garments—sandals, trousers, and a vest that left his chest and thick arms bare. Even before he was handed from the back of the combat car, trussed to immobility in sheets of water-clear hydorclasp, Griffiths could hear him screaming about his rights under the York Constitution of '03.

Didn't the fellow realize he'd been picked up by Hammer's Slammers?

"Yours or mine, Chief?" asked Major Smokey Soames, Griffiths' superior and partner on the interrogation team—a slim man of Afro-Asian ancestry, about as suited for wringing out a mountaineer here on York as he was for swimming through magma. Well, Smokey'd earned his pay on Kanarese. . . .

"Is a bear Catholic?" Griffiths asked wearily. "Go set the hardware up, Major."

216

"And haven't I already?" said Smokey, but it had been nice of him to make the offer. It wasn't that mechanical interrogation *required* close genetic correspondences between subject and operator, but the job went faster and smoother in direct relation to those correspondences. Worst of all was to work on a woman, but you did what you had to do. . . .

Four dusty troopers from A Company manhandled the subject, still shouting, to the command car housing the interrogation gear. The work of the firebase went on. Crews were pulling maintenance on the fans of some of the cars facing outward against attack, and one of the rocket howitzers rotated squealingly as new gunners were trained. For the most part, though, there was little to do at midday, so troopers turned from the jungle beyond the berm to the freshly-snatched prisoner and the possibility of action that he offered.

"Don't damage the goods!" Griffiths said sharply when the men carrying the subject seemed ready to toss him onto the left-hand couch like a log into a blazing fireplace. One of the troopers, a non-com, grunted assent; they settled the subject in adequate comfort. Major Soames was at the console between the paired couches, checking the capture location and relevant intelligence information from Central's data base.

"Want us to unwrap 'im for you?" asked the non-com, ducking instinctively though the roof of the command car cleared his helmet. The interior lighting was low, however, especially to eyes adapted to the sun hammering the bulldozed area of the firebase.

"Listen, me'n my family *never*, I swear it, dealt with interloping traders!" the York native pleaded.

"No, we'll take care of it," said Griffiths to the A Company trooper, reaching into the drawer for a disposable-blade scalpel to slit the hydorclasp sheeting over the man's wrist. Some interrogators liked to keep a big fighting knife around, combining practical requirements with a chance to soften up the subject through fear. Griffiths thought the technique was misplaced: for effective mechanical interrogation, he wanted his subjects as relaxed as possible. Panic-jumbled images were better than no images at all; but only *just* better.

"We're not the Customs Police, old son," Smokey murmured as he adjusted the couch headrest to an angle which looked more comfortable for the subject. "We're a lot more interested in the government convoy ambushed last week."

Griffiths' scalpel drew a line above the subject's left hand and wrist. The sheeting drew back in a narrow gape, briefly iridescent as stresses within the hydorclasp readjusted themselves. As if the sheeting were skin, however, the rip stopped of its own accord at the end of the scored line.

"What're you doing to me?"

"Nothing I'm not doing to myself, friend," said Griffiths, grasping the subject's bared forearm with his own left hand so that their inner wrists were together. Between the thumb and forefinger of his right hand he held a standard-looking stim cone up where the subject could see it clearly, despite the cocoon of sheeting still holding his legs and torso rigid. "I'm George, by the way. What do your friends call you?"

"You're drugging me!" the subject screamed, his fingers digging into Griffiths' forearm fiercely. The mountaineers living under triple-canopy jungle looked pasty and unhealthy, but there was nothing wrong with this one's muscle tone.

"It's a random pickup," said Smokey in Dutch to his partner. "Found him on a trail in the target area, nothing suspicious—probably just out sap-cutting—but they could snatch him without going into a village and starting something."

"Right in one," Griffiths agreed in soothing English as he squeezed the cone at the juncture of his and the subject's wrist veins. The dose in its skin-absorbed carrier—developed from the solvent used with formic acid by Terran solifugids for defense—spurted out under pressure and disappeared into the bloodstreams of both men: thrillingly cool to Griffiths, and a shock that threw the subject into mewling, abject terror.

"Man," the interrogator murmured as he detached the subject's grip from his forearm, using the pressure point in the man's wrist to do so, "if there was anything wrong with it, I wouldn't have split it with you, now would I?"

He sat down on the other couch, swinging his legs up and lying back before the drug-induced lassitude crumpled him on the floor. He was barely aware of movement as Smokey fitted a helmet on the subject and ran a finger up and down columns of touch-sensitive controls on his console to reach a balance. All Griffiths would need was the matching helmet, since the parameters of his brain were already loaded into the data base. By the time Smokey got around to him, he wouldn't even feel the touch of the helmet.

Though the dose *was* harmless, as he'd assured the subject, unless the fellow had an adverse reaction because of the recreational drugs he'd been taking on his own. You could never really tell with the sap-cutters, but it was generally okay. The high jungles of York produced at least a dozen drugs of varying effect, and the producers were of course among the heaviest users of their haul.

By itself, that would have been a personal problem; but the mountaineers also took the position that trade off-planet was their own business, and that there was no need to sell their drugs through the Central Marketing Board in the capital for half the price that traders slipping into the jungle in small starships would cheerfully pay. Increasingly-violent attempts to enforce customs laws on men with guns and the willingness to use them had led to what was effectively civil war—which the York government had hired the Slammers to help suppress.

It's a bitch to fight when you don't know who the enemy is; and that was where Griffiths and his partner came in.

"Now I want you to imagine that you're walking home from where you were picked up," came Smokey's voice, but Griffiths was hearing the words only through the subject's mind. His own helmet had no direct connection to the hushed microphone into which the major was speaking. The words formed themselves into letters of dull orange which expanded to fill Griffiths' senses with a blank background.

The monochrome sheet coalesced abruptly, and he was trotting along a trail which was a narrow mark beaten by feet into the open expanse of the jungle floor. By cutting off the light, the triple canopies of foliage ensured that the real undergrowth would be stunted—as passable to the air-cushion armor of Hammer's Slammers as it was to the locals on foot.

Judging distance during an interrogation sequence was a matter of art and craft, not science, because the 'trip'—though usually linear—was affected by ellipses and the subject's attitude during the real journey. For the most part, memory was a blur in which the trail itself was the major feature and the remaining landscape only occasionally obtruded in the form of an unusually large or colorful hillock of fungus devouring a fallen tree. Twice the subject's mind—not necessarily the man himself—paused to throw up a dazzlingly-sharp image of a particular plant, once a tree and the other time a knotted, woody vine which stood out in memory against the misty visualization of the trunk which the real vine must wrap.

Presumably the clearly-defined objects had something to do with the subject's business— which was none of Griffiths' at this time. As he 'walked' the Slammer through the jungle, the mountaineer would be mumbling broken and only partly intelligible words, but Griffiths no longer heard them or Smokey's prompting questions.

The trail forked repeatedly, sharply visualized each time although the bypassed forks disappeared into mental fog within a meter of the route taken. It was surprisingly easy to determine the general direction of travel: though the sky was rarely visible through the foliage, the subject habitually made sunsightings wherever possible in order to orient himself.

The settlement of timber-built houses was of the same tones—browns, sometimes overlaid by a gray-green—as the trees which interspersed the habitations. The village glowed brightly by contrast with the forest, however, both because the canopy above was significantly thinner and because the place was home and a goal to the subject's mind.

Sunlight, blocked only by the foliage of

very large trees which the settlers had not cleared, dappled streets which had been trampled to the consistency of coarse concrete. Children played there, and animals—dogs and pigs, probably, but they were undistinguished shadows to the subject, factors of no particular interest to either him or his interrogator.

Griffiths did not need to have heard the next question to understand it, when a shadow at the edge of the trail sprang into mental relief as a forty-tube swarmjet launcher with a hard-eyed woman slouched behind it watching the trail. The weapon needn't have been loot from the government supply convoy massacred the week before, but its swivelling base was jury-rigged from a truck mounting.

At present, the subject's tongue could not have formed words more complex than a slurred syllable or two, but the Slammers had no need for cooperation from his motor nerves or intellect. All they needed were memory and the hard-wired processes of brain function which were common to all life forms with spinal cords. The subject's brain retrieved and correlated the information which the higher centers of his mind would have needed to answer Major Soames' question about defenses—and Griffiths collected the data there at the source.

Clarity of focus marked as the subject's one of the houses reaching back against a bole of colossal proportions. Its roof was of shakes framed so steeply that they were scarcely distinguishable from the vertical timbers of the siding. Streaks of the moss common both to tree and to dwelling faired together cut timber and the russet bark. On the covered stoop in front, an adult woman and seven children waited in memory.

At this stage of the interrogation Griffiths had almost as little conscious volition as the subject did, but a deep level of his own mind recorded the woman as unattractive. Her cheeks were hollow, her expression sullen, and the appearance of her skin was no cleaner than that of the subject himself. The woman's back was straight, however, and her clear eyes held, at least in the imagination of the subject, a look of affection.

The children ranged in height from a boy already as tall as his mother to the infant girl looking up from the woman's arms with a face so similar to the subject's that it could, with hair and a bushy beard added, pass for his in a photograph. Affection cloaked the vision of the whole family, limning the faces clearly despite a tendency for the bodies of the children to mist away rather like the generality of trees along the trail; but the infant was almost deified in the subject's mind.

Smokey's unheard question dragged the subject off abruptly, his household dissolving unneeded to the answer as a section of the stoop hinged upward on the end of his own hand and arm. The tunnel beneath the board flooring dropped straight down through the layer of yellowish soil and the friable rock beneath. There was a wooden ladder along which the wavering oval of a flashlight beam traced as the viewpoint descended.

The shaft was seventeen rungs deep, with a further gooseneck dip in the gallery at the ladder's end to trap gas and fragmentation grenades. Where the tunnel straightened to horizontal, the flashlight gleamed on the powergun in a niche ready to hand but beneath the level to which a metal detector could be tuned to work reliably.

Just beyond the gun was a black-cased directional mine with either a light-beam or ultrasonic detonator—the subject didn't know the difference and his mind hadn't logged any of the subtle discrimination points between the two types of fuzing. Either way, someone ducking down the tunnel could, by touching the pressure-sensitive cap of the detonator, assure that the next person across the invisible tripwire would take a charge of shrapnel at velocities which would crumble the sturdiest body armor.

"Follow all the tunnels," Smokey must have directed, because Griffiths had the unusual experience of merger with a psyche which split at every fork in the underground system. Patches of light wavered and fluctuated across as many as a score of simultaneous images, linking them together in the unity in which the subject's mind held them.

It would have made the task of mapping the tunnels impossible, but the Slammers did not need anything so precise in a field as rich as this one. The tunnels themselves had been cut at the height of a stooping runner, but there was more headroom in the pillared bays excavated for storage and shelter. Flashes—temporal alternatives, hard to sort from the multiplicity of similar physical locations—showed shelters both empty and filled with villagers crouching against the threat of bombs which did not come. On one image the lighting was uncertain and could almost have proceeded as a mental artifact from the expression of the subject's infant daughter, looking calmly from beneath her mother's worried face.

Griffiths could not identify the contents of most of the stored crates across which the subject's mind skipped, but Central's data bank could spit out a list of probables when the interrogator called in the dimensions and colors after the session. Griffiths would do that, for the record. As a matter of practical use, all that was important was that the villagers had thought it necessary to stash the material here—below the reach of ordinary reconnaissance and even high explosives.

There were faces in the superimposed panorama, villagers climbing down their own access ladders or passed in the close quarters of the tunnels. Griffiths could not possibly differentiate the similar, bearded physiognomies during the overlaid glimpses he got of them. It was likely enough that everyone, every male at least, in the village was represented somewhere in the subject's memory of the underground complex.

There was one more sight offered before Griffiths became aware of his own body again in a chill wave spreading from the wrist where Smokey had sprayed the antidote. The subject had seen a nine-barrelled powergun, a calliope whose ripples of high-intensity fire could eat the armor of a combat car like paper spattered by molten steel. It was deep in an underground bay from which four broad 'windows'—firing slits—were angled upward to the surface. Preparing the weapon in this fashion to cover the major approaches to the village must have taken enormous effort, but there was a worthy payoff: at these slants, the bolts would rip into the flooring, not the armored sides, of a vehicle driving over the camouflaged opening of a firing slit. Not even Hammer's heavy tanks could survive having their bellies carved that way. . . .

The first awareness Griffiths had of his physical surroundings was the thrashing of his limbs against the sides of the couch while Major Soames lay across his body to keep him from real injury. Motor control returned with a hot rush, permitting Griffiths to lie still for a moment and pant.

"Need to go under again?" asked Smokey as he rose, fishing in his pocket for another cone of antidote for the subject if the answer was 'no.'

"Got all we need," Griffiths muttered, closing his eyes before he took charge of his arms to lift him upright. "It's a bloody fortress, it is, all underground and *cursed* well laid out."

"Location?" said his partner, whose fingernails clicked on the console as he touched keys.

"South by southeast," said Griffiths. He opened his eyes, then shut them again as he swung his legs over the side of the couch. His muscles felt as if they had been under stress for hours, with no opportunity to flush fatigue poisons. The subject was coming around with comparative ease in his cocoon, because his system had not been charged already with the drug residues of the hundreds of interrogations which Griffiths had conducted from the right-hand couch. "Maybe three kays—you know, plus or minus."

The village might be anywhere from two kilometers to five from the site at which the subject had been picked up, though Griffiths usually guessed closer than that. This session had been a good one, too, the linkage close enough that he and the subject were a single psyche throughout most of it. That wasn't always the case: many interrogations were viewed as if through a bad mirror, the images foggy and distorted.

"Right," said Smokey to himself or the hologram map tank in which a named point was glowing in response to the information he had just keyed. "Right, Thomasville they call it." He swung to pat the awakening subject on the shoulder. "You live in Thomasville, don't you, old son?"

"Wha . . . ?" murmured the subject.

"You're sure he couldn't come from another village?" Griffiths queried, watching his partner's quick motions with a touch of envy stemming from the drug-induced slackness in his own muscles.

"Not a chance," the major said with assurance. "There were two other possibles, but they were both north in the valley."

"Am I—" the subject said in a voice that gained strength as he used it. "Am I all right?"

Why ask us? thought Griffiths, but his partner was saying, "Of course you're all right, m'boy, we said you would be, didn't we?"

While the subject digested that jovial affirmation, Smokey turned to Griffiths and said, "You don't think we need an armed recce then, Chief?"

"They'd chew up anything short of a company of panzers," Griffiths said flatly, "and even *that* wouldn't be a lotta fun. It's a bloody underground fort, it is."

"What did I say?" the subject demanded as he regained intellectual control and remembered where he was—and why. "Please, *please*, what'd I say?"

"Curst little, old son," Smokey remarked. "Just mumbles—nothing to reproach yourself about, not at all."

"You're a gentle bastard," Griffiths said.

"Ain't it true, Chief, ain't it true?" his partner agreed. "Gas, d'ye think, then?"

"Not the way they're set up," said Griffiths, trying to stand and relaxing again to gain strength for a moment more. He thought back over the goose-necked tunnels; the filter curtains ready to be drawn across the mouths of shelters; the atmosphere suits hanging beside the calliope. "Maybe saturation with a lethal skin absorbtive like K3, but what's the use of that?"

"Right you are," said Major Soames, tapping the console's preset for Fire Control Central.

"You're going to let me go, then?" asked the subject, wriggling within his wrappings in an unsuccessful attempt to rise.

Griffiths made a moue as he watched the subject, wishing that his own limbs felt capable of such sustained motion. "Those other two villages may be just as bad as this one," he said to his partner.

"The mountaineers don't agree with each other much better'n they do with the government," demurred Smokey with his head cocked toward the console, waiting for its reply. "They'll bring us in samples, and we'll see then."

"Go ahead," said Fire Central in a voice bitten flat by the two-kilohertz aperture through which it was transmitted.

"Got a red-pill target for you," Smokey said, putting one ivory-colored fingertip on the holotank over Thomasville to transmit

the coordinates to the artillery computers.
"Soonest."

"Listen," the subject said, speaking to Griffiths because the major was out of the line of sight permitted by the hydorclasp wrappings, "let me go and there's a full three kilos of Misty Hills Special for you. Pure, I swear it, so pure it'll float on water!"

"No damper fields?" Central asked in doubt.

"They aren't going to put up a nuclear damper and warn everybody they're expecting attack, old son," said Major Soames tartly. "Of course, the least warning and they'll turn it on."

"Hold one," said the trooper in Fire Control.

"Just lie back and relax, fella," Griffiths said, rising to his feet at last. "We'll turn you in to an internment camp near the capital. They keep everything nice there so they can hold media tours. You'll do fine."

There was a loud squealing from outside the interrogators' vehicle. One of the twenty-centimeter rocket howitzers was rotating and elevating its stubby barrel. Ordinarily the six tubes of the battery would work in unison, but there was no need for that on the present fire mission.

"We have clearance for a nuke," said the console with an undertone of vague surprise which survived sideband compression. Usually the only targets worth a red pill were protected by damper fields which inhibited fission bombs and the fission triggers of thermonuclear weapons.

"Lord blast you for sinners!" shouted the trussed local, "what is it you're doing, you blackhearted devils?"

Griffiths looked down at him, and just at that moment the hog fired. The base charge blew the round clear of the barrel and the sustainer motor roared the shell up in a ballistic path for computer-determined seconds of burn. The command vehicle rocked. Despite their filters, the vents drew in air burned by exhaust gases.

It shouldn't have happened after the helmets were removed and both interrogator and subject had been dosed with antidote. Flashback contacts did sometimes occur, though. This time it was the result of the very solid interrogation earlier; that, and meeting the subject's eyes as the howitzer fired.

The subject looked so much like his infant daughter that Griffiths had no control at all over the image that sprang to his mind: the baby's face lifted to the sky which blazed with the thermonuclear fireball detonating just above the canopy—

—and her melted eyeballs dripping down her cheeks.

The hydorclasp held the subject, but he did not stop screaming until they had dosed him with enough suppressants to turn a horse toes-up.

CODE-NAME FEIREFITZ

"*L*ORD, WE GOT ONE!" cried the trooper whose detector wand pointed toward the table that held the small altar. "That's a powergun for sure, Captain, nothing else'd read so much iridium!"

The three other khaki-clad soldiers in the room with Captain Esa Mboya tensed and cleared guns they had not expected to need. The villagers of Ain Chelia knew that to be found with a weapon meant death. The ones who were willing to face that were in the Bordj, waiting with their households and their guns for the Slammers to rip them out. Waiting to die fighting.

The houses of Ain Chelia were decorated externally by screens and colored tiles; but the tiles were set in concrete walls and the screens themselves were cast concrete. Narrow cul-de-sacs lined by blank, gated courtyard walls tied the residential areas of the village into knots of strongpoints. The rebels had elected to make their stand in Ain Chelia proper only because the fortress they had cut into the walls of the open pit mine was an even tougher objective.

"Stand easy, troopers," said Mboya. The householder gave him a tight smile; he and Mboya were the only blacks in the room—or the village. "I'll handle this one," Captain Mboya continued. "The rest of you get on with the search under Sergeant Scratchard. Sergeant—" calling toward the outside door—"come in here for a moment."

Besides the householder and the troops, a narrow-faced civilian named Youssef ben Khedda stood in the room. On his face was dawning a sudden and terrible hope. He had been Assistant Superintendent of the ilmenite mine before Kabyles all over the planet rose against their Arabized central government in al-Madinah. The Superintendent was executed, but ben Khedda had joined the rebels to be spared. It was a common enough story to men who had sorted through the ruck of as many rebellions as the Slammers had. But now ben Khedda was a loyal citizen again. Openly he guided G Company from house to house, secretly he whispered to Captain Mboya the names of those who had carried their guns and families to the mine. "Father," said ben Khedda to the householder, lowering his eyes in a mockery of contrition, "I never dreamed that there would be contraband *here*, I swear it."

Juma al-Habashi smiled back at the small

man who saw the chance to become undisputed leader of as much of Chelia as the Slammers left standing and alive. "I'm sure you didn't dream it, Youssef," he said more gently than he himself expected. "Why should you, when I'd forgotten the gun myself?"

Sergeant Scratchard stepped inside with a last glance back at the courtyard and the other three men of Headquarters Squad waiting there as security. Within, the first sergeant's eyes touched the civilians and the tense enlisted men; but Captain Mboya was calm, so Scratchard kept his own voice calm as he said, "Sir?"

"Sergeant," Mboya said quietly, "you're in charge of the search. If you need me, I'll be in here."

"Sir," Scratchard agreed with a nod. "Well, get the lead out, daisies!" he snarled to the troopers, gesturing them to the street. "We got forty copping houses to run yet!"

As ben Khedda passed him, the captain saw the villager's control slip to uncover his glee. The sergeant was the last man out of the room; Mboya latched the street door after him. Only then did he meet the householder's eyes again. "Hello, Juma," he said in the Kabyle he had sleep-learned rather than the Kikuyu they had both probably forgotten by now. "Brothers shouldn't have to meet this way, should we?"

Juma smiled in mad irony rather than humor. Then his mouth slumped out of that bitter rictus and he said sadly, "No, we shouldn't, that's right." Looking at his altar and not the soldier, he added, "I knew there'd be a—a unit sent around, of course. But I didn't expect you'd be leading the one that came here, where I was."

"Look, I didn't volunteer for Operation Feirefitz," Esa blazed. "And Via, how was I supposed to know where you where anyway? We didn't exactly part kissing each other's cheeks ten years ago, did we? And here you've gone and changed your name even—how was I supposed to keep from stumbling over you?"

Juma's face softened. He stepped to his brother, taking the other's wrists in his hands. "I'm sorry," he said. "Of course that was unfair. The—what's going to happen disturbs me." He managed a genuine smile. "I didn't really change my name, you know. 'Al-Habashi' just means 'the Black', and it's what everybody on this planet was going to call me whatever I wanted. We aren't very common on Dar al-B'heed, you know. Any more than we were in the Slammers."

"Well, there's one fewer black in the Slammers than before *you* opted out," Esa said bitterly; but he took the civilian's wrists in turn and squeezed them. As the men stood linked, the clerical collar that Juma wore beneath an ordinary jellaba caught the soldier's eye. Without the harshness of a moment before, Esa asked, "Do they all call you 'Father'?"

The civilian laughed and stepped away. "No, only the hypocrites like Youssef," he said. "Oh, Ain Chelia is just as Islamic as the capital, as al-Madinah, never doubt. I have a small congregation here ... and I have the respect of the rest of the community, I think. I'm head of equipment maintenance at the mine, which doesn't mean assigning work to other people, not here." He spread his hands, palms down. The fingernails were short and the grit beneath their ends a true black and no mere skin tone. "But I think I'd want to do that anyway, even if I didn't need to eat to live. I've guided more folk to the Way by showing them how to balance a turbine than I do when I mumble about peace."

Captain Mboya walked to the table on top of which stood an altar triptych, now closed. Two drawers were set between the table legs. He opened the top one. In it were the altar vessels, chased brasswork of local manufacture. They were beautiful both in sum and in detail, but they had not tripped a detector set to locate tool steel and iridium.

The lower drawer held a powergun.

Juma watched without expression as his brother raised the weapon, checked the full magazine, and ran a fingertip over the manufacturer's stampings. "Heuvelmans of Friesland," Esa said conversationally. "Past couple contracts have been let on Terra, good products ... but I always preferred the one I was issued when they assigned me to a tribarrel and I rated a sidearm." He drew his own pistol from its flap holster and compared it to the weapon from the drawer. "Right, consecutive serial numbers," the soldier said. He laid Juma's pistol back where it came from. "Not the sort of souvenir we're supposed to take with us when we resign from the Slammers, of course."

Very carefully, and with his eyes on the wall as if searching for flaws in its thick, plastered concrete, Juma said, "I hadn't really . . . thought of it being here. I suppose that's grounds for carrying me back to a Re-education Camp in al-Madinah, isn't it?"

His brother's fist slammed the table. The triptych jumped and the vessels in the upper drawer rang like Poe's brazen bells. "Re-education? It's grounds for being burned at the *stake* if I say so! Listen, the reporters are back in the capital, not here. My orders from the District Governor are to *pacify* this region, not coddle it!" Esa's face melted from anger to grief as suddenly as he had swung his fist a moment before. "Via, elder brother, why'd you have to leave? There wasn't a man in the Regiment could handle a tribarrel the way you could."

"That was a long time ago," said Juma, facing the soldier again.

"I remember at Sphakteria," continued Esa as if Juma had not spoken, "when they popped the ambush and killed your gunner the first shot. You cut 'em apart like they weren't shooting at you too. And then you led the whole platoon clear, driving the jeep with the wick all the way up and working the gun yourself with your right hand. Nobody else could've done it."

"Do you remember," said Juma, his voice dropping into a dreamy caress as had his brother's by the time he finished speaking, "the night we left Nairobi? You led the Service of Farewell yourself, there in the starport, with everyone in the terminal joining in. The faith we'd been raised in was just words to me before then, but you made the Way as real as the tiles I was standing on. And I thought 'Why is he going off to be a soldier? If ever a man was born to lead other men to peace, it was Esa.' And in time, you did lead me to peace, little brother."

Esa shook himself, standing like a centipede in his body armor. "I got that out of my system," he said.

Juma walked over to the altar. "As I got the Slammers out of my system," he said, and he closed the drawer over the powergun within.

Neither man spoke for moments that seemed longer. At last Juma said, "Will you have a beer?"

"What?" said the soldier in surprise. "That's permitted on Dar al-B'heed?"

Juma chuckled as he walked into his kitchen. "Oh yes," he said as he opened a trapdoor in the floor, "though of course not everyone drinks it." He raised two corked bottles from their cool recess and walked back to the central room. "There are some Arab notions that never sat very well with Kabyles, you know. Many of the notions about women, veils and the like. Youssef ben Khedda's wife wore a veil until the revolt . . . then she took it off and walked around the streets like the other women of Ain Chelia. I suspect that since your troops swept in, she has her veil on again."

"*That* one," said the Captain with a snort that threatened to spray beer. "I can't imagine why nobody had the sense to throttle him—at least before they went off to their damned fortress."

Juma gestured his brother to one of the room's simple chairs and took another for himself. "Not everyone has seen as many traitors as we have, little brother," he said. "Besides, his own father was one of the martyrs whose death ignited the revolt. He was caught in al-Madinah with hypnocubes of Kabyle language instruction. The government called that treason and executed him."

Esa snorted again. "And didn't anybody here wonder who shopped the old man to the security police? Via! But I shouldn't complain—he makes my job easier." He swallowed the last of his beer, paused a moment, and then pointed the mouth of the bottle at Juma as if it would shoot. "What about you?" the soldier demanded harshly. "Where do you stand?"

"For peace," said Juma simply, "for the Way. As I always have since I left the Regiment. But . . . my closest friends in the village are dug into the sides of the mine pit now, waiting for you. Or they're dead already outside al-Madinah."

The soldier's hand tightened on the bottle,

his fingers darker than the clear brown glass. With a conscious effort of will he set the container down on the terrazzo floor beside his chair. "They're dead either way," he said as he stood up. He put his hand on the door latch before he added, pausing but not turning around, "Listen, elder brother. I told you I didn't ask to be assigned to this mop-up operation; and if I'd known I'd find you here, I'd have taken leave or a transfer. But I'm here now, and I'll do my duty, do you hear?"

"As the Lord wills," said Juma from behind him.

The walls of Juma's house, like those of all the houses in Ain Chelia, were cast fifty centimeters thick to resist the heat of the sun. The front door was on a scale with the walls, close-fitting and too massive to slam. To Captain Mboya, it was the last frustration of the interview that he could elicit no more than a satisfied thump from the door as he stamped into the street.

The ballistic crack of the bullet was all the louder for the stillness of the plateau an instant before. Captain Mboya ducked beneath the lip of the headquarters dug-out. The report of the sniper's weapon was lost in the fire of the powerguns and mortars that answered it. "Via, Captain!" snarled Sergeant Scratchard from the parked commo jeep. "Trying to get yourself killed?"

"Via!" Esa wheezed. He had bruised his chin and was thankful for it, the way a child is thankful for any punishment less than the one imagined. He accepted Scratchard's silent offer of a fiber-optics periscope. Carefully, the captain raised it to scan what had been the Chelia Mine and was now the Bordj—the Fortress—holding approximately one hundred and forty Kabyle rebels with enough supplies to last a year.

Satellite photographs showed the mine as a series of neatly-stepped terraces in the center of a plateau. From the plateau's surface, nothing of significance could be seen until a flash discovered the position of a sniper the moment before he dodged to fire again.

"It'd be easy," Sergeant Scratchard said, "if they'd just tried to use the pit as a big foxhole. . . . Have Central pop a couple anti-personnel rounds overhead and then we go in and count bodies. But they've got tunnels and spider holes—and command-detonated mines—laced out from the pit like a giant worm-farm. This one's going to cost, Esa."

"Blood and martyrs," the captain said under his breath. When he had received the Ain Chelia assignment, Mboya had first studied reconnaissance coverage of the village and the mine three kilometers away. It was now a month and a half since the rebel disaster at al-Madinah. The Slammers had raised the siege of the capital in a pitched battle that no one in the human universe was better equipped to fight. Surviving rebels had scattered to their homes to make what preparations they could against the white terror they knew would sweep in the wake of the government's victory. At Ain Chelia, the preparations had been damned effective. The recce showed clearly that several thousand cubic meters of rubble had been dumped into the central pit of the mine, the waste of burrowings from all around its five kilometer circumference.

"We can drop penetrators all year," Mboya said, aloud but more to himself than to the non-com beside him. "Blow the budget for the whole operation, and even then I wouldn't bet they couldn't tunnel ahead of the shelling faster than we broke rock on top of them."

"If we storm the place," said Sergeant Scratchard, "and then go down the tunnels after the hold-outs, we'll have thirty per cent casualties if we lose a man."

A rifle flashed from the pit-edge. Almost simultaneously, one of the company's three-barreled automatic weapons slashed the edge of the rebel gunpit. The trooper must have sighted in his weapon earlier when a sniper had popped from the pit, knowing the site would be re-used eventually. Now the air shook as the powergun detonated a bando-lier of grenades charged with industrial explosives. The sniper's rifle glittered as it spun into the air; her head was by contrast a ragged blur, its long hair uncoiling and snapping outward with the thrust of the explosion.

"Get that gunner's name," Mboya snapped

to his first sergeant. "He's earned a week's leave as soon as we stand down. But to get all the rest of them . . ." and the officer's voice was the more stark for the fact that it was so controlled, "we're going to need something better. I think we're going to have to talk them out."

"Via, Captain," said Scratchard in real surprise, "why would they want to come out? They saw at al-Madinah what happens when they faced us in the field. And nobody surrenders when they know all prisoners're going to be shot."

"Don't say nobody," said Esa Mboya in a voice as crisp as the gunfire bursting anew from the Bordj. "Because that's just what you're going to see this lot do."

The dead end of Juma's street had been blocked and turned into the company maintenance park between the time Esa left to observe the Bordj and his return to his brother's house. Skimmers, trucks, and a gunjeep with an intermittent short in its front fan had been pulled into the cul-de-sac. They were walled on three sides by the courtyards of the houses beyond Juma's.

Sergeant Scratchard halted the jeep with the bulky commo equipment in the open street, but Mboya swung his own skimmer around the supply truck that formed a makeshift fourth wall for the park. A guard saluted. "Muller!" Esa shouted, even before the skirts of his one-man vehicle touched the pavement. "What in the name of heaven d'ye think you're about! I told you to set up in the main square!"

Bog Muller stood up beside a skimmer raised on edge. He was a bulky Technician with twenty years service in the Slammers. A good administrator, but his khakis were clean. Operation Feirefitz had required the company to move fast and long, and there was no way Muller's three half-trained subordinates could have coped with the consequent rash of equipment failures. "Ah, well, Captain," Muller temporized, his eyes apparently focused on the row of wall spikes over Esa's head, "we ran into Juma and he said—"

"He *what*!" Mboya shouted.

"I said," said Juma, rising from behind the skimmer himself, "that security in the middle of the village would be more of a problem than anybody needed. We've got some hot-heads; I don't want any of them to get the notion of stealing a gun-jeep, for instance. The two households there—" he pointed to the entrances now blocked by vehicles, using the grease gun in his right hand for the gesture—"have both been evacuated to the Bordj." The half-smile he gave his brother could have been meant for either what he had just said or for the words he added, raising both the grease gun and the wire brush he held in his left hand: "Besides, what with the mine closed, I'd get rusty myself with no equipment to work on."

"After all," said Muller in what was more

explanation than defense, "I knew Juma back when."

Esa took in his brother's smile, took in as well the admiring glances of the three Tech I's who had been watching the civilian work. "All right," he said to Muller, "but the next time clear it with me. And you," he said, pointing to Juma, "come on inside for now. We need to talk."

"Yes, little brother," the civilian said with a bow as submissive as his tone.

In the surprising cool of his house, Juma stripped off the gritty jellaba he had worn while working. He began washing with a waterless cleaner, rubbing it on with smooth strokes of his palms. On a chain around his neck glittered a tiny silver crucifix, normally hidden by his clothing.

"You didn't do much of a job persuading your friends to your Way of Peace," Esa said with an anger he had not intended to display.

"No, I'm afraid I didn't," the civilian answered mildly. "They were polite enough, even the Kaid, Ali ben Cheriff. But they pointed out that the Arabizers in al-Madinah intended to stamp out all traces of Kabyle culture as soon as possible . . . which of course was true. And we did have our own martyr here in Ain Chelia, as you know. I couldn't—" Juma looked up at his brother, his dark skin glistening beneath the lather— "argue with their *military* estimate, after all, either. The Way doesn't require that its followers lie about reality in order to change it—but I don't have to tell you that."

"Go on," said the captain. His hand touched the catches of his body armor. He did not release them, however, even though the hard-suit was not at the moment protection against any physical threat.

"Well, the National Army was outnumbered ten to one by the troops we could field from the backlands," Juma continued as he stepped into the shower. "That's without defections, too. And weapons aren't much of a problem. Out there, any jack-leg mechanic can turn out a truck piston in his back room. The tolerances aren't any closer on a machine gun. But what we didn't expect—" he raised his deep voice only enough to override the hiss of the shower— "was that all six of the other planets of the al-Ittihad al-Arabi—" for Arab Union Juma used the Arabic words, and they rasped in his throat like a file on bars— "would club together and help the sanctimonious butchers in al-Madinah hire the Slammers."

He stepped shining from the stall, no longer pretending detachment or that he and his brother were merely chatting. "I visited the siege lines then," Juma rumbled, wholly a preacher and wholly a man, "and I begged the men from Ain Chelia to come home while there was time. To make peace, or if they would not choose peace then at least to choose life—to lie low in the hills till the money ran out and the Slammers were off on somebody else's contract, killing somebody else's enemies. But my friends would stand with their brothers ... and so they did, and they died with their brothers, too many of them, when the tanks came through their encirclement like knives through a goat-skin." His smile crooked and his voice dropped. "And the rest came home and told me they should have listened before."

"They'll listen to you now," said Esa, "if you tell them to come out of the Bordj without their weapons and surrender."

Juma began drying himself on a towel of coarse local cotton. "Will they?" he replied without looking up.

Squeezing his fingers against the bands of porcelain armor over his stomach, Esa said, "The Re-education Camps outside al-Madinah aren't a rest cure, but there's too many journalists in the city to let them be too bad. Even if the hold-outs are willing to die, they surely don't want their whole families wiped out. And if we have to clear the Bordj ourselves—well, there won't be any prisoners, you know that.... There wouldn't be even if we wanted them, not after we blast and gas the tunnels, one by one."

"Yes, I gathered the Re-education Camps aren't too bad," the civilian agreed, walking past his brother to don a light jellaba of softer weave than his work garment. "I gather they're not very full, either. A—a cynic, say, might guess that most of the trouble-makers don't make it to al-Madinah where journalists can see them. That they die in the desert after they've surrendered. Or they don't surrender, of course. I don't think Ali ben Cheriff and the others in the Bordj are going to surrender, for instance."

"Damn you!" the soldier shouted. "The choice is *certain* death, isn't it? *Any* chance is better than that!"

"Well you see," said Juma, watching the knuckles of his right hand twist against the palm of his left, "they know as well as I do that the only transport you arrived with was the minimum to haul your own supplies. There's no way you could carry over a hundred prisoners back to the capital. No way in . . . Hell."

Esa slammed the wall with his fist. Neither the concrete nor his raging expression showed any reaction to the loud impact. "I could be planning to put them in commandeered ore haulers, couldn't I?" he said. "Some of them must be operable!"

Juma stepped to the younger man and took him by the wrists as gently as a shepherd touching a newborn lamb. "Little brother," he said, "swear to me that you'll turn anyone who surrenders over to the authorities in al-Madinah, and I'll do whatever I can to get them to surrender."

The soldier snatched his hands away. He said, "Do you think I wouldn't lie to you because we're brothers? Then you're a fool!"

"What I think, what anyone thinks, is between him and the Lord," Juma said. He started to move toward his brother again but caught the motion and turned it into a swaying only. "If you will swear to me to deliver them unharmed, I'll carry your message into the Bordj."

Esa swung open the massive door. On the threshold he paused and turned to his brother. "Every one of my boys who doesn't make it," he said in a venemous whisper. "His blood's on your head."

Captain Mboya did not try to slam the door this time. He left it standing open as he strode through the courtyard. "Scratchard!" he roared to the sergeant with an anger not meant for the man on whom it fell. "Round up ben Khedda!" Mboya threw himself down on his skimmer and flicked the fans to life. Over their whine he added, "Get him up to me at the command dugout. Now!"

With the skill of long experience, the captain spun his one-man vehicle past the truck and the jeep parked behind it. Sergeant Scratchard gloomily watched his commander shriek up the street. The captain shouldn't have been going anywhere without the jeep, his commo link to Central, in tow. No point in worrying about that, though. The noncom sighed and lifted the jeep off the pavement. Ben Khedda would be at his house or in the cafe across the street from it. Scratchard hoped he had a vehicle of his own and wouldn't have to ride the jump seat of the jeep. He didn't like to sit that close to a slimy traitor.

But Jack Scratchard knew he'd done worse

things than sit with a traitor during his
years with the Slammers; and, needs must,
he would again.

The mortar shell burst with a white flash.
Seconds later came a distant *chunk*! as if a
rock had been dropped into a trash can.
Even after the report had died away, fragments continued ricocheting from rock with
tiny gnat-songs. Ben Khedda flinched beneath the clear night sky.

"It's just our harrassing fire," said Captain Mboya. "You rag-heads don't have
high-angle weapons, thank the Lord. Of
course, all our shells do is keep them down
in their tunnels."

The civilian swallowed. "Your sergeant,"
he said, "told me you needed me at once."
Scratchard stirred in the darkness at the
other end of the dugout, but he made no
comment of his own.

"Yeah," said Mboya, "but when I cooled
off I decided to take a turn around the perimeter. Took a while. It's a bloody long
perimeter for one cursed infantry company
to hold."

"Well, I," ben Khedda said, "I came at
once, sir. I recognize the duty all good citizens owe to our liberators." Firing broke
out, a burst from a projectile weapon answered promiscuously by powerguns. Ben
Khedda winced again. Cyan bolts from
across the pit snapped overhead, miniature
lightning following miniature thunder.

Without looking up, Captain Mboya keyed

his commo helmet and said, "Thrasher Four
to Thrasher Four-Three. Anybody shoots
beyond his sector again and it's ten days in
the glass house when we're out of this cop."
The main unit in Scratchard's jeep purred
as it relayed the amplified signal. All the
firing ceased.

"Will ben Cheriff and the others in the
Bordj listen to you, do you think?" the captain continued.

For a moment, ben Khedda did not realize the officer was speaking to him. He swallowed again. "Well, I . . . I can't say," he
blurted. He began to curl in his upper lip as
if to chew a moustache, though he was clean
shaven. "They aren't friends of mine, of
course, but if God wills and it would help
you if I addressed them over a loudspeaker
as to their true duties as citizens of Dar
al-B'heed—"

"We hear you were second in command
of the Chelia contingent at Madinah," Mboya
said inflexibly. "Besides, there won't be a
loudspeaker, you'll be going in in person."

Horror at past and future implications
warred in ben Khedda's mind and froze his
tongue. At last he stammered, "Oh no,
C-captain, before G-god, they've lied to you!
That accurst al-Habashi wishes to lie away
my life! I did no more than any man would
do to stay alive!"

Mboya waved the other to silence. The
pale skin of his palm winked as another
shell detonated above the Bordj. When the
echoes died away, the captain went on in a

voice as soft as a leopard's paw, "You will tell them that if they all surrender, their lives will be spared and they will not be turned over to the government until they are actually in al-Madinah. You will say that I swore that on my honor and on the soul of my house."

Ben Khedda raised a hand to interrupt, but the soldier's voice rolled on implacably, "They must deposit all their arms in the Bordj and come out to be shackled. The tunnels will be searched. If there are any hold-outs, three of those who surrendered will be shot for each hold-out. If there are any boobytraps, ten of those who surrendered will be shot for every man of mine who is injured."

Mboya drew a breath, long and deep as that of a power lifter. The civilian, tight as a house-jack, strangled his own words as he waited for the captain to conclude. "You will say that after they have done as I have said, all of them will be loaded on ore carriers with sun-screens. You will explain that there will be food and water brought from the village to support them. And you will tell them that if some of them are wounded or are infirm, they may ride within an ambulance which will be air-conditioned.

"Do you understand?"

For a moment, ben Khedda struggled with an inability to phrase his thoughts in neutral terms. He was unwilling to meet the captain's eyes, even with the darkness as a cushion. Finally he said, "Captain—I, I trust your word as I would trust that of no man since the Prophet, on whom be peace. When you say the lives of the traitors will be spared, there can be no doubt, may it please God."

"Trust has nothing to do with it," said Captain Mboya without expression. "I have told you what you will say, and you will say it."

"Captain, Captain," whimpered the civilian, "I understand. The trip is a long one and surely some of the most troublesome will die of heat stroke. They will know that themselves. But there will be no . . . general tragedy? I must live here in Ain Chelia with the friends of the, the traitors. You see my position?"

"Your position," Mboya repeated with scorn that drew a chuckle from Scratchard across the dug-out. "Your position is that unless you talk your friends there out of the Bordj—" he gestured. Automatic weapons began to rave and chatter as if on cue. "Unless you go down there and come back with them, I'll have you shot on your doorstep for a traitor, and your body left to the dogs. That's your position."

"Cheer up, citizen," Sergeant Scratchard said. "You're getting a great chance to pick one side and stick with it. The change'll do you good."

Ben Khedda gave a despairing cry and stood, his dun jellaba flapping as a lesser shadow. He stared over the rim of the dug-out into a night now brightened only by stars and a random powergun bolt, harrassment like that of the mortars. He turned and shouted at the motionless captain, "It's easy for you—you go where your colonel sends you, you kill who he tells you to kill. And then you come all high and moral over the rest of us, who have to make our own decisions! You despise me? At least I'm a man and not somebody's dog!"

Mboya laughed harshly. "You think Colonel Hammer told us how to clear the back country? Don't be a fool. My official orders are to co-operate with the District Governor, and to send all prisoners back to al-Madinah for internment. The colonel can honestly deny ordering anything else—and letting him do that is as much a part of my job as co-operating with a governor who knows that anybody really sent to a Re-education Camp will be back in his hair in a year."

There was a silence in the dug-out. At last the sergeant said, "He can't go out now, sir." The moan of a ricochet underscored the words.

"No, no, we'll have to wait till dawn," the captain agreed tiredly. As if ben Khedda were an unpleasant machine, he added, "Get him the hell out of my sight, though. Stick him in the bunker with the Headquarters Squad and tell them to hold him till called for. Via! but I wish this operation was over."

The guns spat at one another all through the night. It was not the fire that kept Esa

Mboya awake, however, but rather the dreams that plagued him with gentle words whenever he did manage to nod off.

"Well," said Juma, scowling judiciously at the gun-jeep on the rack before him, "I'd say we pull the wiring harness first. Half the time that's the whole problem—grit gets into the conduits and when the fans vibrate, it saws through the insulation. Even if we're wrong, we haven't done anything that another few months of running on Dar al-B'heed wouldn't have required anyway."

"You should have seen him handle one a' these when I first knew him," said Bog Muller proudly to his subordinates. "Beat it to hell, he would, Via—bring her in with rock scrapes on both sides that he'd put on at the same time!"

The Kikuyu civilian touched a valve and lowered the rack. His hand caressed the sand-burnished skirt of the jeep as it sank past him. The joy-stick controls were in front of the left-hand seat. Finesse was a matter of touch and judgment, not sophisticated instrumentation. He waggled the stick gently, remembering. In front of the other seat was the powergun, its three iridium barrels poised to rotate and hose out destruction in a nearly-continuous stream.

"You won't believe it," continued the Technician, "but I saw with my own eyes—" that was a lie—"this boy here steering with one hand and working the gun with the other. Bloody miracle that was—even if he did give Maintenance more trouble than any three other troopers."

"You learn a lot about a machine when you push it, when you stress it," said Juma. His fingers reached for but did not quite touch the spade grips of the tribarrel. "About men, too," he added and lowered his hand. He looked Muller in the face and said, "What I learned about myself was that I didn't want to live in a universe that had no better use for me than to gun other people down. I won't claim to be saving souls . . . because that's in the Lord's hands and he uses what instruments he desires. But at least I'm not taking lives."

One of the younger Techs coughed. Muller nodded heavily and said, "I know what you mean, Juma. I've never regretted getting into Maintenance right off the way I did. Especially times like today. . . . But Via, if we stand here fanning our lips, we won't get a curst bit of work done, will we?"

The civilian chuckled without asking for an explanation of 'especially times like today.' "Sure, Bog," he said, latching open the left-side access ports one after another. "Somebody dig out a 239B harness and we'll see if I remember as much as I think I do about changing one of these beggars." He glanced up at the truncated mass of the plateau, wiping his face with a bandanna. "Things have quieted down since the sun came up," he remarked. "Even if I weren't— dedicated to the Way—I know too many people on both sides to like to hear the shooting at the mine."

None of the other men responded. At the time it did not occur to Juma that there might be something about his words that embarrassed them.

"There's a flag," said Scratchard, his eyes pressed tight to the lenses of the periscope. "Blood and martyrs, Cap—there's a flag!"

"No shooting!" Mboya ordered over his commo as he moved. "Four to all Thrasher units, stand to but no shooting!"

All around the mine crater, men watched a white rag flapping on the end of a long wooden pole. Some looked through periscopes like those in the command dugout, others over the sights of their guns in hope that something would give them an excuse to fire. "Well, what are they waiting for?" the captain muttered.

"It's ben Khedda," guessed Scratchard without looking away from the flag. "He was scared green to go out there. Now he's just as scared to come back."

The flag staggered suddenly. Troopers tensed, but a moment later an unarmed man climbed full height from the Bordj. The high sun threw his shadow at his feet like a pit. Standing as erect as his age permitted him, Ali ben Cheriff took a step toward the Slammers' lines. Wind plucked at his jellaba and white beard; the rebel leader was a patriarch in appearance as well as in simple fact. On his head was the

green turban that marked him as a pilgrim
to al-Meccah on Terra. He was as devotedly
Moslem as he was Kabyle, and he—like most
of the villagers—saw no inconsistencies in
the facts. To ben Cheriff it was no more
necessary to become an Arab in order to
accept Islam than it had seemed necessary
to Saint Paul that converts to Christ first
become Jews.

"We've won," the captain said as he
watched the figure through the foreshorten-
ing lenses. "That's the Kaid, ben Cheriff. If
he comes, they all do."

Up from the hidden tunnel clambered an
old woman wearing the stark black of a
matron. The Kaid paused and stretched back
his hand, but the woman straightened without help. Together the old couple began to
walk toward the waiting guns.

The flagstaff flapped erect again. Gripping it like a talisman, Youssef ben Khedda
stepped from the tunnel mouth where the
Kaid had shouldered aside his hesitation.
He picked his way across the ground at increasing speed. When ben Khedda passed
the Kaid and his wife, he skirted them
widely as if he were afraid of being struck.
More rebels were leaving the Bordj in single
file. None of them carried visible weapons.
Most, men and women alike, had their eyes
cast down; but a red-haired girl leading a
child barely old enough to walk glared
around with the haughty rage of a lioness.

"Well, no rest for the wicked," grunted
Sergeant Scratchard. Settling his subma-

chinegun on its sling, he climbed out of the
dugout. "Headquarters Squad to me," he
ordered. Bent over against the possible shock
of a fanatic's bullets, experienced enough to
know the reality of his fear and brave enough
to face it none the less, Scratchard began to
walk to the open area between pit and siege
lines where the prisoners would be immo-
bilized. The seven men of HQ Squad followed; their corporal drove the jeep loaded
with leg irons.

One of the troopers raised his powergun
to bar ben Khedda. Scratchard waved and
called an order; the trooper shrugged and
let the Kabyle pass. The sergeant gazed after him for a moment, then spat in the dust
and went on about the business of searching and securing the prisoners.

Youssef ben Khedda was panting with
tension and effort as he approached the dug-
out, but there was a hard glint of triumph
in his eyes as well. He knew he was de-
spised, by those he led no less than by those
who had driven him; but he had dug the
rebels from their fortress when all the men
and guns of the Slammers might have been
unable to do so without him. Now he saw a
way to ride the bloody crest to permanent
power in Ain Chelia. He tried to set his flag
in the ground. It scratched into the rocky
soil, then fell with a clatter. "I have brought
them to you," ben Khedda said in a haughty
voice.

"Some of them, at least," said Mboya, his
face neutral. Rebels continued to straggle

from the Bordj, their faces sallow from more than the day they had spent in their tunnels. The Kaid had submitted to the shackles with a stony indifference. His wife was weeping beside him, not for herself but for her husband. Two of the nervous troopers were fanning the prisoners with detector wands set for steel and iridium. Anything the size of a razor blade would register. A lead bludgeon or a brass-barreled pistol would be ignored, but there were some chances you took in the service of practicality.

"As God wills, they are all coming, you know that," ben Khedda said, assertive with dreamed-of lordship. "If they were each in his separate den, many of them would fight till you blew them out or buried them. All are willing to die, but most would not willingly kill their fellows, their families." His face worked. "A fine joke, is it not?" If what had crossed ben Khedda's lips had been a smile, then it transmuted to a sneer. "They would have been glad to kill me first, I think, but they were afraid that you would have been angry."

"More fools them," said the captain.

"Yes . . . ," said the civilian, drawing back his face like a rat confronting a terrier, "more fools them. And now you will pay me."

"Captain," said the helmet speaker in the first sergeant's voice, "this one says he's the last."

Mboya climbed the four steps to surface level. Scratchard waved and pointed to the Kabyle who was just joining the scores of

his fellows. The number of those being shackled in a continuous chain at least approxi-
mated the one hundred and forty who were
believed to have holed up in the Bordj.
Through the clear air rang hammer strokes
as a pair of troopers stapled the chain to
the ground at intervals, locking the prisoners even more securely into the killing
ground. The captain nodded. "We'll give it
a minute to let anybody still inside have
second thoughts," he said over the radio.
"Then the search teams go in." He looked
at ben Khedda. "All right," he said, "you've
got your life and whatever you think you
can do with it. Now, get out of here before I
change my mind."

Mboya gazed again at the long line of
prisoners. He was unable not to imagine
them as they would look in an hour's time,
after the Bordj had been searched and their
existence was no longer a tool against potential hold-outs. He could not have broken
with the Way of his childhood, however,
had he not replaced it with a sense of duty
as uncompromising. Esa Mboya, Captain,
G Company, Hammer's Regiment, would
do whatever was required to accomplish
the task set him. They had been hired to
pacify the district, not just to quiet it down
for six months or a year.

Youssef ben Khedda had not left. He was
still facing Mboya, as unexpected and unpleasant as a rat on the pantry shelf. He
was saying, "No, there is one more thing
you must do, as God wills, before you leave

Ain Chelia. I do not compel it—" the soldier's face went blank with fury at the suggestion—"your duty that you talk of compels you. There is one more traitor in the village, a man who did not enter the Bordj because he thought his false god would preserve him."

"Little man," said the captain in shock and a genuine attempt to stop the words he knew were about to be said, "don't—"

"Add the traitor Juma al-Habashi to these," the civilian cried, pointing to the fluttering jellabas of the prisoners. "Put him there or his whines of justice and other words and his false god will poison the village again like a dead rat stinking in a pool. Take him!"

The two men stood with their feet on a level. The soldier's helmet and armor increased his advantage in bulk, however, and his wrath lighted his face like a cleansing flame. "Shall I slay my brother for thee, lower-than-a-dog?" he snarled.

Ben Khedda's face jerked at the verbal slap, but with a wave of his arm he retorted, "Will you now claim to follow the Way yourself? There stand one hundred and thirty-four of your brothers. Make it one more, as your duty commands!"

The absurdity was so complete that the captain trembled between laughter and the feeling that he had gone insane. Carefully, his tone touched more with wonder than with rage until the world should return to focus, the Kikuyu said, "Shall I, Esa Mboya, order the death of Juma Mboya? My brother, flesh of my father and of my mother . . . who held my hand when I toddled my first steps upright?"

Now at last ben Khedda's confidence squirted out like blood from a slashed carotid. "The name—" he said. "I didn't *know*!"

Mboya's world snapped into place again, its realities clear and neatly dove-tailed. "Get out, filth," he said harshly, "and wonder what I plan for you when I come down from this hill."

The civilian stumbled back toward his car as if his body and not his spirit had received the mortal wound. The soldier considered him dispassionately. If ben Khedda stayed in Ain Chelia, he wouldn't last long. The Slammers would be out among the stars, and the central government a thousand kilometers away in al-Madinah would be no better able to protect a traitor. Youssef ben Khedda would be a reminder of friends and relatives torn by blasts of cyan fire with every step he took on the streets of the village. Those steps would be few enough, one way or the other.

And if in the last fury of his well-earned fear ben Khedda tried to kill Juma—well, Juma had made his bed, his Way . . . he could tread it himself. Esa laughed. Not that the traitor would attempt murder personally. Even in the final corner, rats of ben Khedda's stripe tried to persuade other rats to bite for them.

"Captain," murmured Scratchard's voice

over the command channel, "think we've waited long enough?"

Instead of answering over the radio, Mboya nodded and began walking the hundred meters to where his sergeant stood near the prisoners. The rebels' eyes followed him, some with anger, most in only a dull appreciation of the fact that he was the nearest moving object on a static landscape. Troopers had climbed out of their gun pits all around the Bordj. Their dusty khaki blended with the soil, but the sun woke bright reflections from the barrels of their weapons.

"The search teams are ready to go in, sir," Scratchard said, speaking in Dutch but stepping a pace further from the shackled Kaid besides.

"Right," the captain agreed. "I'll lead the team from Third Platoon."

"Captain—"

"Where are the trucks, unbeliever?" demanded Ali ben Cheriff. His voice started on a quaver but lashed at the end.

"—there's plenty cursed things for you to do besides crawling down a hole with five pongoes. Leave it to the folks whose job it is."

"There's nothing left of this operation that Mendoza can't wrap up," Mboya said. "Believe me, he won't like doing it any less, either."

"Where are the trucks to carry away our children, dog and son of dogs?" cried the Kaid. Beneath the green turban, the rebel's face was as savage and unyielding as that of a trapped wolf.

"It's not for fun," Mboya went on. "There'll be times I'll have to send boys out to be killed while I stay back, safe as a staff officer, and run things. But if I lead from the front when I can, when it won't compromise the mission if I do stop a load—then they'll do what they're told a little sharper when it's me that says it the next time."

The Kaid spat. Lofted by his anger and the breeze, the gobbet slapped the side of Mboya's helmet and dribbled down onto his porcelain-sheathed shoulder.

Scratchard turned. Ignoring the automatic weapon slung ready to fire under his arm, he drew a long knife from his boot sheath instead. Three strides separated the noncom from the line of prisoners. He had taken two of them before Mboya caught his shoulder and stopped him. "Easy, Jack," the captain said.

Ben Cheriff's gaze was focused on the knifepoint. Fear of death could not make the old man yield, but neither was he unmoved by the approach of its steel-winking eye. Scratchard's own face had no more expression than did the knife itself. The Kaid's wife lunged at the soldier to the limit of her chain, but the look Scratchard gave her husband dried her throat around the curses within it.

Mboya pulled his man back. "Easy," he repeated. "I think he's earned that, don't you?" He turned Scratchard gently. He did not point out, nor did he need to do so, the three gun-jeeps which had swung down to fifty meters in front of the line of captives. Their crews were tense and still with the weight of their orders. They met Mboya's eyes, comprehending but without enthusiasm.

"Right," said Scratchard mildly. "Well, the quicker we get down that hole, the quicker we get the rest of the job done. Let's go."

The five tunnel rats from Third Platoon were already squatting at the entrance from which the rebels had surrendered. Captain Mboya began walking toward them. "You stay on top, Sergeant," he said. "You don't need to prove anything."

Scratchard cursed without heat. "I'll wait at the tunnel mouth unless something pops. You'll be out of radio contact and I'll be curst if I trust anybody else to carry you a message."

The tunnel rats were rising to their feet, silent men whose faces were in constant, tiny motion. They carried detector wands and sidearms; two had even taken off their body armor and stood in the open air looking paler than shelled shrimp. Mboya cast a glance back over his shoulder at the prisoners and the gun-jeeps beyond. "Do you believe in sin, Sergeant?" he asked.

Scratchard glanced sidelong at his superior. "Don't know, sir. Not really my field."

"My brother believes in it," said the captain, "but I guess he left the Slammers before you transferred out of combat cars. And he isn't here now, Jack, I am, so I guess we'll have to dispense with sin today."

"Team Three ready, sir," said the black-haired man who probably would have had sergeant's pips had he not been stripped to the waist.

"Right," said Mboya. Keying his helmet he went on, "Thrasher to Club One, Club Two. Let's see what they left us, boys." And as he stepped toward the tunnel mouth, without really thinking about the words until he spoke them, he added, "And the Lord be with us all."

The bed of the turbine driving Youssef ben Khedda's car was enough out of true that the vehicle announced its own approach unmistakably. Juma wondered in the back of his mind what brought the little man, but his main concentration was on the plug connector he was trying to reeve through a channel made for something a size smaller. At last the connector shifted the last two millimeters necessary for Juma to slip a button-hook deftly about it. The three subordinate Techs gave a collective sigh, and Bog Muller beamed in reflected glory.

"Father!" ben Khedda wheezed, oblivious to the guard frowning over his powergun a pace behind, "Father! You've got to ... I've got to talk to you. You must!"

"All right, Youssef," the Kikuyu said. "In a moment." He tugged the connector gently through its channel and rotated it to mate with the gun leads.

Ben Khedda reached for Juma's arm in a fury of impatience. One of the watching Techs caught the Kabyle's wrist. "Touch him, rag-head," the trooper said, "and you better be able to grow a new hand." He thrust ben Khedda back with more force than the resistance demanded.

Juma straightened from the gun-jeep and put an arm about the shoulders of the angry trooper. "Worse job than replacing all the fans," he said in Dutch, "but it gives you a good feeling to finish it. Run the static test, if you would, and I'll be back in a few minutes." He squeezed the trooper, released him, and added in Kabyle to his fellow villager, "Come into my house, then, Youssef. What is it you need of me?"

Ben Khedda's haste and nervousness were obvious from the way his car lay parked with its skirt folded under the front from an over-hasty stop. Juma paused with a frown for more than the mechanical problem. He bent to lift the car and let the skirt spring away from the fan it was probably touching at the moment.

"Don't *worry* about that," ben Khedda cried, plucking at the bigger man's sleeve. "We've *got* to talk in private."

Juma had left his courtyard gate unlatched since he was working only a few meters away. Before ben Khedda had reached the door of the house, he was spilling the words that tormented him. "Before God, you have to talk to your brother or he'll kill me, Father, he'll kill *me!*"

"Youssef," said the Kikuyu as he swung his door open and gestured the other man toward the cool interior, "I pray—I have been praying—that at worst, none of our villagers save those in the Bordj are in danger." He smiled too sadly to be bitter. "You would know better than I, I think, who may have been marked out to Esa as an enemy of the government. But he's not a cruel man, my brother, only a very—determined one. He won't add you to whatever list he has out of mere dislike."

The Kabyle's lips worked silently. His face was tortured by the explanation that he needed to give but could not. "Father," he pleaded, "you *must* believe me, he'll have me killed. Before God, you must beg him for my life, you *must!*"

Ben Khedda was gripping the Kikuyu by both sleeves. Juma detached himself carefully and said, "Youssef, why would my brother want you killed—of all the men in Ain Chelia? Did something happen?"

The smaller man jerked himself back with a dawning horror in his eyes. "You planned this with him, didn't you?" he cried. His arm thrust at the altar as if to sweep away the closed triptych. "This is all a lie, your prayers, your *Way*—you and your butcher brother trapped me to bleed like a sheep on Id al-Fitr! Traitor! Liar! Murderer!" He threw his hands over his face and flung himself

down and across a stool. The Kabyle's sobs
held the torment of a man without hope.

Juma stared at the weeping man. There
was something unclean about ben Khedda.
His back rose and fell beneath the jellaba
like the distended neck of a python bolting
a young child. "Youssef," the Kikuyu said
as gently as he could, "you may stay here
or leave, as you please. I promise you that I
will speak to Esa this evening, on your behalf as well as that of ... others, all the
others. Is there anything you need to tell
me?"

Only the tears responded.

The dazzling sun could not sear away
Juma's disquiet as he walked past the guard
and the barricading truck. Something was
wrong with the day, with the very silence.
Though all things were with the Lord.

The jeep's inspection ports had been
latched shut. The Techs had set a pair of
skimmers up on their sides as the next project. The civilian smiled. "Think she'll float
now?" he asked the trooper who had grabbed
ben Khedda. "Let's see if I remember how
to put one of these through her paces. You
can't trust a fix, you see, till you've run her
under full load."

There was a silence broken by the whine
of ben Khedda's turbine firing. Juma managed a brief prayer that the Kabyle would
find a Way open to him—knowing as he
prayed that the impulse to do so was from
his mind and not at all from his heart.

"Juma, ah," Bog Muller was trying to

say. "Ah, look, this isn't—isn't our idea, it's the job, you know. But the captain—" none of the four Techs were looking anywhere near the civilian—"he ordered that you not go anywhere today until, until ... it was clear."

The silence from the Bordj was a cloak that smothered Juma and squeezed all the blood from his face. "Not that you're a prisoner, but, ah, your brother thought it'd be better for both of you if you didn't see him or call him till—after."

"I see," said the civilian, listening to his own voice as if a third party were speaking. "Until after he's killed my friends, I suppose ... yes." He began walking back to his house, his sandaled feet moving without being consciously directed. "Juma—"called Muller, but the Tech thought better of the words or found he had none to say.

Ben Khedda had left the door ajar. It was only by habit that Juma himself closed it behind him. The dim coolness within was no balm to the fire that skipped across the surface of his mind. Kneeling, the Kikuyu unlatched and opened wide the panels of his altar piece. It was his one conscious affectation, a copy of a triptych painted over a millenium before by the Master of Hell, Hieronymous Bosch. Atop a haywain rode a couple. Their innocence was beset by every form of temptation in the world, the World. Where would their Way take them? No doubt where it took all Mankind, saving the Lord's grace, to Hell and the grave—good intentions be damned, hope be damned, innocence be damned. . . . Obscurely glad of the harshness of the tiles on which he knelt, Juma prayed for his brother and for the souls of those who would shortly die in flames as like to those of Hell as man could create. He prayed for himself as well, for he was damned to endure what he had not changed. They were all travellers together on the Way.

After a time, Juma sighed and raised his head. A demon faced him on the triptych; it capered and piped through its own blue snout. Not for the first time, Juma thought of how pleasant it would be to personify his own weakness and urgings. Then he could pretend that they were somehow apart from the true Juma Mboya, who remained whole and incorruptible.

The lower of the two drawers beneath the altar was not fully closed.

Even as he drew it open, Juma knew from the lack of resistance that the drawer was empty. The heavy-barreled powergun had rested within when ben Khedda had accompanied the search team. It was there no longer.

Striding swiftly and with the dignity of a leopard, Mboya al-Habashi crossed the room and his courtyard. He appeared around the end of the truck barricade so suddenly that Bog Muller jumped. The Kikuyu pointed his index finger with the deliberation of a pistol barrel. "Bog," he said very clearly, "I need to call my brother at once or something terrible will happen."

"Via, man," said the Technician, looking away, "you know how I feel about it, but it's not my option. You don't leave here, and you don't call, Juma—or it's my ass."

"Lord blast you for a fool!" the Kikuyu shouted, taking a step forward. All four Technicians backed away with their hands lifting. "Will you—" But though there was confusion on the faces watching him, there was nothing of assent, and there was no time to argue. As if he had planned it from the start, Juma slipped into the left saddle of the jeep he had just rewired and gunned the fans.

With an oath, Bog Muller grappled with the civilian. The muscles beneath Juma's loose jellaba had shifted driving fans beneath ore carriers in lieu of a hydraulic jack. He shrugged the Technician away with a motion as slight and as masterful as that of an earth tremor. Juma waggled the stick, using the vehicle's skirts to butt aside two of the younger men who belatedly tried to support their chief. Then he had the jeep clear of the repair rack and spinning on its own axis.

Muller scrambled to his feet again and waited for Juma to realize there was not enough room between truck and wall for the jeep to pass. If the driver himself had any doubt, it was not evident in the way he dialed on throttle and leaned to bring the right-hand skirt up an instant before it scraped the courtyard wall. Using the wall as a running surface and the force of his turn to hold him there, Juma sent the gun-jeep howling sideways around the barricade and up the street.

"Hey!" shouted the startled guard, rising from the shady side of the truck. "Hey!" and he shouldered his weapon.

A Technician grabbed him, wrestling the muzzle of the gun skyward. It was the same lanky man who had caught ben Khedda when he would have plucked at Juma's sleeve. "Via!" cried the guard, watching the vehicle corner and disappear up the main road to the mine. "We weren't supposed to let him by!"

"We're better off explaining that," said the Tech, "than we are telling the captain how we just killed his brother. Right?"

The street was empty again. All five troopers stared at it for some moments before any of them moved to the radio.

Despite his haste, Youssef ben Khedda stopped his car short of the waiting gun-jeeps and began walking toward the prisoners. His back crept with awareness of the guns and the hard-eyed men behind them; but, as God willed, he had chosen and there could be no returning now.

The captain—his treacherous soul was as black as his skin—was not visible. No doubt he had entered the Bordj as he had announced he would. Against expectation, and as further proof that God favored his cause, ben Khedda saw no sign of that damnable first sergeant either. If God willed it, might they both be blasted to atoms somewhere down in a tunnel!

The soldiers watching the prisoners from a few meters away were the ones whom ben Khedda had led on their search of the village. The corporal frowned, but he knew ben Khedda for a confidant of his superiors. "Go with God, brother," said the civilian in Arabic, praying the other would have been taught that tongue or Kabyle. "Your captain wished me to talk once more with that dog—" he pointed to ben Cheriff. "There are documents of which he knows," he concluded vaguely.

The non-com's lip quirked nervously. "Look, can it wait—" he began, but even as he spoke he was glancing at the leveled tribarrels forty meters distant. "Blood," he muttered, a curse and a prophecy. "Well, go talk then. But watch it—the bastard's mean as a snake and his woman's worse."

The Kaid watched ben Khedda approach with the fascination of a mongoose awaiting a cobra. The traitor threw himself to the ground and tried to kiss the Kaid's feet. "Brother in God," the unshackled man whispered, "we have been betrayed by the unbelievers. Their dog of a captain will have you all murdered on his return, despite his oaths to me."

"Are we to believe, brother Youssef," the Kaid said with a sneer, "that you intend to die here with the patriots to cleanse your soul of the lies you carried?"

Others along the line of prisoners were

peering at the scene to the extent their irons permitted, but the two men spoke in voices too low for any but the Kaid's wife to follow the words. "Brother," ben Khedda continued, "preservation is better than expiation. The captain has confessed his wicked plan to no one but me. If he dies, it dies with him—and our people live. Now, raise me by the hands."

"Shall I touch your bloody hands, then?" ben Cheriff said, but he spoke as much in question as in scorn.

"Raise me by the hands," ben Khedda repeated, "and take from my right sleeve what you find there to hide in yours. Then wait the time."

"As God wills," the Kaid said and raised up ben Khedda. Their bodies were momentarily so close that their jellabas flowed together.

"And what in the blaze of Hell is *this*, Corporal!" roared Sergeant Scratchard. "Blood and martyrs, who told you to let anybody in with the prisoners?"

"Via, Sarge," the corporal sputtered, "he said—I mean, it was the captain, he tells me."

Ben Khedda had begun to sidle away from the line of prisoners. "Where the hell do you think *you're* going?" Scratchard snapped in Arabic. "Corporal, get another set of leg irons and clamp him onto his buddy there. If he's so copping hot to be here, he can stay till the captain says otherwise."

The sergeant paused, looking around the

circle of eyes focused nervously on him. More calmly he continued, "The Bordj is clear. The captain's up from the tunnel, but it'll be a while before he gets here—they came up somewhere in West Bumfuck and he's borrowing a skimmer from First Platoon to get back. We'll wait to see what he says." The first sergeant stared at Ali ben Cheriff, impassive as the wailing traitor was shackled to his right leg. "We'll wait till then," the soldier repeated.

Mboya lifted the nose of his skimmer and grounded it behind the first of the waiting gun-jeeps. Sergeant Scratchard trotted toward him from the direction of the prisoners. The non-com was panting with the heat and his armor; he raised his hand when he reached the captain in order to gain a moment's breathing space.

"Well?" Mboya prompted.

"Sir, Maintenance called," said Scratchard jerkily. "Your brother, sir. They think he's coming to see you."

The captain swore. "All right," he said, "if Juma thinks he has to watch this, he can watch it. He's a cursed fool if he expects to do anything *but* watch."

Scratchard nodded deeply, finding he inhaled more easily with his torso cocked forward. "Right, sir, I just—didn't want to rebroadcast on the Command channel in case Central was monitoring. Right. And then there's that rag-head, ben Khedda—I caught him talking to green-hat over there and thought he maybe ought to stay. For good."

Captain Mboya glanced at the prisoners. The men of Headquarters Squad still sat a few meters away because nobody had told them to withdraw. "Get them clear," the captain said with a scowl. He began walking toward the line, the first sergeant's voice turning his direction into a tersely-radioed order. Somewhere down the plateau, an aircar was being revved with no concern for what pebbles would do to the fans. Juma, very likely. He was the man you wanted driving your car when it had all dropped in the pot and Devil took the hindmost.

"Jack," the captain said, "I understand how you feel about ben Khedda; but we're here to do a job, not to kill sons of bitches. If we were doing that, we'd have to start in al-Madinah, wouldn't we?"

Mboya and his sergeant were twenty meters from the prisoners. The Kaid watched their approach with his hands folded within the sleeves of his jellaba and his eyes as still as iron. Youssef ben Khedda was crouched beside him, a study in terror. He retained only enough composure that he did not try to run—and that because the pressure of the leg iron binding him to ben Cheriff was just sharp enough to penetrate the fear.

A gun-jeep howled up onto the top of the plateau so fast that it bounced and dragged its skirts, still under full throttle. Scratchard turned with muttered surprise. Captain Mboya did not look around. He reached into the thigh pocket of his coveralls where he kept a magnetic key that would release ben Khedda's shackles. "We can't just kill—" he repeated.

"Now, God, *now!*" ben Khedda shrieked. "He's going to *kill me!*"

The Kaid's hands appeared, the right one extending a pistol. Its muzzle was a gray circle no more placable than the eye that aimed it.

Mboya dropped the key. His hand clawed for his own weapon, but he was no gunman, no quick-draw expert. He was a company commander carrying ten extra kilos, with his pistol in a flap holster that would keep his hand out at least as well as it did the wind-blown sand. Esa's very armor slowed him, though it would not save his face or his femoral arteries when the shots came.

Behind the captain, in a jeep still skidding on the edge of control, his brother triggered a one-handed burst as accurate as if parallax were a myth. The tribarrel was locked on its column; Juma let the vehicle's own side-slip saw the five rounds toward the man with the gun. A single two-centimeter bolt missed everything. Beyond, at the lip of the Bordj, a white flower bloomed from a cyan center as ionic calcium recombined with the oxygen from which it had been freed a moment before. Closer, everything was hidden by an instant glare. The pistol detonated in the Kaid's hand under the impact of a round from the tribarrel.

That was chance—or something else, for only the Lord could be so precise with certainty. The last shot of the burst hurled the Kaid back with a hole in his chest and his jellaba aflame. Ali ben Cheriff's eyes were free of fear when they closed them before burying him, and his mouth still wore a tight smile. Ben Khedda's face would have been less of a study in virtue and manhood, no doubt, but the two bolts that flicked across it took the traitor's head into oblivion with his memory. Juma had walked his burst on target, like any good man with an automatic weapon; and if there was something standing where the bolts walked—so much the worse for it.

There were shouts, but they were sucked lifeless by the wind. No one else had fired, for a wonder. Troops all around the Bordj were rolling back into dug-outs they had thought it safe to leave.

Juma brought the jeep to a halt a few meters from his brother. He doubled over the joy-stick as if he had been shot himself. Dust and sand puffed from beneath the skirts while the fans wound down; then the plume settled back on the breeze. Esa touched his brother's shoulder, feeling the dry sobs that wracked the jellaba. Very quietly the soldier said in the Kikuyu he had not, after all, forgotten, "I bring you a souvenir, elder brother. To replace the one you have lost." From his holster, now unsnapped, he drew his pistol and laid it carefully down on the empty gunner's seat of the jeep.

Juma looked up at his brother with a terrible dignity. "To remind me of the day I slew two men in the Lord's despite?" he asked formally. "Oh, no, my brother; I need no trinket to remind me of that forever."

"If you do not wish to remember the ones you killed," said Esa, "then perhaps it will remind you of the hundred and thirty-three whose lives you saved this day. And my life, of course."

Juma stared at his brother with a fixity by which alone he admitted his hope. He tugged the silver crucifix out of his jellaba and lifted it over his head. "Here," he said, "little brother. I offer you this in return for your gift. To remind you that wherever you go, the Way runs there as well."

Esa took the chain. With clumsy fingers he slipped it over his helmet. "All right, Thrasher, everybody stand easy," the captain roared into his commo link. "Two-six, I want food for a hundred and thirty-three people for three days. You've got my authority to take what you need from the village. Three-six, you're responsible for the transport. I want six ore carriers up here and I want them fast. If the first truck isn't here loading in twenty, that's two-zero mikes, I'll burn somebody a new asshole. Four-six, there's drinking water in drums down in those tunnels. Get it up here. Now, *move!*"

Juma stepped out of the gun-jeep, his left hand gripping Esa's right. Skimmers were already lifting from positions all around the

Bordj. G Company was surprised, but no one had forgotten that Captain Mboya meant his orders to be obeyed.

"Oh, one other thing," Esa said, then tripped his commo and added, "Thrasher Four to all Thrasher units—you get any argument from villagers while you're shopping, boys . . . just refer them to my brother."

It was past midday now. The sun had enough westering to wink from the crucifix against the soldier's armor—and from the pistol in the civilian's right hand.

THE FIFTEEN-YEARS'
AFTERWORD

*I*N THE SUMMER of 1970, I had occasion to watch a seventeen-year-old girl die. She'd taken a bullet from a fifty-caliber machine-gun through the abdomen, so it was really pretty amazing that she'd survived the short helicopter flight that brought her to us.

We were at a firebase somewhere north-west of Saigon, a squadron headquarters (battalion level, in effect), and the medical facilities weren't the fanciest in Military Region III. They were the closest, though, and the medics had enough experience and *cared* enough to be pretty damned good. Not that it mattered. Nothing was going to save the girl by the time she got to a place that somebody could try.

The bullet was half an inch in diameter, weighed just under two ounces, and must have had a velocity of about twenty-five hundred feet per second when it hit her—

spitting distance from the armored vehicle that fired it.

She was wearing black trousers and a beige ao dai, the attractive "skirt" with knee-length panels front and back which is traditional garb for Vietnamese women. There was some blood on the right front of the garment and a great deal on the left rear where the bullet had exited, but the resilience of flesh had puckered closed the lips of both wounds. The bleeding that killed her was internal, where a wide track through her torso had been jellied by hydrostatic shock.

It was a big bullet, that cal fifty, and it was probably going as fast on the other side of her frail body as it had been when it hit her.

The medics were pissed. They were too good and they cared too much to like losing a patient, even though they knew the girl couldn't have been saved. More specifically, they were pissed at me for trying to question the kid as they worked on her. I'd been ordered to do things I liked more, to tell the truth; but that was my job, and I got through a lot at that time by doing my job.

The girl didn't care, any more than she cared that somebody in the line troop which killed her had stolen her green-sequined shoes. She was in a coma from the time she reached the firebase to the time she died, not long after.

We got the story a few hours later, from the girlfriend who'd been captured in the same action. The two of them had been recruited by the VC a few weeks before—or abducted, if you prefer, since the girls wanted as little part of the war as I did or any of the other draftees I knew in Nam. Sometimes it's hard to draw lines.

The girls had been grabbed to transport rice from villages to local VC units. That was what they'd been doing that afternoon, each of them pushing a bicycle with a hundred-kilo bag of rice balanced on the frame, under escort of a VC soldier with an automatic rifle. While they were walking along the trail, they met an armored platoon on routine patrol.

That shouldn't have caused any problem. The platoon's half dozen ACAVs and Sheridans made enough noise to wake the dead, between diesel engines, the squeal and ringing of their tracks, and the assorted other noises of ten- and twenty-ton metal boxes moving down a path beaten through the jungle by water buffaloes. There was plenty of time for the trio to get themselves and the two massively-overburdened bicycles into concealment at the trail's edge.

They did that, and it would all have been fine—except that the escort panicked and popped a couple shots toward the vehicles as they came abreast. He ran like hell, then, showing a great deal better judgment than he had when he pulled the trigger. For all I know, he's still alive. Certainly he got through that afternoon uninjured.

The girls crouched down while the platoon opened up with everything it had, firing into the undergrowth on both sides. Cannon, more than a dozen machineguns, and the odd grenade launcher and automatic rifle, all spraying the immediate vicinity. Just thinking about it, the amazing thing is that only one round from all that storm of fire hit anybody. That's what happened, though; and of course, one was plenty for the kid who caught it.

So this isn't a story about an atrocity. The victim was in the active service of the enemy and, while nobody could see well enough to shoot at her as an individual, there would have been ample reason to do so on the information the gunners had. As for the shoes—both pairs, though we got the survivor's back for her—talk to me about that when somebody's put a couple rounds past *your* head and you've behaved like a perfect gentleman afterwards.

All things considered, it worked out about as well as it had any right to do. Only . . . it gives me problems sometimes to think about a world in which seventeen-year-old girls are gutshot as a matter of course. Maybe there isn't a better way, maybe it's part of the makeup of the species. Certainly there's enough evidence to support that view.

But I sort of wish that more of the people who talk so blithely about "conflict" had had a chance to watch a kid or two bleed out on a stretcher.

A lot of fictional violence has been cleaned up. When I was a kid, I watched Davy Crockett shoot an Indian into a neat, bloodless swan dive from a tree branch. Nowadays you can see a lot of the equivalent thing on TV, folks using fully-automatic weapons which do even less obvious injury than Davy's flintlock had. In prose, the normal technique is for the victim to fall over, out of the story-line, and permit the author to get on to matters of greater interest.

And that's fine, no problem, we all do what we do. . . . But for my part, I don't want kids joining the Marines—or politicians voting to deploy those Marines—because at the back of their minds they have the no-tion that real violence is clean and cute.

Violence is sometimes necessary? Maybe; I won't advocate unilateral national disar-mament until I'm willing to disarm myself, which at the moment I'm not. But the look and sound and *smell* of the results of people killing one another—that should be clear to everybody.

Everybody who might be asked some day to kill, or might vote that other people go out and kill for them.

—Dave Drake